INHERITANCE

INHERITANCE

A Story Of Our Times

Len Manwaring

The Book Guild Ltd
Sussex, England

First published in Great Britain in 2004 by
The Book Guild Ltd
25 High Street
Lewes, East Sussex
BN7 2LU

Typesetting in Baskerville by
Acorn Bookwork, Salisbury, Wiltshire

Printed in Great Britain by
Antony Rowe Ltd, Chippenham, Wiltshire

A catalogue record for this book is available from
The British Library.

ISBN 1 85776 816 7

FOR
G A Y E
my daughter, who never saw the farm where
I was born, although my mother told her
many stories about the place.

CONTENTS

AUTHOR'S NOTE

The farm at Lydden is no more, having been sold off into small lots. In the Local Collection at Margate Public Library there are maps of Lydden that indicate a hamlet of several roads. However, this was never built, so much of the area remains as it was when I knew it.

I wish to acknowledge the help and encouragement of my wife, Joan, who suggested important changes in the story.

1

Return to Roots

I had moved away from Margate years ago and although now only just turned 45 had decided not to work for a while – at least not for anyone else. Looking back, I suppose many of my subsequent decisions arose from the accident that had taken the lives of my mum and dad and my dear wife, Anne. Like most true accidents, it couldn't have been foreseen or prevented, and it's true that those who are left behind suffer most. A series of unrelated events had caused a backlog at air traffic control and one plane coming in to land suddenly caught fire and veered off the approach. With its under-carriage already down and locked but with no power to go round again it did actually land, although the pilot was unable to control events from then on. Apparently in an effort to land away from the main runway, it hit two other planes that had already landed, and burst into flames. The fires had been quickly extinguished but among many others, Anne, mum and dad had perished.

I watched helplessly from the airport. I had gone to meet them on their return from a holiday in Canada, where they had been visiting my son, Alex. At the time I hadn't realised it was their plane that was involved, only that it had landed. The authorities reckoned everyone had died instantly but who can tell. It's best not to dwell on these things. Anne was buried at Cambridge, where we then lived. Two days later I travelled to Margate to say farewell to mum and dad. That was five years ago and now here I was back in Margate again to bury yet another member of my family – my grandfather. I was on my own. June, my daughter, was in Scotland and I thought she needn't travel all the way down south to attend the funeral. Alex and his wife were in Canada and I didn't consider it necessary to drag them all the way to England either.

As for me, in a way, I welcomed the excuse. A year ago I'd decided to sell the family home just outside Cambridge. It was a beautiful house but now far too large for me. I got a good price for it, put the money in the bank and spent a happy six months looking for a smaller property. Finally I decided to have one built, not too large yet big enough in case the family arrived en masse to visit me. In the meantime, with nowhere to live and the furniture in store, I'd invested in a motor home which was quite comfortable and big enough for my present needs provided I remembered to put things away and not just down. My new motor home was a marvellous machine. It was American, although it had right-hand drive and ran on petrol. It seated four very comfortably and if necessary could take more. Both front seats swivelled to face the other passengers. It could sleep four and was equipped with many stowage compartments. It also had a small shower, toilet, cooker and fridge. Even so, it was not much bigger than a small van.

My grandfather had died a week earlier but because I had a temporary address it had taken a few days for the news to reach me. Our family solicitor, Nigel Crompton, had written informing me of his death, the date of the funeral and that he had already taken care of the funeral arrangements according to my grandfather's wishes.

There were still friends living nearby who had grown

2

up with me – shared youthful adventures and a few indiscretions. I remember once we'd been caught taking a shortcut to the sea across private property and cornfields. The policeman waiting for us as we emerged from a small copse was our local bobby and a friend of my dad. He let us off with a caution and not even a clip round the ears.

Funny, how just remembering that incident triggered off other memories – some old, others more recent and a few which with the passage of time just don't come through with any clarity. A few remembered snippets, wishful thinking and imagined happenings all blend in to create a hotchpotch of make-believe based only on a small amount of truth. It's strange, too, that if you repeat such memories often enough they are recalled as factual events. Everyone says it's a mistake to return to places where one has been happy. It's not always so.

So I drove down, attended the funeral and chatted to the few friends who had come to pay their respects. Old Dr Hedges was there, also Nigel Crompton, who was a year or so older than grandad. His hair was completely white yet he carried himself upright and when he spoke his voice was strong and comforting. He had a ready smile and a twinkle in his eyes.

We spoke briefly and as I left to begin the long journey back to Higham he said, 'I'll be in touch. Give me a week and I'll write to you.' I gave him my poste restante address and said goodbye. That week had long since passed and I began to think the old man had joined my grandfather. A month after the funeral Nigel Crompton's letter arrived. It was more like a summons yet friendly enough. So here I was back in Margate to see the solicitor and to take the opportunity to visit my best childhood friend, Eric Harding, with whom I had shared so many adventures.

I wanted to see Eric and his wife Sandra. Somehow in my move I had mislaid the address where they now lived with their two children, who were also my godchildren. I had written to his mother, telling her of my intended visit. She hadn't replied, or maybe she'd written to my old address. As I drew up outside in my motor home I could see that the house in Arlington Gardens was still occupied. Standing in the drive was the family car, now some ten years old, yet still looking in good shape.

The front door opened and there she was with a smile on her face and arms outstretched in welcome. Eric's mum hadn't changed much in all the years I'd known her – maybe she was a little greyer but her bubbly nature was there just the same. Mind you, it must have been hell living with someone who always seemed so full of life. Possibly her husband had learned to switch off.

Now, memories again. I recall Eric, his father and me in the shed at the bottom of their garden, tinkering with the lawn mower. Eric's mother had called saying it was time to come in. We'd all heard her and again a few minutes later when she repeated the summons. His father smiled, put his finger to his lips and said quietly, 'Sorry dear, I can't hear you.'

A few minutes later, she had appeared at the shed. 'Didn't you hear me calling?'

Even then Mr Harding had affected not to hear her and then suddenly turned to face his wife. 'Hello dear. Is it tea time?' he asked with an angelic smile on his face. We kids could scarcely keep straight faces as we all trudged back to the house.

Anyway, here I was back with my childhood friend, or at least with his mother. It was as though I had never been away as I entered their home. I thought it might be awkward as I hadn't seen her for a few years. Perhaps I even felt a bit guilty about not visiting more often. But then if one moves away new friendships are forged and life takes a different direction. It doesn't mean that old friendships are forgotten. Someone once described such a situation as putting it on the back burner to simmer gently until required. That time was now.

I hung my coat on the old familiar hall stand. By its side was the full-length mirror where, as lads, Eric and I had made faces at each other. For a moment I was tempted to do so now. I looked at myself, now on the wrong side of the year when life is supposed to begin. I didn't feel any older and I suppose life had been kind to me. I still had a good head of dark hair. Long gone were the pencil marks on the wall where Eric and I had measured our heights as we grew. I reckoned my present height at five foot eight would remain for some time yet. For many years I had maintained a weight of about 11 stone. Active life during my army days had kept me fit and even when I returned to civilian life I hadn't exactly been stuck at a desk.

I made my way into the lounge and sat down in one of the old familiar armchairs. The only change I could see was that the open fire on which we used to roast chestnuts and make toast had been replaced by a gas fire with make-believe coal. The warmth was there but somehow it wasn't the same.

Almost at once Alice Harding returned from the kitchen with two cups of tea and buttered toast on which she had spread some Marmite, and we sat down to exchange news. 'Sorry to hear about your grandfather, although I suppose he was a good age. Arthur has just gone next door to help Mrs Jennings. He should be back soon. Shall I give him a call?'

I thought of other times when he had not always obeyed her summons. 'No, leave him for the moment. As for my grandfather he'd had a good innings and I think right up to the last he was out in the fields. I gather he managed to reach the farmhouse and make a telephone call to his doctor. Old Doc Hedges arrived fairly soon and spoke to my grandad but in a matter of minutes it was all over. I'm told it was quite peaceful.'

'All the same, it must have been a shock to you and the rest of his family.'

'Only me left now, although both my children are alive and married. Gran died some years ago. Both her children had already passed on. Grandad was a bit of a ladies man and there have been stories of a couple of love children although he never mentioned them to me.'

Surprisingly, Alice seemed to accept this. There was no condemnation in her voice as she replied, 'All families have their skeletons. I only met your grandfather a few times and I liked him. He always looked after his family, whatever else he may have done.'

It seemed that Eric was away for a few days but would be back at the weekend. So I had a few days to kill. Alice asked if I'd liked to stay there but since I'd come down in my motor home I declined her kind offer with the excuse that I'd be wandering around, coming back at odd times and didn't wish to put her out. I promised to call back on Saturday to see Eric and said cheerio. Her parting shot was, 'Well, if the weather gets bad or you get lonely do come back.'

I knew of a nice quiet spot in the Northdown Park area. If I fancied a drink I could call in at the Wheat-sheaf or the more upmarket Old King Charles, where they used to serve quite passable meals. Surprisingly, I found my spot after all these years without difficulty. My dad told me that during the war several Nissen huts had housed a detachment of anti-aircraft gunners and other troops. The huts had been removed but the concrete bases on which they had stood remained more or less intact although willow herb and all manner of weeds and brambles had taken over.

I did go for my drink in the Wheatsheaf that evening and mentioned to the landlord where I had parked. 'It's not as safe as you might imagine,' was his warning. 'Kids play hide and seek there among the shrubs and throw stones at anything. You could park in the back yard here if you are only staying for a few days.'

I thanked him and the next morning took up residence at my new parking lot. Although I did go out each day I spent quite a few evenings at the pub. It seemed that the Wheatsheaf had also gone upmarket. Among his clientele there seemed to be a good cross-section from the local community – pretty young women with far too much makeup and dresses far too short, drinking with their boyfriends or husbands or someone else's husband. There were also a couple of stockbrokers who travelled up to London three times each week and a few local farmers, the present day landed gentry.

I spent a few nights there and got to know the landlord quite well. Landlords must be a special breed for almost wherever you go they are a friendly lot. I suppose it's part of the job, although it's not one I should like, having to be at everyone's beck and call. His son was the chef and produced excellent meals, while his daughter and wife helped at the bar. I asked him once if he ever had time off. 'Only with great difficulty,' he replied. He had a cousin in the trade who occasionally came over to take his place, although for him it must have been a busman's holiday.

2

Home Truths

I went to see Nigel Crompton at 10 o'clock on Tuesday morning. That seemed to be the time when most solicitors are awake enough to advise their clients. Nothing much had changed in all the years I had known him – the same old desk, still cluttered up with files leaving just enough room for him to write. Bookshelves covered two walls from floor to ceiling, the top ones being reached by a moveable ladder on rollers. Just inside the door there were six sets of filing cabinets and a huge fireplace. On the fourth wall was a window that went from floor to ceiling and a door that opened out on to a walled garden.

He rose from his chair and came forward to greet me. 'Very nice to see you again, David. We might have done all this by letter but I'm sure you'll have some questions so it will be quicker in the long run. We'll talk first and then I'll get my secretary to take down a draft of our deliberations. It will probably take some time so we'll have a break for lunch.'

I wondered what on earth could warrant such a lengthy discussion. I assumed that since grandad had no other living relatives I was probably the only beneficiary of the estate, but in all honesty I didn't think it could amount to much.

He began, 'Your grandfather and I grew up together, went to school together, went into the army at the same time and both came out without a scratch. That luck stayed with him all his life and, as you can see, I'm also fairly fit myself. I don't do as much now but coming in each day keeps me alive and I love it. So it was with Charlie. He worked until he died and wouldn't have had it any other way.'

Well, I knew that and wondered for what purpose this long preamble was meant to prepare me. In retrospect I think it was just his way of coming to terms with the loss of his friend.

'Charlie Holden was an honest man all his life. He took risks but they paid off. When he and I came out of the army in 1935 he had his farm at Lydden and I came back to this firm. We were both concerned when government promises didn't always materialise and many ex-servicemen failed to get jobs. There were still many people unemployed, left over from the 1914–1918 war. I managed to employ a couple here in somewhat menial jobs. Your grandfather took on a few at his farm as he gradually built it up and expanded.

'He also persuaded other farmers to take on a few. For most it was a meagre existence, being given food, somewhere to stay and a bit of pocket money. And of course within a few years we had another war. At the end of that, Charlie's farm prospered in spite of the fact that food prices were so low. He enlarged his farm, renting several acres from neighbours and buying more when he could. On two occasions when we were unable to establish the owners he merely extended his boundaries. However, all this is documented and an acceptable price was put into a trust to be paid, plus interest, whenever the rightful owners were found.

'I mention this to show how honest your grandfather was. Once the statutory time had elapsed he owned all the land, and it has been so registered. However, when good men become prosperous there are always those who are jealous and tend to make trouble. A young man, Tony Locke, lived with his wife in one of the cottages on the farm. He suddenly became ill and within a month had died. This was when you were about a year old and your sister was on the way.

'Charlie really needed that cottage for another couple but was loath to put the young widow out into the street, so he suggested that she move into the big farmhouse to help your mum. Jennifer Locke was happy with this arrangement and she, your mum and your gran got along very well. In return for her board and lodging and a small financial allowance she would look after the house and help your mum with you and your sister Margaret when she was born.

'It was only a couple of months after your sister was born that Jennifer also gave birth to a baby boy. You can imagine the tongues began to wag, although not within earshot of your grandparents. They accepted the new addition as a matter of course and Jennifer remained at the farm for a number of years, long after you and your sister and your parents had moved into town. Other babies were born in other houses on the farm and it wasn't long before rumours began that your grandfather might be responsible, all the more so as he often visited his workers in their homes. He usually took a few goodies, especially at Christmas, and your gran often went round for birthdays.

'All in all it was a happy place to be. Your grandparents were very hurt when the rumours surfaced but they thought it was best to say nothing, although I'm not so sure. One jolly good row would have cleared the air. They were happy with each other, rose above the stories and prospered.

'Then Jennifer Locke was called back to her home to

look after her own mother, who was ill. Charlie drove her all the way to Norwich and left her enough money to get the train back. As you know, Edward stayed at the farm and went to school with you and your sister. Again the rumours started and worse was to follow. Jennifer stayed with her mother until she died but unfortunately she herself was struck down and died soon after. Charlie consulted me about adopting Edward but I advised against it. In the end, of course, he stayed on at the farm and seemed to accept his lot.

'He grew up, and at one time, you remember, it looked as though he and your sister might eventually get married. That was after he got his first job away from home at Chatham with the Civil Service. Then he was promoted and moved to London.' The old man seemed scarcely to pause for breath as he continued.

'Nearly at the end now, but I felt you should know the background and the reason why there is a bequest for Edward Locke in your grandfather's will. It amounts to £3,000 and I have to see him and explain in much the same way as I have told you.'

He stopped talking and I started to take it all in. Of course I remembered Edward – Ed, or Eddie, as we all called him. We'd played together, had mock battles against each other and had gone to the same school. We'd always thought he was some relative of a forgotten uncle. He left school about the same time as I did, while Margaret stayed on for another year. Within a couple of years she had married and moved away. I joined the army and got married myself. Only three years after her wedding Margaret died. Her husband was a nice enough fellow, though I only saw him a few times. There had been various family get-togethers from time to time until that dreadful accident when my mum, dad and Anne were killed.

11

I felt I should say something. 'Thanks for telling me the potted history. You know, I also heard the rumours but could never quite believe them. Gran and grandad seemed such a devoted couple. When you see Eddie ask him to write to me here and you could forward it to me, if you would. I haven't seen him for years now.'

Nigel Crompton was speaking again. 'Well, David, that's by the way. The main reason for your visit is to tell you about your legacy. With the exception of a bequest of £2,000 to each family living at the farm and a similar amount to three local charities, the remainder of the estate is yours. There's the farm at Lydden, the main farmhouse and some 500 acres. There are four old cottages and four newer ones that Charlie had built. There's also a caravan park of some 50 acres out on the road to Manston that is rented out during the summer months and brings in £200 a week. You will have to decide what you'd like done with it all.

'My suggestion would be to leave things ticking over, at least until probate has been proved. The farm manager, Ray Sneddon, is quite competent. He got on well with Charlie and he'll make sure that the farm comes to no harm. I don't think he's in a position to make an offer for the farm himself. You could rent it out as a going concern, although there are a few farm workers on the farm and a newcomer may not wish them all to remain. Also, there will be something like £100,000 in cash.

'There is another property which you may know nothing about – Wakefield Place, the estate at Chapel Hill of about 100 acres. There are also two cottages at Cliffsend, together with about ten acres. One of these is rented out, the other is vacant at present, and the adjoining fields are rented out for sheep grazing. There's a small copse at one edge of the land.'

I did remember the place at Chapel Hill, in south

Margate, just beyond a small housing estate. I don't know why this part of Ramsgate Road was called Chapel Hill, for there was certainly no evidence of any place of worship. The main house was enclosed on three sides by a high wall with wrought-iron gates allowing access from the road. When I had first seen it the house and woodland had extended to a further 100 acres, where the new housing estate had been built. The main house and gardens remained and it must be this, together with the land and little bit of woodland, that I had now inherited.

My mind went back over many years to the time when we were kids – young Eric Harding, myself and our gang. In those days the house was not occupied and had been left in a sorry state. One of the wrought-iron gates was off its hinges, and many of the windows on the ground floor were broken and had been boarded up. We kids had a lovely time playing cops and robbers or cowboys and Indians in the grounds. Our greatest find had been the summer house at the back, about 50 yards from the house and almost hidden by a screen of trees and overgrown with brambles.

As I sat there I became aware that the old man had finished. It didn't look as though we were going to get our break for lunch and he made no effort to ring for his secretary so I decided I'd better make a move.

'Thanks very much, Mr Crompton. This is all too much to take in at once. I'm hoping to stay down for a few days and see a few friends. May I call in again?'

'Of course, David. When it's all sorted out I'll need you to sign some papers. In the meantime congratulations. Your grandfather was very fond of you.'

I made my way to a snack bar in the High Street, although I wasn't really hungry.

This part of Margate had changed a lot in the last few

years. A brand new library had been built on the site of a cinema and theatre that had been bombed during the Second World War. The pedestrian precinct was also new and led from Cecil Square to the old High Street. I sat down at a table for two in a corner, watched the world go by for a few minutes and then ordered a bowl of soup, beans on toast and a cup of tea.

3

Early Memories

My new status as a wealthy landowner would take some getting used to. I had never been short of funds, although I had always had to earn my keep. I'd done very well in the army and after only 18 years had left with the rank of major and a reasonable pension. I had been with the gunners and among other things had become an expert in electronics. When I left the army a large firm at Cambridge welcomed me and my knowledge into their research complex.

A few years down the line they were taken over by a huge Dutch firm. They asked me to head up a new research project but it would have meant moving to Holland and I didn't want to work abroad. They had been very good about it and had given me a handsome financial leaving present on the understanding that I did not divulge my knowledge to a rival firm, so I was really quite comfortable in a financial sense.

A few months after leaving the firm I had come up with a modification that improved tracking facilities. I'd actually gone over to Holland and explained my ideas. Another researcher had already thought of something similar but mine was simpler and easier to produce. Six months later when it had been perfected they sent me a cheque for £5,000. And now I really was rich.

My grandfather's farm was at Lydden, a few miles outside Margate. I had been born there, although a couple of years later we had moved into town. I remember my mother speaking of my adventures on the farm. Once, as a baby who had just started to walk, I was discovered in the chicken pen sharing their corn. Another escapade found me in the stable with one of the horses, Rosie, who was the most gentle of creatures. But I came to no harm on the farm and suffered no ill effects from hobnobbing with the chickens or the horse.

In any case, I don't really remember those adventures. What still lingers with me is the smell of the hot potatoes, bran and no doubt other ingredients that were fed to the chickens each evening. The rabbits also came in for their share of this mash. They were kept in hutches along one side of a storage shed. Even though the rabbits were cleaned out each day, the stink inside was at times overpowering.

When my children were born and got into similar scrapes, my mother told them of my time on the farm. My children in turn reminded me. 'Remember the time you almost fell down the well and when you let the cows out to get greener grass?' Of course I nodded, though I never did remember.

When my sister was born I took a temporary back seat, although once the problems and joys of a new baby had subsided we were both treated with equal love and affection. Soon, however, especially after I had moved from the infant school I was off with my classmates and enjoyed the games and make-believe that all young boys experience. The long summer holidays were the best, and once our gang had acquired a variety of old bicycles we spent hours away from our homes. Soon after breakfast we'd set off, taking a few sandwiches and a bottle of water or a fizzy drink. We would return late in the afternoon or just in time for an evening meal.

Sometimes these day trips took us to the seaside about

a mile from where we lived all fairly close to each other. There were nine miles of beach where we could explore, and if you discount the built-up areas of Margate, Westgate and Birchington that still left a lot of places that remained wild. When the tide was out we searched among the rock pools. As the tide came in we retreated to one of the many caves eroded out of the chalk cliffs. The best cave was actually man-made. It started at the beach and extended in a long gradual slope all the way to the top of the cliffs. At intervals there were openings on the cliff face that allowed light to enter the darker interior and show us the way.

We imagined smugglers had used the caves, and for all we knew, some of the hoards of silk, brandy and rum were still hidden – though we never found any. There were four major players in our gang, Roger, Eric, Bob Simmonds and me, although others joined from time to time. One summer we neglected the beach for pastures new, more than a mile from home and in the opposite direction. There were a number of farms, some quite small, while others extended for miles, and they all held a fascination for small boys. Occasionally the farmers told us to clear off. A few gave us apples or eggs and let us wander around. And then one day we discovered the house at Chapel Hill.

Wakefield Place was a Georgian mansion with a façade of equal proportions, typical of that period. It had seen a number of changes, for the most part blending in with the original building. Leading out from one of the rooms on the west side was a short glazed passage that led into a small orangery. Pipes carrying hot water ran all round the sides and down the middle. A large central area probably had seats at one time but I imagine it must have been rather too warm to stay for long. Again on the west side but leading out from a room towards the front of the house, the Victorian owners at the time had built one of those typical conservatories with stained glass panels.

Whereas the glass in the orangery remained more or less intact, that in the conservatory was broken in many places where the tropical plants had grown too big and forced their way upwards. As a consequence of this and neglect by the owners, the pineapple plants and banana trees were now very poor specimens. Somehow they had survived, although there was no evidence that they had ever borne fruit.

The large coach house on the other side of the house had moved with the times. It had been converted and was now capable of housing three cars. With the self-contained flat above that ran the whole length it would now be worth a small fortune.

The whole property was completed by a walled garden, so I imagine the people who had lived there were largely self-sufficient. The annual flowers had seeded themselves over the years and were now so overcrowded they scarcely had room to grow. The fruit trees were a wonderful source of food for the birds, squirrels, bees and people who had broken in over the years.

Some distance from the house and the more formal gardens was a small section of woodland. It too was now so overgrown that it presented an impenetrable barrier to all but rabbits and other small mammals.

At the main road there was a long high wall of flint, topped with vicious bits of broken glass with entrance through a pair of quite large gates. Each gate had a coat of arms that formed part of the intricate wrought iron. They were different, and we supposed that one belonged to the man of the house while the other was for the lady. The name of the place was emblazoned across both gates

– WAKEFIELD PLACE. A bell still clanged if you pulled the handle on the right. Set into the left hand pillar was a letter-box and a bell push that no longer worked. A brick wall continued along both sides of the estate although the rear had only open fencing panels.

The house itself was set back from the road about 50 yards and was reached by a winding drive. Trees and overgrown shrubs partially obscured the house, but even in its somewhat dilapidated condition it was obvious that it had been a substantial and elegant mansion.

We returned there many times but that first occasion will always remain in my memory. We pretended we had been called in by Scotland Yard to solve the mystery of the owners who had disappeared without trace. Even so, they had managed to board up the ground floor windows. Our job was to find where they had gone.

To us it was obvious that some crime or even murder had been committed. Possibly the servants had killed the owners for failing to pay their wages. We needed to gain access and look for clues. Fortunately a flap in the back garden close to the house gave entry via the cellar. Bob Simmonds, our leader at the time, always had a supply of matches. These gave off sufficient light as he led the way down and then up the stairs at the other side of the cellar to a door into the hall. It opened quite easily and there in spite of the ground floor windows being covered, we saw a magnificent hall illuminated from above by a huge glass dome.

To one side was an elegant circular staircase that led to the next floor. All was quiet. There was no smell of dead bodies, not that we would have known even if there had been. It was obvious that further investigation was needed, so we went into each room in turn. The first, at the front of the house, revealed nothing, not even so much as a stick of furniture or a picture on the wall.

19

There could be a hidden safe behind the walls, so we persevered tapping them every few yards. A large hole where the fireplace had been suggested that thieves had been at work. After checking the second room at the front of the house we became bolder and split our forces into two teams. Bob and I checked the rooms on one side and half way along the back, while Eric and Roger tackled the others.

The only noises we heard were the movements from the other team as we looked for clues. Each room was much the same, with fireplaces ripped out and chandeliers that must have hung from the high ceilings no longer in place. Most of the rooms were covered with rich flock wallpaper except around the fireplaces. Small alcoves revealed no hidden passages, while double doors leading into the next room held no exciting cavities. The walls between each room must have been almost two feet thick yet when we tapped them no hollow sound came forth.

The kitchen at the back was huge. There were two sinks, yet when we turned on the taps only rusty water came out and finally ceased. It was here that we came across some furniture – a large kitchen table, two small chairs and two large carvers. Drawers in the kitchen revealed nothing, though plates still hung in the racks near the windows above the sinks. Leading off from the kitchen were two big larders. One had marble shelves and two empty boxes. The second had shelves all round and three boxes which were packed full of kitchen utensils, pots, pans, kettles and so on.

There was a large building in the rear garden that we hadn't yet entered. We resolved to leave it and the other floors for another visit. We left the house by the way we had entered, collected our cycles and went home. Whatever secrets were in the mansion our tea was waiting for us.

4

Eric and Friends

Eric Harding and I had grown up together. We lived a few doors from each other and because our names were close together in the alphabet we often sat next to each other at school. When we later went to the grammar school we cycled the three or four miles to Ramsgate together, occasionally we made a race of it and went by different routes.

We developed a system of mutual assistance with our homework. Eric was always good at maths, while I excelled in languages. We helped each other with ideas for essays, and in physics and chemistry we were often better at explaining things to each other than our teachers.

Eric played cricket for the school XI, I was more interested in soccer and rugby. We were both members of the school dramatic society that put on a play each year. Eric was also in the school orchestra and practised twice a week after school. I was not gifted in that way though I did learn to play the piano. Thinking back, I now wonder how we ever managed to find time for other activities, but we did.

Now, back in the present, I kept to my intended programme of visits. On Wednesday I drove over to Birchington and was pleasantly surprised to see that Roger Howerd still ran his petrol station and repair shop. He was a redhead and the smallest of our gang, though immensely strong for his size.

Roger no longer got his hands dirty but he obviously missed solving problems with car engines. Now his time was taken up with looking after his string of garages in east Kent. For the most part he concentrated on good-quality second-hand cars. He said there was more profit in them and he usually sold half a dozen each week at each of his five outlets.

I was impressed with his garage at Birchington. As well as the pumps in the front and workshops at the rear, he had a sales office at one side with *Car of the Week* on display. In a compound at the back were a dozen other cars waiting to be sold. On the other side of the forecourt a small café dispensed hot drinks and snacks all day long as well as selling a useful range of convenience foods.

His garages had all moved with the times – engine diagnostics and car maintenance systems were all now computerised. It was only for the really old or classic cars that he was asked for his advice or needed to consult one of the many manuals he kept in his office. Very occasionally he still had to make or adapt a replacement part.

He told me all his premises were built in the same general pattern. At this one he employed six people and had a reserve of local part-time staff he could call on in an emergency. I must say he looked prosperous enough, and when I suggested we walk into Birchington for lunch he was quite happy to drop everything. Over the meal he filled me in with all the local news since I'd last seen him. We decided it must be all of five years yet the old easy friendship was still there. First-hand information like this was far better than the scribbled notes at the end of Christmas card greetings. I resolved to make my next visit much sooner.

We walked back to the garage and looked in the shops on the way. Everyone seemed to be thriving but the relaxed pace of the village had gone. Like so many other places, it was rush, rush, rush with little time for the courtesies of old.

Roger didn't know that my grandfather had died but said he was sorry. As a lad Roger had often ridden out with me to Lydden. Sometimes we went just for the ride to look round the farm and see the animals. On other occasions we'd earned pocket money helping to pick soft fruit. Grandad allowed us to eat as many strawberries as we liked but after the first five or six we'd had enough. Blackcurrants were too sour and so were loganberries, though the worst to pick were gooseberries. The thorns were really sharp and it was awkward wearing gloves.

Possibly the easiest crop was potatoes. A plough set off at one end of the field and dug up several rows at a time, while we came along behind and gathered the tubers into pails. When these were full we ran back to the edge of the field, tipped them into sacks and just about made it into position before the plough came back digging up another section of spuds. It was a never-ending process and quite tiring. However, the pocket money was always useful. We managed this for several years until we went to grammar school, when such menial tasks were beneath us. I blush when I think back to such snobbish behaviour.

The farm hands worked long hours in all sorts of weather and were glad of additional help in the really busy times, harvesting the potatoes and other crops throughout the year. Many of their families, especially those who lived on the farm, also helped and appreciated the additional money. In real emergencies other people came each day by car from Margate and Ramsgate.

Roger remembered these times and remarked, 'I could never get my kids to help anywhere in the garage but they still wanted pocket money and every new toy. Of course they've left home now.'

'That's progress,' was all I could reply. I told him the

reason for my visit to Margate though not the full amount of the legacy, and this started off a new round of questions as to where I might go and what I might do.

'Well, to be honest, I haven't given it much thought. I don't think it's sunk in yet.'

'Why don't you come over on Sunday and have dinner with us? Mary will be pleased to see you.'

I thanked him and explained that I was seeing Eric Harding on Saturday or Sunday.

'That's all right. Bring him and his wife. I'll see if Frank Thompson and his wife are free. I'm sure Kath would love to see you again. She always had a soft spot for you. Here's my card. Give us a call after you've seen Eric.'

I explained that I was on my way to Sarre to see Frank. He and his younger brother had been at grammar school with me, and his father had a big farm at Sarre. Sometimes he brought the boys to school in one of his lorries but most of the time they came by bus. If they missed it they had to wait half an hour for the next, so in winter they often missed roll call and the first lesson. The old man had now retired so Frank ran the farm, mostly arable, though the last time I'd been there he had a few cows and rented some of his fields out for sheep rearing.

His house was set back from the main road and faced west across the low lying ground. When Thanet was an island there was a four mile channel at Sarre. Now all that remained was a small stream. As I drove through the farm entrance, Frank was there in the yard, having just lifted off a bale of straw as though it weighed just a few pounds. He was always a big lad – I'd forgotten just how big – and now with middle age approaching he was positively huge. He recognised me at once, threw down another bale and came over to greet me.

'Welcome, stranger. Thought you were dead.'

'No. That was my grandfather.'

24

I supposed, being in the farming community, he would have heard. I mentioned that I'd just been to see Roger and that he would be getting in touch regarding dinner, and Frank seemed pleased that we would all be seeing each other soon. Then I briefly told him I'd inherited a farm and might be asking for his advice.

Although Frank had not been a member of our youthful gang, we had known each other at school. Later we both joined the army at different times, were in different units and actually met up again in the Falklands. Since then we had more or less kept in touch. I'd wondered at the time why he had joined the army, especially after a lengthy apprenticeship to learn modern farming techniques. When his father retired, somewhat early, Frank obtained an early release from Her Majesty's Forces. He seemed content with getting up earlier than in his army days and working longer hours.

It would be good to talk of old times, and it would be nice to see Kathleen again. I had originally met her when my grammar school and hers did a joint cavalcade of history at Ramsgate one summer. We'd also played tennis together. But I didn't seriously remember that Kathleen had seen me as anything other than a friend. There were several in our immediate group who went around together, both boys and girls.

Most of the boys were in the church choir and we all belonged to the youth club. Then there were church socials, where we took our first hesitant steps in dancing. Kate had a good contralto voice and I think at one time she contemplated taking professional singing lessons but she never did. However, at Christmas, Easter and Whitsun she sang solos accompanied by the church choir and was very popular. I'd forgotten all that until now. Even so, I'm sure Kathleen and I never progressed beyond the occasional kiss and holding hands.

5

New Friends

The Isle of Thanet is not heavily wooded. In fact there are very few patches of woodland, so the occasional copse left in the middle of ploughed fields or a belt of trees for a windbreak is a welcome sight. The old golf course at Shottendane, in south Margate, had a few lines of trees as windbreaks, although the club has long since gone and sheep now graze where once there had been bunkers. This was another place we visited as kids and helped golfers to find their lost balls. The old club-house now serves as a storage barn for the farm. More trees are to be found on the way to the North Foreland at Kingsgate, where there is a thriving golf course. On a bright sunny day this presents a perfect picture of well-cut fairways and brighter greens at every hole, all set within a gently undulating course surrounded by trees. The North Foreland lighthouse can be seen peeping over the trees, while the blue sea in the distance completes the picture of tranquillity. It's a different story in winter or when the wind and rain do their best to keep the golfers inside.

On Thursday I drove out to Kingsgate and went down to the beach below Kingsgate Castle. It is not all that old, although it gives the appearance of having been built in mediaeval times. A local story, printed in the *Isle of Thanet Gazette*, suggested that John Buchan's *The 39 Steps* was partially based on the fact that at high water there are 39 steps covered by the sea on a stairway from the beach to the castle. I can't remember that we ever bothered to count them.

The castle, originally built by Lord Holland in the 18th century, is not the only fake building in the area. A number of follies on the cliff tops have provided interest for visitors over the years. The tide was out and I was able to see again some of the places we had discovered as kids. Very little had changed here. When the sun was out and the wind was in the right direction this little bay was a veritable sun-trap. Today, with the wind from the north and the white horses on the waves as they came in, it was not conducive to sitting on the sands.

I made my way to the pub and ordered a hot lunch at the bar. A few other customers were also sheltering from the cold wind. One couple sat down next to my table. The girl smiled and I raised my glass of beer in their direction.

The couple were joined by an older woman. She seemed a little flustered, apologised for her late arrival and explained that her car had broken down and a passing motorist had given her a lift. I don't usually listen to the conversation of other people but the tables were so close together that unless I moved away it was impossible not to hear what they said.

It seemed that the woman was the girl's mother and had come to meet her daughter's latest boyfriend on neutral ground, so to speak. The girl caught me looking in her direction, so I merely smiled. She returned my smile and the mother turned round, so I saw her full face for the first time. She wasn't pretty yet she had a likeable face, very little makeup and darkish hair which was very well groomed except for a couple of wisps that had escaped but which only added to the charm of her features. She also smiled and then turned once more to her daughter.

Over coffee, the older woman opened a small handbag and took out a packet of cigarettes, offered one to the boyfriend, who declined, and then attempted to light hers. The lighter failed a couple of times and I decided to assist. Although I don't smoke I usually carry a box of matches so I took the two steps to their table and muttered the time honoured introduction, 'Please allow me,' struck a match and held it towards her.

Also in the time-honoured way they do in films, she held my hand, pulled it towards her lips and lit the cigarette. She must have guessed what I was thinking for she suddenly laughed and said, 'Yes. I saw the film too. Thanks.'

The daughter was quick off the mark. 'Are you on your own?' And before I could answer followed up with, 'Do come and join us for another coffee.'

Well, I wasn't in any real hurry so I did just that. 'I'm Joyce Carlyle, this is my fiancé, John Matthews, and my mother, Helen.'

'David Holden of no fixed abode.' That intrigued them I could see, but for the moment I wasn't going to tell them much more. I merely explained that I was between houses and just visiting old friends. It's very odd how some people tell complete strangers their life story. Joyce explained that John Matthews was her third boyfriend in as many years. He, poor fellow, looked suitably embarrassed and said little other than he felt lucky to have met Joyce. They were going down to Chichester to meet his parents and were anxious to get off, so I volunteered to take the mother back to her car.

Helen and I remained for a few minutes until I suggested we make a move. If I couldn't get her car moving I could at least tow it to the nearest garage. She seemed quite relieved to let me take charge although she hesitated a bit when she saw my motor home until I

28

laughed and said, 'My other car's a Porsche,' and went on to explain why I was driving a bedroom. When we reached her car it was obvious once I'd opened the bonnet what the trouble was. The fan belt had broken. I refrained from asking her to take off her tights, having remembered I had a useful device in my toolkit. Within ten minutes I'd got the car going. I explained it was only a temporary measure, that I would follow her home and that she should get it properly fixed as soon as possible.

I followed her to Northdown Way, where she lived, and as we drove up a long drive I was most impressed by the house that came into view. However, we continued round the side and she stopped outside a small detached house at the back.

'Thanks so much. You really have been a knight errant. I'm grateful. Would you like to come in and wash?'

I was tempted but declined, saying that I was a bit late for a meeting but could I call her later to see how she got on? I also volunteered to fix the car if she couldn't get the garage to do it. Helen gave me her telephone number, and I returned to the Wheatsheaf. From the pub I telephoned Alice Harding, and was surprised when Eric answered. He recognised my voice at once.

'Greetings. I heard you were in town. I've only just got back from Holland. I called in at mum's to drop off her bottle of gin I'm just on my way home to see Sandra and the kids. Come round to see us. We now live at The Old Rectory, St Mark's Lane, St Peters.'

'I'll leave it for a couple of hours if I may and on Sunday both of you are invited for dinner at Roger's place in Birchington. No doubt he'll be ringing you.'

'Sure. That's fine. Mum says you're carrying your house on your back but you're welcome to stay here.' Again the past few years fell away as though they had never been. We slipped again into that easy friendship that only special friends enjoy and that cannot be defined.

'I mustn't keep you away from your family any longer. I'll see you soon. We have lots to talk about. Love to Sandra.'

I walked over to the bar and ordered a whisky. The observant bartender noticed I had changed my tipple so I replied, 'Yes, and I'll have another. I've got a lot to think about.'

And indeed I had. My original plan had been to apprise Eric of my newly acquired properties and for us both to have a look round Wakefield Place. This time I had a key to the front gates and to the front door so we need not sneak in through the back way. What on earth was I going to do with such a big house. I'd only recently got rid of one and bought a plot of land at Higham, a few miles east of Matlock, I was having a much smaller place built. While it was being built I intended to visit many of the places of my youth and other places I'd never seen. I would then have a wealth of memories to keep me happy in my old age. It was now going to be a busy few days until I returned to see how my new home was progressing.

I gave Eric time to get home, wash away the grime of his foreign travel and tell his wife of my imminent visit. He opened the front door to my ring and there he was, large as life. They say that people who spend a lot of time together often grow to look alike. In our case we were very similar in appearance right from the start. We both had dark hair and were of medium height. When young we were both slim and of athletic build. I am one of those people who can eat anything and not put on an ounce of weight but Eric was already showing signs of middle age spread. Even so, I could still see much of myself in Eric's outward appearance. As kids we'd often wrestled each other. I didn't much fancy my chances against him now, with all the excess weight he was carrying. Yet he seemed fit enough. I expect that too much comfortable travel and good food, and too many drinks, can play havoc with even a good body.

We shook hands and gave each other a hug for old times' sake. 'Come in. You know you're always welcome here.' I know he meant it and later Sandra repeated the offer, only in her voice I sensed almost a pleading note as though she needed me to stay. Over a mug of tea and biscuits we slowly told each other what had happened since our last meeting. The really important details would follow at a more leisurely pace. Now in the space of an hour or so we were up to date.

'So what on earth are you going to do with all those properties,' Eric and Sandra wanted to know, as did I.

'Haven't got a clue as yet. It's too much all at once. Trouble is, I do need to sort something out. The farm at Lydden will tick over quite happily and the manager there is very competent and I'd like to retain all the staff. It's the other big place in Ramsgate Road that is the real problem. If I sell it, what am I going to do with all the money? I was wondering if with all your business sense you might think about some options.'

Eric considered this for a moment before replying. 'When you have all the details we can go over them together. I'm sure we can come up with something.'

I didn't stay long but it was good to know I'd be seeing them both again quite soon. On the way back to my parking lot I thought again about the adventures Eric and I had enjoyed. He had never been the leader of our gang but to my mind he had the best brain of all of us. Partly because of that, and because he would usually volunteer if a teacher wanted anything done, he was well liked by the teachers and occasionally disliked by his fellow pupils. But he was never a crawler. He once said to me, 'I don't mind helping out. There'll come a time when I might need their help.'

6

The Old Summer House

My intended visit to Wakefield Place led me to think about the last time I had been there as a kid. For some reason our gang had been reduced to only two, Eric Harding and me. It was almost a month after our previous visit and this time we brought extra torches and an additional supply of sandwiches and lemonade for an all-day exploration. Access to the grounds was as easy as on the earlier visit and it didn't look as though anyone else had found our secret house. So in through the door at the back we went, up through the cellar and then climbed up the large winding staircase to the floor above.

At the front of the house was one huge room with similar ones via connecting doors at each end. This was either a ballroom or the largest sitting room we had ever seen. Leading off from the ballroom and at the back was another kitchen, while along both sides of the house were other rooms, possibly bedrooms and bathrooms. All the rooms were empty, though here in the larger rooms the fireplaces were still intact and each had beautiful marble surrounds. At the end of this floor there was another staircase that led up to the servants' quarters. The rooms on the top floor were quite large and each had windows and a door that opened out onto small sections of the flat roof. It must have been very pleasant in the summer, that is, if servants got any time to themselves.

In the north-east corner of the roof we found the remains of a gun emplacement. Made to look like part of the roof, it was a small square building with its own roof. Any guns that may have been there had long since been taken away, although several broken sandbags were still in evidence and a few were intact. The site was a wonderful vantage point; anyone approaching from the harbour could be seen long before they saw the house. A similar observation post was located in the south west corner of the roof so that all approaches were covered.

Well, we knew about Home Guard outposts, but surely they had all gone. The war had been over for years but the very fact that this place was still deserted may be the reason why nobody had bothered to remove these observation posts.

There was nothing of any interest to us here – no hidden rooms or passages behind oak panels. So with a last look round the house we made our way out and went towards the summer house. Nothing had changed here since our last visit. Again we went in by the door, using the key that still hung from a hook in a small box outside. I don't know how long it takes a place to acquire a really neglected look but at the rate brambles grow I suppose a couple of years would achieve the result which met our eyes.

I wondered why such a place had been built. Maybe it was used as a surplus dormitory for weekend guests or maybe the family used it when the weather was warm. It was the luxury of a bygone age.

Inside, it was darkish because of the overgrown shrubs but it felt quite warm. There were no broken windows and we could see no bird nests, droppings from rabbits or holes made by squirrels. Moreover, there was furniture: four chairs and two armchairs made of greenish cane. The four chairs, all with cushions, were placed around a wicker table with a glass top, and even this was intact. The armchairs, again complete with cushions, were arranged each side of the fireplace.

The main room was about 15 feet by 15. Shutters at the windows still functioned when Eric pulled on one of the cords. Leading off this room was a kitchen containing another table and a couple of chairs. Yet another room was obviously the bedroom, complete with wardrobes but no bed, and leading off from this was a bathroom. We assumed the owners had died or more likely gone abroad without telling anyone. Maybe they had died overseas of some horrible tropical disease.

There were no letters anywhere in here or indeed in the main house and not even any old papers or magazines. Most of the furniture and the curtains and carpets had also been removed from the main house. Only in the summer house were there bits of furniture. We supposed that nice though they were, they were hardly worth selling. We could find no hidden panels anywhere, that is until we opened a pair of double doors in the wardrobe. It was a huge walk in affair and the base had a hollow ring to it. Lifting up the bottom revealed a trap-door and beneath that a flight of steps that must have led directly outside and probably into the garden.

The discovery of a secret passage, the very thing we had been hoping for, was almost too much for our young minds to take in. We literally stopped in our tracks and decided to have our sandwiches and a drink while we considered our next move. Part of us wanted to continue down the steps and part wished for guidance from an older person. In the end we decided to go outside to see if we could find an outhouse or covered way where the tunnel might emerge.

We searched carefully all over the back garden until

we came to the boundary fence but could find nothing that looked like an escape exit. We even levered up several paving slabs and looked in the greenhouse but drew a blank. We returned to the wardrobe and wished that more of our gang had been with us. We could have used their moral support.

I recall we were quite methodical in our approach to the next part of the investigation. We wrote a note for anyone to find if we didn't return and left it just outside the wardrobe. On it we wrote our names, addresses and something to the effect that we were investigating the disappearance of the owners. So in our minds we were back in our role of Scotland Yard detectives in pursuit of villains and missing persons.

We went down the steps in the wardrobe, opened a door at the bottom and found ourselves in another room underground. This room also had furniture in it – of a kind. Against one wall there were two pairs of bunk beds, complete with mattresses, pillows and blankets. Above each of the top bunks were several storage lockers. Each contained roughly the same items: several pounds of dried fruit, tins of spam, packets of candles, matches, tins of fruit and vegetables as well as four tins of stewed steak. There were tins of sugar that had now formed into a solid mass, tins of condensed milk, tea, cocoa and powdered milk. In one cardboard box we found an assortment of tin plates, enamel mugs, cutlery and cooking pots.

On the walls opposite the beds were more storage cupboards. One of these held lots of clothing, boots, socks, groundsheets, shovels, axes, several pounds of nails and several bundles of wood for kindling. There were also several buckets of coal. The greatest discovery was in the big cupboard near another doorway on the far side of the room. This contained several sten guns and pistols, hundreds of rounds of ammunition, hand grenades, bottles of oil and some rags. We also discovered a couple of tilley lamps, four bottles of paraffin, two paraffin stoves, more matches and candles as well as several bottles of water. In yet another cupboard we found wellington boots, tin hats, capes and army-type gas masks.

It was a treasure house such as small boys dream about but which rarely materialise. But what on earth could we do with it? The food was probably rotten and we were well aware that guns and ammunition were not toys. Who on earth did they belong to and, more to the point, who had hidden them and for what purpose?

Between the bunk beds another door opened inwards, and beyond that a dark passage-way that led to yet another door. We went up a flight of steps and came to a trapdoor set above. We pulled gently on a handle. It opened quite easily and we found ourselves in the greenhouse that we had already searched.

I think we were a bit scared of what we had found. Our imagination began to run riot. In the end we put back everything as we had found it, shut the wardrobe door and got out. We retrieved our note and cycled home for tea.

It was several weeks later and into the summer holidays before we had time for another visit. This time the main gate had been re-hung and we could find no easy way in. Still, kids are resourceful for we merely cycled the long way round to the back, left our bikes in the hedge, walked along the old railway track and climbed over the back fence.

The key to the summer house was in its usual place and as we entered we could see that someone had been there. The furniture was still roughly in the same place but the room itself looked as though it had been cleaned.

However, the wardrobe was still in place and its base still lifted up to reveal the trapdoor and the steps leading down to the secret room. Every piece of ammunition, all the guns and the stores had gone. We kicked ourselves for not having nicked anything on our earlier visit, not even a single cartridge. We left quickly, rode back home and got on with our young lives. Happy memories.

Now, many years later, as I recalled those earlier visits, I wondered why I had not remembered it until now. Actually, that's not quite true. When I first joined the army we young recruits training to become officers often tried to outdo each other when recounting our previous adventures, and I had told about the arms dump at Wakefield Place.

I tried to make it sound exciting and the others had listened with growing interest until the actual moment when I told them about the guns, ammunition and stores. They didn't believe any of it and reckoned that I had strung them along. I kept quiet after that.

7

Helen

I had a leisurely breakfast, then walked over to the pub and phoned Helen. It was only nine o'clock but I reckoned she'd be up.

The phone was answered at the second ring.

'Good morning, Mrs Carlyle. It's David Holden.'

'Oh, hello. I was just thinking about you.'

'Really? Well, I'm ringing to find out if you managed to get your car fixed.'

'Not yet. The garage said they couldn't fit me in until Monday. Not to worry, but thanks for asking.'

I thought I could get it done sooner than that. 'Let me see if I can locate a new fan belt. If I can I'll drop over this morning and fit it. Will you be in?'

'Yes. I'm just going down to the local shops to get a few bits and pieces but I'll be back by ten o'clock.'

'O.K. I'll see you then.'

Now all I had to do was get hold of a fan belt. After a quick look in Yellow Pages, the first place I tried did have the correct size. I had half an hour to kill so I phoned Roger. He wasn't there but Mary, his wife, answered the phone.

'I'm sorry if I lumbered you with putting on a big dinner for Sunday. Is there anything you'd like me to bring?'

'No, just yourself. Eric rang earlier. He brought back lots of wine from his recent trip so he'll bring us a couple of bottles. Dinner is no big deal especially when we're all friends. In fact we're all a bit cross that you live so far away. You should come and visit us more often.'

I could only mutter, 'Ah well, you know how it is. Lots to do. People to see.'

'Well, how are you really?'

'Very well thanks. I'm gradually coming to terms with everything and beginning to look ahead. I'll tell you all about it on Sunday. By the way, would you mind if I brought along a friend – just to make up the numbers?'

'Come on, David. There's got to be more to it than that. Who is she and where did you meet her?'

'Well, I met her yesterday and to be honest I haven't mentioned that I'm having dinner out on Sunday. In fact I've only just thought of bringing her.'

'No problem but we shall need to know chapter and verse before we meet her so you'd better do something pretty quick. Give me a ring this afternoon.'

'OK, and thanks. Let Roger know and tell him not to make any wisecracks.'

'We'll see. Don't forget to let me know just how much about you I may let out of the bag.'

I let that last crack go, said cheerio and hung up. I changed into a different pair of slacks, shirt and pullover, drove down to the auto-shop and then made my way to Helen's house. She opened the door almost at once and there she was, a smile on her face, outstretched hand in welcome and a friendly 'Hello'. She was wearing slacks and a matching top with a bright green scarf around her neck. She looked very elegant but still that wisp of hair had managed to escape.

'Good morning, Helen. May I call you that? Done your shopping?'

'Yes please do. I've just bought a few bits to keep me going. Good morning yourself.'

40

'Right, let's get to work on your car.'

She opened the garage doors and handed me the car keys. 'How long will you be? I'll have a cup of coffee ready when you've finished.'

'Well, if there are no snags, say half an hour. Or I could spin it out like the garages usually do and charge twice as much.'

As she turned and went inside the house I wondered how old she was. It's always difficult to judge a woman's age. I imagined that Joyce must be in her early twenties so Helen might be 43, but she could have had her daughter early.

I got to work, and in just a few minutes I'd fitted the replacement belt to the correct tension and started the engine. I checked oil, water and petrol and decided to give it a short test run. Helen came out of the front door as I drove past. I gave her a toot on the horn and she waved back with a question forming on her lips, thought better of it and realised I was merely checking my handiwork.

I was back in five minutes. I know I had a self-satisfied grin on my face as she let me in. She smiled and said, 'What took you so long? Do come in and have a coffee.'

I handed back her keys. 'There you are, madam. You shouldn't have any more trouble but if you do, just give me a ring.'

'You must let me pay you. How much?'

'This one's on me.'

'Are you sure? I ought at least to pay for the part.'

'Well, on second thoughts, that would be handy. I'm just a bit short of cash until I go to the bank. If you really want to pay, it's £8.'

'Thanks very much, David. Would you like to wash your hands here or in the bathroom?'

'Here will do, thanks.'

I followed her into the kitchen and we sat on stools drinking our coffee. There was a pleasant smell of cooking and then a buzzer sounded. Helen excused herself, put on a pair of oven gloves and took out two tins of sultana buns. She left them for a while, and then prised them out onto a wire tray.

'Would you like one? They don't always come out so well. When they don't my daughter says that only proves I'm human.'

So we sat on our stools a little longer while we had two each. It must have been years since I'd done that. Probably in Cambridge when Anne was still alive.

I intended to have a quick look round my new properties at Cliffsend, so I asked Helen if she'd like to accompany me. She said she'd like to come and should we take her car to make sure it was all right. I looked directly at her and she blushed as she realised the implied criticism of my workmanship. But I wasn't offended and she could see that I didn't mind her faux pas.

She was a careful driver as she chauffeured me to my two cottages overlooking Pegwell Bay. I took out the map that the solicitor had given me and gave Helen directions as we approached our destination. She didn't ask the purpose of my visit but probably thought I was looking for somewhere to live.

At Pegwell Bay the tide goes out a long way, leaving acres of mud flats with small boats and yachts flopped over on their sides. It comes in quickly – too fast at times for the unwary. There is only a small raised beach and the road to Sandwich that prevents the sea from coming right over the land. If this happened the old Wantsum Channel of Roman times would be four miles and Thanet would once again be an island. My few acres were also low lying but the two cottages were built on slightly higher ground. Even so, if serious flooding occurred and the water rose more than 20 feet the sea would be lapping at the back doors.

As we got closer to the hoverport Helen remarked, 'When I was a good deal younger we used to catch the bus to Ramsgate and then walk out here for a picnic. If the tide was out we played on the beach, though there wasn't much sand – mostly mud. If the tide was in we walked inland over the marshes looking for frogs and tadpoles.'

'You're not going to believe this but I also used to come here. That was before the hoverport was built, and there used to be lavender fields nearby.' We chatted some more about times past until we reached our destination. It seemed that Helen and I were about the same age.

The cottages stood close together separated by a low brick wall. One was occupied but the other one to which I had the key was empty. Even so the front garden was neat, the lawn had been recently cut and there were curtains up at the windows. This surprised me as Nigel Crompton had not indicated that he had hired anyone to look after the garden. This was the first time I had seen the property and I quite liked the location. It was in the countryside, not really isolated and with Ramsgate only a few miles away there were shops and entertainment.

The more I thought about it the more I considered it might be a temporary resting place for me. On the other hand I had a brand new place in the course of construction, so I put thoughts of moving down to Kent firmly from my mind.

8

Cliffsend

I turned to Helen, 'Would you like to have a look round?'

'Yes. Are you thinking of buying?'

'Well no. Both cottages belong to me. My grandfather left them to me in his will.'

'Who's a lucky boy then,' was her only comment.

I suppose the cottages must have been a hundred years old, well built and not all that small. In recent years someone had brought them up to date and put them on mains water, electricity and gas. They had the usual pattern of entrance hall and one room at the front, then a kitchen and a sort of scullery or store-room down one side with a bathroom and separate WC on the other side of the passage. There were two rooms along the back. One of these was the dining room, the other was a sitting room.

In the old days the large room at the front would have been the sitting room, used only on Sundays. The rear of the house faced south and was a sun-trap. Someone had added a sunroom or conservatory, and attached to this was a garage and workshop that jutted out from the side of the house. Always on the lookout to improve things, I could see that another bedroom could be built above, providing the foundations were strong enough.

A staircase at the front led up from the narrow hall to

the first floor. At the front was a large bedroom with en-suite. A small bedroom looked out over the back garden, as did another bedroom also with its own toilet facilities. The view from downstairs was passable, while that from the back bedroom, although not exactly breathtaking, was certainly interesting. Across the bay and the marshes we could see countless numbers of birds. The only blots on the landscape were the massive cooling towers of the old generating station.

Helen was interested to see everything so we went out into the back garden. It was a calm day but if the wind blew it would not be pleasant to sit outside for long. Then I noticed a screen of bushes that extended up each side of the back garden, so maybe the previous tenant had taken care of the wind. All manner of vegetables were growing in the garden and the fruit trees were heavy with the promise of a bumper crop later on.

In the right-hand corner behind the screen of bushes I caught sight of a wartime pillbox or observation post. Slightly intrigued, I wondered why it hadn't been removed long ago. As I got closer I could see why. It was really a massive structure and during the war had probably been manned by the army or the Home Guard. Just a hundred yards or so to the north the railway line ran from Ramsgate to Minster and beyond. The railway embankment was probably the only solid object across the marshes. The army post had been sited in a good position as it commanded a wide view over the low-lying ground towards Sandwich. It had worn well, was pretty solid and still had a turf roof. Its wooden door opened to reveal it was now used as a garden shed. The gun openings had been glazed over and with a raised wooden floor it was completely dry inside.

My mind returned to many years ago when our gang had found a similar outpost at Wakefield Place. I

45

wondered if there could be a link since I now owned both properties.

'Did your grandfather live here then?' Helen enquired.

'Well no. In fact I didn't know he owned it until recently. He had a farm out at Lydden that I knew about but at some time he must have acquired this and the cottage next door.'

Just at that moment a middle-aged man called over from next door, 'Good morning. Are you thinking of moving in?'

'Hello. I'm David Holden. We're just having a look round.'

'I'm keeping an eye on the place. In fact, since the couple moved away from here I've been looking after the garden too.'

'I must say you're doing a good job. I expect it's a lot of work as well as looking after your own.'

'Well, not too bad. I hate to see gardens and houses go to waste. Would you and your wife like to come round and have some tea?'

For some reason, neither Helen nor I corrected the man as to our relationship. Helen merely said, 'That would be lovely if it's not too much trouble.' So round we went. Helen whispered to me, 'You had better tell him you're the landlord.'

'OK, if necessary.'

So here we were, two strangers who had met only yesterday, posing as husband and wife about to take tea with our neighbours. The house next door had a similar layout and was comfortably furnished. The man from the back garden welcomed us. 'I'm John Bull – no cracks please – and this is my wife, Janet.'

We shook hands and then I introduced Helen and myself. We chatted about mundane things but somehow it was all very friendly. I hadn't the heart to tell him I

46

was their new landlord. In the end it was Helen who broached the subject.

'We're glad we've met you both. David has something to tell you.'

So I was lumbered but didn't really object.

'As a matter of fact this house and the one next door belonged to my grandfather, who died recently and left them to me in his will. I'm only down here for a few days so I thought I'd come over and see them. I'm not sure what I shall do with the one next door. In the meantime, Mr Bull, if you'd like to continue to keep an eye on the place and the garden I'd be grateful. Can I give you a key, or would you prefer not to have the responsibility.'

John Bull was all for looking after the place but his wife thought that it should be done properly through the solicitor, and I agreed. 'You're absolutely right, Mrs Bull. I'll write to him and no doubt he'll be in touch.'

Mrs Bull seemed reassured by my ready answer and asked if we'd like more tea.

'No, thanks. That was lovely. We'd better go. It was nice to meet you both and thanks for looking after next door.'

As John Bull and I, at his insistence, went to see his greenhouse, I said, 'Mr Bull, if you are happy to continue to look after next door until someone moves in I'd be most grateful. Don't take this the wrong way, but would you like to suggest an amount which would compensate for your time?'

'I'll think about it,' was all I could get him to agree.

We left soon after and headed for the hotel on the coast. We went inside and took our places for lunch as though this was what we had always intended. It was a strange feeling as though someone was guiding our steps.

47

Since leaving the Bulls neither of us had mentioned the fact that they had assumed that Helen and I were married. I had no idea what Helen was thinking but even at this early stage in our relationship I viewed that possibility with a certain pleasure and hoped that Anne would understand and approve. Then I dismissed such thoughts from my mind. For all I knew, Helen was happily married and in any case I would soon be returning to Higham and my new home.

9

Lunch at Pegwell Bay

As we sat down Helen said, 'Say something, David, or pinch me. It's all so unreal.'

Just then a waitress dropped a knife and the dream or whatever was broken and we both laughed. As I handed the menu to her I said, 'I had intended to ask you to have lunch at the Captain Digby, but will this do as well?'

'This will be just fine, and before you say anything this is my treat. I know you're a poor chap who hasn't got much money.' And so the jokey conversation continued.

While we waited for our lunch we compared notes regarding our early years. Helen had also gone to the grammar school in Ramsgate, probably a couple of years later than me, although she did remember the pageant when Kathleen and I had dressed up as part of Britain's history. I now remembered that Kathleen had gone as a British Red Cross nurse and I had been a British Tommy, wounded in action. I hadn't remembered that in ages and now wondered if that small episode had set me on my career in the army.

We didn't say much over lunch. Over the fruit salad Helen mentioned that the old Theatre Royal in Margate had been refurbished, and that she had a couple of tickets for a performance of *An Inspector Calls*. Would I like to accompany her? The tickets were for Saturday and she apologised for the short notice.

'That's perfectly all right,' I remarked. 'You couldn't

have given me much notice. Do you realise, it's less than two days since we first met.' I was happy to accept, and asked what time I should call for her.

'Well seven o'clock would be fine. That will just give us time to find a parking spot.'

'I've got a better idea. Why don't I order a taxi. May I use the phone when we get back to your place.'

Helen insisted on paying for lunch and then drove me back to collect my transport. I ordered the taxi and asked if I might make another local call. I rang Roger and asked, 'Everything all right for Sunday?'

'Yes, everyone's coming. We'll kill the fatted calf.'

'Would you mind if I brought a friend?'

'No, of course not. What's her name?'

'How do you know it's a her?'

'I know you, matey. If it had been a bloke you'd have just turned up, and in any case Mary's already told me.'

'Well, it is a young lady I met just the other day but I haven't asked her yet. In fact I'm ringing from her home now.' As soon as I'd said it I regretted the implication.

His reply was predictable. 'OK feet already under the table! I'll say no more.'

I ignored that remark and continued, 'Her name is Helen Carlyle. I don't expect you know her.'

I could tell from the long silence that he was talking to Mary and sure enough the next voice I heard was hers.

'I thought we'd already agreed. Yes, do bring her and I'll tell you after ten minutes if she's good enough.'

'It's nothing like that. It's a sort of repayment. Cheerio.'

'I don't believe a word of it,' she replied. The phone clicked and she had hung up. I could imagine the conversation going on in the Howerd household and the phone calls to various other Sunday guests that David Holden had got a girlfriend.

50

I'd just replaced the phone when it rang again. Without thinking I picked it up, somehow expecting it would be for me. Of course it wasn't. Joyce was phoning her mother to tell her some news so I apologised and called Helen.

Later Helen told me why she had phoned. Their journey yesterday to Chichester had been somewhat tedious but she had been made very welcome by John's parents. Joyce had kept the most important news until the end. She and John were getting married. I heard Helen's reply to this announcement: 'Wonderful, darling. I know you'll be very happy. I quite took to John when we met the other day.'

I felt I was intruding on a family affair, so I collected my coat from the hall and said, 'I'll get away now and see you again at seven o'clock.'

'Thanks for your help. You don't have to go but I'll understand if you have things to do.'

I just had time for a quick visit to Lydden, but instead of turning right to go to Lydden I turned left, which would take me back to my parking lot. It had been a strange day up till now, so I turned off the engine and sat for a while, going over the events of the day.

As I sat in my car I had a strange feeling that a new chapter in my life was about to begin. It had happened twice before. The first time was when we'd been suddenly recalled from exercises in the West Indies prior to going to the Falklands. Well, that wasn't so much a change as a continuation of the old only this time there had been real bullets. Like most others, I'd just got on with the job.

The second occasion had been when I left the army. Now that certainly had been a new beginning and I had looked forward with a certain satisfaction as I joined my wife and family as a civilian. And it had been a good chapter until the accident that had left three of my family dead.

Now that feeling was with me again and I knew something would happen, though I had no idea what it might be. Even at that moment although I'd only known Helen for two days, I hoped she would be part of my new life.

10

Lydden Farm Memories

Once back in the silence of my motor home at the back of the Wheatsheaf, I got out my suit from the wardrobe, the one I had worn to the funeral and to the solicitor's. A quick press with my travel iron, clean socks, shoes polished and I was as ready as I'd ever be for this evening's theatre trip. I hadn't been in ages. In fact I rarely went out these days. Cinemas always seemed noisy and although I could easily afford it the price was exorbitant. As for theatres, I felt that at least the entrance fee went to support real live people trying to earn a crust. Few actors were in the financial bracket of film stars.

I lay on my bunk and although I hadn't intended to sleep I did just that and woke up with a start an hour later. During my sleep I had dreamed that I was back on the farm as a boy feeding the rabbits and chickens. The aroma of mash, bran and potatoes was all around.

Then Eric and I were on the farm again helping grandad. My sister was also there and wanted to help but did not want to spoil her summer frock. Once our chores had been completed we were free to roam the farm. In those days it was much larger. In my dream we went out of the side gate along the lane until the road petered out into a long leafy cart track and a small stream that helped to drain the land. A little to one side were several haystacks and, as we watched, all manner of animals came out to play. Mice caused a fair amount of damage but we enjoyed their antics. It was the rats we detested with their bright darting eyes. We chased them with sticks but they always got away.

The wild rabbits seemed tame by comparison and we caught a baby one which Margaret then wanted. As soon as she had it in her hand and it wriggled, she screamed and dropped it. The hares we only saw from a distance. A few foxes walked casually by in my dream. In reality there were always foxes about and I was surprised that grandad had not lost more chickens to them.

Even in the summer there was water in the stream and it was here that we saw a great variety of birds. Now there were all manner of exotic ones that I had never seen before, not even in books. In my dream the stream had dried up completely, a few fish were dead at the bottom and the birds were queuing up for a drink at the few muddy pools that remained. I soon found where the water had gone – an enormous hole had appeared. Looking down over the edge, I could see torrents of water some 50 feet below rushing by in an underground tunnel. I scrambled back to safety and woke up.

I hadn't felt in any danger at the time and as I lay there half awake I reviewed the dream in slow motion. If my gran had been alive and I had told her of my dream she would have provided some explanation. She was one of those women, the epitome of a grandmother, a big cuddly woman who never seemed to get angry. She had an enormous wealth of stories, some of which she read from books and some she remembered. Many more she made up and they usually had happy endings. Nothing ever seemed to bother her and she had time for everyone. I don't know that I ever believed my gran's interpretations but it was always fascinating to listen to her.

My own mother I recall as a much more practical

person, aware of what went on in the real world. I suppose different ages and times have different priorities and different answers to similar problems.

Now fully awake, I began to think about all my properties. Whatever was I going to do with them? Both my children had well paid jobs and would be unlikely to need anything I left behind. Besides, Alex and Angela lived in Canada – he was in the oil business and fast moving up the executive ladder – and June was married to Arthur Coleman, a lecturer at St Andrews. My closest friends were all pretty well set up. The bungalow I was having built was all I really needed. I resolved to see the solicitor and ask if he had any suggestions. I really didn't want the bother of looking after the properties, yet if I disposed of them, what would I do with all the proceeds; and just think of the tax bill.

I made a list of my newly acquired wealth. Lydden Farm with 500 acres and the cottages was probably worth getting on for a million pounds. If part of it could be sold for housing it would realise even more. The cottages and land at Pegwell Bay might be a problem. One had a sitting tenant but the other could be worth £90,000. Wakefield Place, by far the largest of the houses would probably be the most difficult to sell. Even so, if sold as it stood, it was likely to fetch £450,000. If I sold only part of the extensive grounds for building purposes it would realise at least another £250,000 and maybe a good deal more.

It was a happy state to be in yet a worrying one. Another thought intruded – where on earth had grandad acquired the money to purchase them all?

I roused myself from my thoughts, took a quick walk down to the first few shops in Northdown Road and bought a small box of chocolates to give to Helen at the theatre. I started back and passed the other pub, The

Old King Charles. It had been built in a mock Tudor style many years ago and now, probably to cater for a younger clientele, it had changed its image, for the worse in my opinion. The old-style tea garden had been turned into a beer garden, while another part, once reserved as a family area, now sported all manner of miniature helter-skelter contraptions and noisy merry-go-rounds. There were hundreds of coloured lights hung all over the façade, while loud music blared out from four speakers. If they had guests staying overnight, I hoped they were issued with ear-plugs.

I continued on my way back to the Wheatsheaf. Even with all the money I had recently acquired I was down to my last few pounds in actual cash. I did something I'd never done before. I asked the landlord if he could cash a cheque for me. He did and I was a bit embarrassed. I wrote out a cheque for £50 and asked him to give me £40 and keep the remainder for letting me park in his back yard and the occasional use of electricity. He demurred at first but agreed when I asked if I could stay on for a few more days. 'Stay as long as you like,' he replied.

My cheese on toast went down a treat. It's marvellous what you can cook on these small stoves, and that reminded me to get some more gas cylinders and recharge my battery for the fridge. The visit to Lydden would have to wait. So too would my look around Wakefield Place. I still wondered why grandad had acquired it, and how. No doubt all would be revealed in time.

Thinking about Lydden Farm, I tried to recall my time there as a very young child but nothing would materialise with any clarity. I was forced to rely on the memories that my mother had provided and I soon realised that many of those were false. I didn't see how I could have had many adventures as a baby for I knew that by the time I was two we had moved into town, even though there had still been occasional visits to see gran and grandad.

From the age of five until about eleven I visited the farm during school holidays. I remembered there was one time when Eric and I spent a whole weekend at the farm. We had cycled out directly after school one Friday, intending to write about the work on the farm for an essay. Friday evening had gone quite well. We had changed into working clothes and done the evening rounds of feeding the animals. The following morning we were woken quite early to do much the same, followed by milking the cows and then mucking out.

After what had seemed a long morning we were glad of a rest and breakfast but horrified to discover it was only 7.30. After a short break the work started all over again this time gathering in vegetables, collecting eggs and making sure that the flowers and the salad stuff in the greenhouses had the right amount of water. The midday break happened whenever there was a lull in the work routine.

Work continued in the afternoon and any time not given over to looking after the animals or plants was devoted to repairing broken fences and making sure there were sufficient boxes for market the following day. We were tired that night – too tired to make any notes for our intended essay. Sunday was much the same and we were glad to escape at about five o'clock to cycle home.

11

The Theatre Royal

I arrived at Helen's and rang the bell. Joyce answered and invited me in. 'Mum's almost ready. She doesn't like to keep people waiting.'

'Well, there's plenty of time and the taxi is not due until ten past.'

'If I'd known I could have driven you. I still could if you like.'

'No, it's all right but thank you.'

Helen came down looking elegant in a short black dress. She carried a small clutch bag and a cashmere shawl. She saw me, smiled and I could tell she approved of my suit although she said nothing. The taxi was prompt. We heard the tyres on the drive, Joyce opened the door and as we went out said, 'Enjoy yourselves. Don't stay out too late.'

Ten minutes later I paid off the taxi and we were in the foyer of the Theatre Royal and then shown to our seats in a box. Classical music via the sound system was loud but not obtrusive. The theatre looked positively sumptuous: the old seats had been removed and the new ones looked very comfortable and weren't crammed together. The four seats in our box were more like armchairs and I wondered how Helen had managed to acquire the tickets.

I whispered to her, 'You could have sold the other two seats and made a vast profit.' Her only reply was, 'Now why didn't I think of that.' I wondered if the padded benches up in the gods had also gone upmarket.

Helen and I chatted quietly. I handed her the chocolates and she remarked, 'I could get used to this.'

The music ended, the lights dimmed, the stage curtains opened and the play began. I'd seen *An Inspector Calls* before, so I knew what was coming. Even so, it did not detract from the performance and I'm sure a few extra twists had been added to the original plot.

At the end of the second act there was an interval. I'd always assumed that drinks at the bar were pricey in order to swell the coffers of the company and pay for the upkeep of the theatre. Here they weren't and as I sat with Helen at a table, waiters and waitresses moved quickly to dispense drinks. This arrangement seemed ideal although there were still those who crowded against the bar.

A voice suddenly asked, 'Do you mind if we join you?' I knew that voice. I looked up and saw Mary and Roger grinning down at us. I got up and made the introductions, and we chatted for a few minutes.

The two girls seemed to be getting along fine. Then I heard Mary say, 'We're having a small dinner party on Sunday. David is coming and I wonder if you would like to join us.'

Helen turned to me with a questioning look on her face. I smiled and said, 'What a good idea.' Helen agreed, so in the space of a few minutes it looked as though Sunday evening had been taken care of. I had intended to invite Helen, of course, but hadn't known when to do so without being too pushy. Here it had been done in a most innocent way. Then a discreet bell warned us it was time to return to our seats.

Afterwards, when we got outside we had both momentarily forgotten that we had no transport. Roger and

Mary came to our rescue. 'Our car is just round the corner. Would you like a lift?' So while Roger went to get the car Mary chatted with us.

'David's a dark horse. He's kept you well hidden,' she began. I didn't doubt that within a few more minutes at least part of my life story would have been exposed.

Fortunately Helen replied politely but firmly. 'Well, no. He hasn't hidden me away because we only met on Thursday. He fixed my car and I'm just repaying a kindness.'

If she felt put down Mary didn't show it. 'We haven't seen him for ages and suddenly out of the blue we meet him at the theatre and with a girlfriend. Sorry if I got it wrong. Shall we start again?'

'It's easily done. Forget it.'

We drove back to Northdown Way in silence for the first few minutes. Roger sensed that something was amiss and started to talk about the play. Soon everything was all right again.

'See you for dinner tomorrow,' said Roger, as he dropped us off at the beginning of the drive.

'Of course. I'm looking forward to meeting more of David's friends.' Then we were alone to walk slowly down the drive.

'Sorry about that. She means well.'

'Don't worry, David. I think I'll be able to take care of myself.'

'You don't have to come on Sunday, but I'd like you to. Please say you will.'

'Of course.'

'Well, I'll get off. Thanks for the theatre. Say goodnight to Joyce for me.'

'Won't you come in for coffee? It's still early and it would round off a pleasant evening.'

I thought so too and followed Helen into the living

room. Joyce was watching the television, but turned it off as we entered, and asked about the play. We chatted for a few minutes and then she made coffee. Helen explained that she'd been invited to a dinner party on Sunday. 'Hope you don't mind being on your own.' Joyce didn't mind, and asked where her mother was going.

'Roger Howerd's house at Birchington.'

'He runs a string of garages and has a big house on the seafront,' I added.

I congratulated Joyce on her forthcoming wedding and she showed me the engagement ring. We chatted a bit about Chichester and she said, 'We went over to Bosham for tea. It's a very quaint place and there are no railings by the sea walls so it would be easy to fall in after coming out of one of the pubs if you were a bit tiddly.'

Joyce continued, 'We'll get married soon but I've decided to stay on here a bit longer, if that's all right, Mum, until we find somewhere to rent. There's no point in buying yet until John has settled in at Frentons.'

'That's fine, darling. Stay as long as you like.'

'They'd like to invite you down soon. Maybe they want to look you over too. No. That's not the reason. They are really very nice and made me feel at home.'

I suggested that it was time I left. 'And where are you staying, Mr Holden?' Joyce wanted to know.

'I'm at the Wheatsheaf. Actually in the yard at the back in my motor home. It's convenient and only a temporary measure.'

They both saw me to their door and amid a chorus of goodbyes I drove off.

12

Wakefield Place and Lydden Farm

I woke early on Sunday morning and couldn't decide whether to take another look round the house at Chapel Hill or make a quick trip out to Lydden, or whether I might just be able to see both properties before I needed to get ready for dinner in the evening. In the end that decision was made easy as Jim Stokes, the landlord of the pub, came round to see me. I invited him in and we had a cup of coffee. He had really come over to ask me about my home on wheels. Apparently he and his wife had been thinking about getting one for some time but wondered if they would ever get enough use out of it.

I explained that in my case it was most convenient and even when my new house had been completed I'd probably hang on to it. I suggested he should hire one in the first instance or even think about sharing the cost with a friend. I could see he was anxious to have a go in mine so I invited him for a short drive. He accepted at once, went off to tell his wife and returned wearing a pair of shoes instead of his slippers.

After a while we changed seats and Jim Stokes took over. He'd driven all manner of cars and lorries so he quickly got the hang of it and was surprised at the ease with which it handled. We found ourselves out on the road to Sandwich and once down by the coast, he put his foot down, again surprised at the quick response.

I was content for him to enjoy himself. On the

Sandwich bypass we reached the roundabout went completely round and headed back towards Margate. 'Thanks very much. I enjoyed that and my mind is made up. My wife and I could do with a break. We've been like prisoners in the pub far too long. With one of these we'd be free to go whenever we could get someone to take over from us.'

The morning had been taken care of so that left me with just time for a quick visit to Lydden after lunch. I called in at the manager's house and apologised for not warning him of my visit. He didn't seem to mind. Roy Sneddon and I had met briefly at the funeral so he recognised me straight away. I explained that I didn't want to alter anything and that if changes ever were in the offing, he would be asked to advise on the future of the farm. My present call was merely to have a look round the farmhouse where I had been born.

'No problem,' he assured me. 'I'll just go and ask Tom Baldwin.'

It was Mrs Baldwin who answered and she was only too pleased to show me round. During recent years she had apparently been over quite often to prepare food and do the odd bit of cleaning for my grandfather. Eventually she took on the job full-time. She and her husband moved in and occupied half the house, leaving my grandfather with the remainder.

Tom Baldwin was an important man on the farm, looking after all the farm machinery, tractors and other vehicles. It seemed he could turn his hand to anything, even doing the milking when necessary. His son was growing up fast and when he left school he would no doubt stay on at the farm and help his father.

The house was somewhat smaller than I remembered. Mrs Baldwin was interested that I had lived there years ago and I explained that it had only been for a couple of years or so, but as a young lad I and my friends had often called over to play or help. The main reason for my visit now was to see the old stable, the site of a very young escapade.

'It's still there,' she said. 'Go and have a look. No one uses it now. It was used as a store but we've now got two more purpose-built barns.' She handed me a key and I walked down the old familiar brick path to the stable. The path, laid by my grandfather, had lasted well and on each side there was still a broad strip that in earlier years had grown dozens of different plants that were used as cut flowers and sold to local florists throughout the year.

The door opened easily and inside there was now electric light and a wooden floor – but nothing else. This too was smaller than I remembered. However, at the back was the stall where Rosie had rested and at the side the manger that had held her feed. As I looked closer I could see that the complete section was really a door, and when I pressed on a bolt head larger than most, the whole contraption opened inwards to reveal another chamber, larger than the stable.

In this part of the farm the ground rose quite steeply so that in effect the stable and this new chamber had been carved out of the hillside. The subsoil, just a matter of inches below the surface, was chalk, so it would have been relatively easy to dig a chamber or even a tunnel.

I don't know what I expected to find. I assumed it might be another secret post from the war years. If there had been food and explosives at one time like those at Wakefield Place they had long since been removed. However, the room was not empty. I was scarcely prepared for what I discovered. On the original racks and shelves that may have held the old army stores and equipment there were now dozens of boxes. Those at the bottom were quite sturdy cartons and labelled BRANDY,

WHISKY, GIN. Above were more cartons containing thousands of cigarettes. If I expected to find bolts of cloth or silk on the opposite wall I was disappointed. Here, too, were boxes and cartons containing whisky, gin, brandy, cigarettes and tobacco.

The years rolled away as I stood looking round this treasure house. I felt the same fear and excitement now as I had as a young lad when Eric Harding and I had found the ammunition and weapons at Wakefield Place. I had not touched anything and was careful to flick a handkerchief over the floor to remove my footprints as I left the room and returned to the normality of the old stable.

I put everything back as I had found it, made my way up the external steps by the side of the stable and was now standing virtually on top of it. I came across two vent pipes and a rusty old drinking trough and I suspected that if I moved it I would find a secret exit.

At this point the ground was probably about 12 feet higher than the remainder of the farm. The extra height gave me a substantial view over the area. I walked over to the road that ran alongside the farm boundary, leading from the Ramsgate road to Manston airport. A little further on from where I stood was the entrance to the caravan park. I wondered how anyone had managed to hide stuff in the old stable without some of the farm workers knowing about it.

I scrambled down the steep bank, walked along the road, turned left into the farm lane and was soon back at the farmhouse.

Mrs Baldwin had made me a cup of tea and I hadn't the heart to refuse. She wanted to talk about my grandfather and the good old days. I sat there listening and drinking but it was a one-sided conversation. To break it, I told her of my recent dream about the farm but realised at once that it was a mistake. Like my grandma, she reckoned she could interpret dreams.

'You must be very careful, Mr Holden, in any new projects you undertake. People are not always as friendly or honest as they first appear. Also, a new friend could turn out to be treacherous, or it could be an old acquaintance you have recently met after many years.'

Well, to my mind that covered all the options and I wished now I'd never mentioned my dream.

Mrs Baldwin was off again. 'The dried up stream and the hole in the ground are clear indications that you must be very careful of where you go and who you trust. Just look after yourself.'

I was about to leave when she stopped me. 'Give me your teacup and saucer.'

I knew before she started that as well as an interpreter of dreams she also read tea leaves. To humour her, I did as she suggested. She picked up the cup, turned it round three times and tipped the dregs out into the saucer. Somehow a few still remained in the cup and it seemed that the pattern they made merely confirmed what my dreams had already implied. I must be wary of my friends and be careful where I walked.

I thanked Mrs Baldwin for the tea and her comments. If I'd been at all inclined to believe these words, her warnings might have made me extra careful or afraid to do anything, and that additional care or hesitation might well have caused an accident. I drove slowly back towards the Wheatsheaf.

I was in a similar situation as I had been as a lad, excited yet worried and not knowing whether to share my discoveries with a friend or the police. At least this time I had a legitimate reason to be there. It belonged to me. And that being so, I might be responsible for it and all that it implied. I would need to consider my position carefully. And just as I had reached that decision another thought entered my head. Did the secret room at Wakefield Place also contain contraband? I must check it out as soon as possible.

As I drove my mind was in a whirl. If modern-day smuggling was going on, there must surely be better and more secure places to hide the loot than at Lydden. Then I remembered that just over the hill was Manston, an old RAF station, and although the RAF still used part of it, the base was becoming an international airport. Then another thought struck me. If the secret room at Wakefield Place had become another storage depot, it was not that far away. Moreover, with the hoverport at Cliffsend and the enlarged port at Ramsgate, all manner of goods were arriving in England and maybe some of them were not passing through customs.

My mind was wandering as I drove back to Margate, so I drew into the side of the road to reflect quietly on what I had discovered. On a scrap of paper I quickly made a rough sketch of the layout of the bolt-hole. Memories of years ago when I was a young boy came flooding back. I couldn't be sure but this secret room looked very similar to the underground room Eric and I had discovered at Wakefield Place. I wondered if that one was still there. I could easily find out, for I now owned it and there would be no need for me to clamber in though the back way to gain entrance via the cellar.

There was also an old pillbox at the end of the lane close to the farm. I could appreciate the need for an army outpost there. Lydden was not far from Manston and if the Germans had invaded, Manston might well have been one of their first objectives. I wondered who had taken advantage of these old sites and put them to use now. There was also the pillbox at Cliffsend, although that appeared not to contain any contraband. I would have to make another inspection of all the places that I now owned.

Back at my motor home, I got myself ready. At the last moment I remembered to get a huge bouquet of flowers for Mary. I was lucky the shop in Northdown Road had remained open on a Sunday. I had completely forgotten what day it was. The days were passing by so quickly.

On only two previous occasions had I lost track of the days. The first had been on the way to the Falklands. The days on the long voyage had been full, practising as best we could for the fight that was inevitable once we landed. True, the weeks had been punctuated by a church service each Sunday but they were quickly forgotten as the daily practice continued. The second time had been when Anne had died. There had been so much to be done so quickly that the days just rolled into one.

13

Dinner Party

Helen surprised me again. This time she wore a sort of loose-fitting two-piece that suited her perfectly and I guess she looked good in whatever she wore. There seemed to be no man in her life. Joyce hadn't mentioned a father, living, dead or divorced from her mother and I hadn't noticed any photographs in either of the two rooms I'd been in at their home. They would tell me when necessary and that time had not yet arrived. Perhaps it never would, as in a few days I would be leaving. This was just a pleasant interlude.

Joyce waved goodbye and called out, 'Enjoy yourselves. Don't be late back.'

I smiled and remarked to Helen, 'What's that, role reversal?'

'Sort of. I suppose it's comforting to think my baby is now prepared to look out for me.'

'I take it I've passed the initial test.'

Helen just smiled and made no reply. As we drove the few miles to Birchington I filled her in regarding my relationship with our hosts and the others we would be meeting. It was surprising how much we had accomplished since growing up together. We had all done quite well in our totally different jobs.

Roger lived at the edge of the village, overlooking the cliffs. The lights were on in every room in the front of the house and I could see that Frank was already there. I parked my car next to his.

The front door was open and there was the sound of music. Mary came down as we arrived. We kissed, and I handed her the flowers and introduced Helen again. The two girls disappeared as convention seems to demand on these occasions and I wandered into the front room, joined Roger, Kathleen and Frank and was just drinking my first sherry when Mary and Helen returned. Mary did the introductions and when she came to me she said, 'I believe you have already met David. He's a special friend. He was a bit wild when younger but like all of us he's calmed down quite a bit.'

Kathleen took over and guided Helen away to a window seat, 'Do come and see the sunset. Do you know there are not many places where you can see the sun rise and set in the sea in this country. This is one of them. Isn't it glorious.' I thought I'd leave Helen to her own devices and when I looked a few minutes later the two women were deep in conversation. Eric and Sandra arrived soon after and we sat down to dinner. I suppose it must have taken a good deal of preparation although everything was done in an accomplished, unhurried way. Soup or melon was followed by meat, which Roger carved like an expert, and there was a choice from several different vegetables. This was followed by a variety of ice creams, fruit salad and then cheese and biscuits.

Roger got up towards the end of the meal, 'Do carry on, but I thought this is such a unique occasion it warranted some mention. First of all, thank you for coming and at such short notice. You know who to blame – David. We are of course delighted that he's here with us again if only for a brief visit. I hope you'll all impress on him that we need to see more of him. I hope you've all had some of this dessert wine, specially brought back from Holland by Eric. Perhaps we should persuade him to go back and bring a case with him next time. Welcome to Helen, our new friend. We're glad you could join us. That's all, folks.'

Everyone clapped. Roger sat down and we all drank some more wine. The buzz of conversation rose in a crescendo until Mary got up. 'If anyone wants coffee we'll have it in the lounge. If it's not too cold you may like to wander round the garden. I believe Roger has planned a surprise if the weather holds.'

The meal had done its work. We stayed at the table until finally Eric made a move towards the coffee. I excused myself from Helen and left her chatting to Frank and went after him. 'Nice wine. I'm only down here for a few more days and then I have to go up north. I wonder if you can spare a few hours to discuss my newly acquired property and what on earth I should do with it all.'

'No problem. Give me a ring any time and we can sort something out.'

I began to tell him about the bequests I had just received. 'I've acquired two cottages at Pegwell Bay as well as the farm at Lydden ...'

Further conversation was interrupted by the arrival of the other guests so I decided to let them all know about my inheritance. I mentioned it first to Roger as the host and he asked everyone to hush, 'David's got a bit of news he'd like to share with us. The floor is yours, David. Don't take too long as we're all going out.'

'I'll be quick. Full details later on for anyone who's interested. You all know my grandfather died recently. Well, he's left me his farm at Lydden and a couple of cottages overlooking Pegwell Bay. Lord knows what I'm going to do with it all. It seems that apart from a few local bequests he's left it all to me.'

For the life of me I still don't know why I didn't reveal the exact name and location of my largest property. Maybe I felt too embarrassed at owning so much. Or had Mrs Baldwin's words really sunk in? Surely I could trust my oldest friends. For whatever reason, I kept it all vague as I heard myself continuing, 'There is also another place on the way to Ramsgate. It's quite large, an old house, I believe, although I haven't seen it since I was told about it on Tuesday.' At least that part was true enough. I watched carefully for any sign of recognition on their faces but could detect none.

There was a moment of silence as the news sunk in and then smiles followed by congratulations. Suddenly Kathleen said, 'Don't worry David. I know what to do. I'll get a divorce from Frank and help you look after all of it.'

'Over my dead body,' said Frank and everyone laughed.

It was all a bit embarrassing. I turned to Roger and said, 'Did you say we were going out?'

He replied, 'Hold on, everyone. If you'd all like to go out for an hour or so we can go along to the Smugglers Retreat. Its only a mile or so and there's live music, a bit of dancing. Nothing too rowdy and a few games. We'll just take two cars.' Frank and Kathleen took me and Helen while the others went off in Eric's car. I sat with Frank and I could hear the two girls talking in the back.

Frank leaned towards me and said, 'I might know of someone who would take the farm off your hands either to rent or possibly purchase.'

'Well, that's good news. I'm going to see the solicitor on Monday just to make sure there are no clauses that prevent me from doing what I want. I'll keep it in mind.' We continued along the road towards Canterbury.

'Remember the old chalk pit just before the roundabout? Austin Reynolds bought it about a couple of years ago.'

'How much do you pay for a hole in the ground?'

'Peanuts I should think, but they've done a marvellous job. You wouldn't recognise it.'

Frank slowed down as he approached the entrance, drove through a gateway and then along a gravel road from where we could see, 30 feet below, a well-lit wooden arena with a few couples dancing, while at the side there were several tables with waiters carrying drinks to the seated guests.

I remembered this old chalk pit, one of the largest in the area. The farmers of old used to dig out the chalk, burn it to make lime and spread it on their fields. The stark white sides had been covered with green mesh and the effect was quite stunning. Multicoloured lights were strung up everywhere. The gradual descent to the bottom of the pit had been well thought out. Guard rails prevented cars from falling over the edge and I could see a similar road on the far side of the chalk pit for cars to exit.

'OK Everyone out. We'll stay here for an hour or so.'

Someone showed us to a table. We ordered a few drinks and while they were arriving Frank and Kathleen took to the dance floor. The others quickly followed and I turned to Helen. 'I really didn't know about this. Would you like to dance?'

'I'd love to. I wonder why it's called the Smugglers Retreat.'

'I've no idea. Maybe they hid their loot here.' She was as light as a feather in my arms. Well that's not true, but we danced so well together it was as though we had done it many times before. The music stopped when we'd only done a couple of turns so we returned to our table, sat down and had our drinks. We all chatted together and when the band started again Eric took Helen off to do the rumba. They danced well together and I must confess I was a little jealous, not that they were dancing together but because I knew I couldn't perform as well. I mentioned this to Sandra. She said, 'Yes. He's very good. Lord knows what he gets up to when he goes abroad. I try not to think about it.'

It seemed as though Sandra wanted me to give her some assurance that Eric did not stray. Well, I no longer really knew him although I felt sure I could trust him. I laughed and suggested she was mistaken.

Other couples on the dance floor tried to emulate Eric and Helen but in the end gave up and almost everyone stood around and watched. When the dance ended there was applause as they made their way back to our table. Roger came back from the cashier's office and gave each of us 12 old pennies. 'Come and see what our old folks used to enjoy.' We followed him to a large section of the chalk pit that was protected from the elements by a large canvas awning.

All round the sides were dozens of old fashioned penny slot machines ranging from *What the Butler Saw* to a *Visit to the Dungeons, Hangman's Noose, Punch and Judy* and *Escape from a Burning House*. There were at least three miniature cranes where people were trying to get prizes but ended up only with jelly-beans. Most people seemed to be at a roll-a-penny circular table. If the penny landed completely within a numbered square the croupier handed over the equivalent number of pennies, and so on. Towards the centre of the board were spaces for ten shillings, five shillings and a pound, though while we watched none of these was won.

We played for a few minutes. Some of us won although most did not. At the end we handed back our pennies to Roger, who exchanged them for real money at 10p for each old penny.

I suppose we stayed there for a couple of hours but as Frank needed to get up early in the morning our party then broke up. As he and Kathleen were already part way to their home at Sarre they went directly there, and the rest of us piled into Eric's car for the return journey to Birchington. Once there, Helen and I bade them farewell and headed back to Margate.

I thought the evening had gone well and said as much to Helen as we drove the few miles back to Northdown Way.

'Yes,' was her reply. 'I quite like your friends. I can imagine you all together in your teens. We'll have to compare notes one day. I don't remember Sandra or Kathleen from the grammar school, either.'

14

The Past Revealed

I dropped Helen off at her home, declined her offer to go in for a coffee but told her I intended to stay down a bit longer and asked if I could call her the next evening.

'Yes. Of course. Not too early as I have to go to work.' She answered my unspoken question: 'I'll tell you all about it later and you can tell me more about yourself. That is, if you want to.'

'Yes, I'd like that. May I call about eight?'

'That will be fine. Don't phone. Just call round.'

I returned to my parking space at the back of the Wheatsheaf and hoped the landlord would let me stay there for another three days. I was asleep almost as soon as my head touched the pillow. Dreams came and went although I don't remember any of them in detail – just that they were pleasant.

The solicitor's secretary said he was busy until 2.30. So there was another half-day wasted. I couldn't really begin to plan anything until I had sorted things out with him. Then I remembered Frank Thompson saying he knew someone who might be interested in the farm. When I phoned he suggested I go over and discuss the matter. I got there about ten o'clock as he returned from the fields, so while he had a late breakfast I joined him for a coffee.

A cousin of his, Gerald Hunter, was actively seeking larger premises and he already had a smallholding not far from my farm. Frank reckoned that Gerald would definitely like to rent Lydden in the first instance and it seemed that he already knew the present manager, Ray Sneddon, and occasionally went drinking with him.

'It would certainly be a weight off my mind if it went to someone we know. Of course I'll have to clear it with the solicitor. He was a friend of my grandfather and I think he'd like to make sure it went to the right person.'

'That's the best way. Let the lawyers sort it out. We pay them enough. Now tell me more about Helen Carlyle. Where did you meet her and what does she do?'

'I can tell you where I met her.' I explained the circumstances. 'But what she does I haven't a clue, but I'll find out tonight as I'm seeing her again.'

Kathleen, who had so far said nothing smiled. 'I could tell you what she does but you'll have to wait, young man. All I will say is she's a bit of a high flyer and I like her.'

'One thing, Frank, before we get down to business – were there any army posts or Home Guard outposts on your farm in 1940?' I felt sure there must have been. Sarre itself is not an important place, having only one pub and no shops, but my army training told me it was a useful junction on the way to Ramsgate and Margate.

Frank confirmed my reasoning. 'My old man said there used to be a pillbox on each side of the road to Ramsgate. At the top of the hill behind this house there was another that covered the way to Birchington and looked out over the marshes to the coast. In the small chalk pit at the top I gather they had a big stores dump. Why do you ask?'

'Well, at the cottages which I've just inherited at Cliff-send there was one at the bottom of the garden. There was another, and a secret room, at Lydden.'

'There were certainly lots of army people around here,

and of course the Home Guard. At one time they reckoned that the Germans might invade this part of the country. Being so flat, there were not many natural defences. I've heard rumours of a secret army, highly trained to defend the coastal areas. Personally I can't believe it, not immediately after Dunkirk. My dad was in the Home Guard and of course he was in a reserved occupation. Maybe your solicitor can tell you. He's old enough and both he and your grandfather were in the army. They only came out in 1935.'

Kathleen caught my eye, 'Is Eric all right? Do you know if he has any worries?'

'Sorry, not to my knowledge. Why do you ask?'

'We don't see him all that often but somehow he never seems to look you in the eye. Frank thinks I imagine it and it's not something you can ask right out.'

'No, that's true. I'm seeing him later on and I'll let you know if anything is mentioned.' I suddenly remembered I had a sneaking feeling that Sandra seemed as though she wanted to confide in me.

On my way back to Margate, I stopped off briefly at Birchington to thank Mary for the nice time on Sunday. Of course she wanted to know all about Helen but I could tell her only what she knew already. I drove slowly back to keep my appointment with Nigel Crompton. He would know some of the answers. He was certainly the right age.

His greeting was friendly as before, although he confused me with all that was involved with my inheritance. 'It's a lot to take in all at once. I don't want to influence you in any way. However, it always seems a pity when someone dies that their estate and all their hard work which went into it is sold off.'

'Yes, I agree. Frank Thompson said he might know someone willing to rent or possibly purchase the farm. If

I hadn't already decided to build a new place for myself I might have been tempted to have the cottage at Cliffsend. Wakefield Place is the real problem. I'd like to know what happened there, why it is now empty and how long my grandfather owned it. Also, there are two other things which I hope you can throw some light on.'

'Of course. Let's get the plans and deeds so we know what we are talking about.'

I told him about our early discoveries at Wakefield Place, the fact that on a subsequent visit everything had been removed and that I intended to find out more about the history of that period. I also mentioned that at Lydden there was a similar secret room. The solicitor considered my words for a moment and then replied.

'I can tell you something and although at the time it was all hush-hush, by the end of the war it was no longer on the secret list. Briefly, as well as Home Guard units that were in evidence here in south-east Kent and indeed all over the country, there was a secret army. Local people, usually in reserved occupations, were secretly recruited to form a defence force. They were very well trained in unarmed combat and had huge numbers of weapons, ammunition and supplies. Their task, if the Germans invaded, was to go into hiding and later emerge to create havoc with the invading army but to return to their underground shelters and then to their homes to continue their jobs. I understand they operated in coastal areas up to twenty miles inland.

'They carried on with their normal jobs during the daytime and came out during the hours of darkness. They went away occasionally for training at a secret depot and generally they kept to themselves. Each patrol had no more than nine people and often they were not aware of who was in their next nearest patrol. Towards the end of the war they were disbanded. All their hideouts were destroyed and their weapons returned to the army. It seems that a few were missed and that probably accounts for your find at Wakefield Place. I did know about the one at Lydden, In fact, because he was an old soldier, your grandfather was the patrol leader there. It's a pity he never recorded what went on in those days and I suppose later when the threat of invasion had vanished he just got on with looking after his farm.'

I suspected that Nigel Crompton had also been in this secret army and soon he volunteered the information that he had indeed been a patrol leader. Almost as though he was glad to talk about it, he continued, 'It's a long time ago and I only know about this local area. By the time the LDV was formed in June 1940, later known as the Home Guard, our local patrol had been in existence for six months. We later learned that the idea had been approved as long ago as 1935. That's the year Charlie and I left the army. Of course we didn't know anything about the secret army at that time but I believe even then there were a few hundred men up and down the country. Mind you, there were so many secret things going on and so much that the public were never told. I often think it would have been better if we had been told. The authorities knew that there were dozens of enemy agents in the country before the war but most of them had been rounded up. Even so, it's virtually impossible to stop everyone getting into the country.

'The secret army had various names like Stay Behinds, Do or Dies and so on, but their proper designation was Auxiliary Units. Throughout the whole country they were formed into three battalions, then into smaller groups in each coastal county and finally into patrols. Soon after the fall of France a few thousand women were also recruited, not to be part of the secret army but to be a covert system for communications. I keep meaning to find out more about these people but I never seem to find the time.'

It was such a wild story I reckoned that most of it was true, and in any case I had seen for myself at least two of the Auxiliary Unit bolt-holes. I determined to find out more, locally if possible. If not I would need to visit the Public Records Office in London.

Of course this didn't answer my present question, although it was a fascinating bit of history. At last I took Nigel Crompton into my confidence about the contraband I had found at Lydden and was glad I had done so. He listened carefully to my story, in its way as interesting as the one he had just told me.

'There is only one thing to be done, and we must keep your name out of any enquiries that may arise.'

Of course I wanted to know why, and his next words gave me the answer that I didn't want to hear.

'The press have a way of finding out names and, once recorded, you could be a marked man. Whatever goods are involved, if criminals can avoid paying for them or get out of paying tax or duty you can be sure it's big business, and big business often means ruthless behaviour. It may seem a bit like a TV drama but for anyone who interferes, first come warnings, then there could be injuries and finally disappearance.'

'Should we tell the police?'

'No, at least not the local police. Leave it with me, David. I know a man who knows a man. I'll be in touch.'

I glanced in his direction, wondering if he was having a joke at my expense, but he merely smiled, touched the side of his nose with his finger and winked. He still had not told me how grandad had acquired Wakefield Place.

That would have to keep for another day. In my haste to get away I forgot to tell him about my intended visit to the summer house at Wakefield Place. I wish now I had taken him completely into my confidence.

15

Contraband

It was almost 4.30 as I drove through the gates of Wakefield Place. Everything seemed in perfect order, with the gates in place and no boards at the windows. The pieces of broken glass that had previously adorned the top of the walls had been removed. As a sign of more benevolent times, they had been replaced by small sections of wrought iron that matched the main gates and increased the height of the walls by 12 inches. That feature alone must have cost a small fortune.

I didn't go directly to the summer house but looked around outside and then went right down to the rear boundary. There was a gate that I hadn't noticed on previous visits and a sloping track just wide enough for a van leading down to the old railway track. On the far side of the track the hedge that separated the old railway from the road had been broken down, so it would have been a simple matter to drive from the road, across the track and on to my property.

Many years ago, in the heyday of the railways, Margate had two stations and two railway companies. There was the present one and another much closer to the sands and next to Dreamland. In fact that space is now used as a terminus and parking lot for the numerous coaches that visit Margate. The old railway ran from there to Ramsgate Town station. The rails and sleepers had long since been removed but the way itself was still there. If

Wakefield Place turned out to be a smugglers' storage depot, the loot could easily be brought across the old railway track and few people would be any the wiser.

At this point my nerve almost failed but I was determined to have a look in that room. After all, it was my property. I was about to leave the boundary fence when a man with a dog appeared, walking down the track. He looked up when he became aware of me and I could swear he hesitated before coming up the rise to where I stood.

'Good afternoon. Not often I see anyone here,' he remarked.

I returned his greeting, It was then that I noticed the gun he carried casually but broken over his arm and added, 'Been shooting?'

'Nothing so far. I let the rabbits alone. It's the grey squirrels I can't abide.'

For the life of me I couldn't understand why I thought it necessary to explain my presence to a stranger but I did. 'Has this place been empty for long, do you know? I'm thinking I might buy it.'

'No idea,' was his reply. 'I only ever come along the track. I live at Westwood about a mile away. It's just a nice stroll for me and the dog. Cheerio.'

With that he moved on in the direction of Margate and I wished I'd said nothing. On the face of it everything could be quite normal, yet in my heightened state I was prepared to believe he was a lookout for the gang and as soon as it became dark another load of contraband would find its way into my summer house. Although I hadn't yet been there, I was convinced some loot was already in the secret room. I watched the man until he disappeared.

I retraced my steps to the summer house. Having come this far I was determined to check it out, but first I went to my car and retrieved the long handle of the wheel jack to use as a weapon if needed. Once inside, everything looked quite undisturbed so I continued to the wardrobe, down the steps and into the secret room. I don't know what I expected to find. I guessed there wouldn't be any guns or ammunition and part of me didn't really expect to see any brandy, whisky or anything else.

I was mistaken. The old shelves and bunk beds were still in place and they were full of merchandise, very similar to those I had seen at Lydden. On the back of an old envelope I made a few notes of the contents of this treasure house. I didn't open the cartons of cigarettes but I imagine that each one held several packs of 100s and 200s. I guessed each large box contained 40,000 cigarettes, and along one wall I counted 60 such boxes – and they were just the English makes.

Against the opposite wall was a similar amount of American brands. At the top of each pile of cigarettes there were boxes containing tobacco. I'd never smoked a pipe so I couldn't guess how much was stacked there. Along the central part of the room were dozens of bottles of spirits and several boxes of wine, mostly French and German. Seeing so much contraband, I began to get a little apprehensive. While I thought I could give a good account of myself on a one-to-one basis, I didn't fancy my chances if more than one smuggler suddenly arrived.

I didn't stop to see the extent of the loot but retraced my steps to my motor home, carefully making sure that I left no tell-tale footmarks. Before leaving, I went into the house by the front door, just in case anyone was keeping an eye on my activities. I comforted myself with the knowledge that unless they'd got carefully hidden cameras they could not have seen me checking out the secret room. The sooner I got rid of this place, the better, I decided. I must get to a phone and tell the solicitor of my latest discovery.

The thought crossed my mind that two out the three properties I had recently inherited had secret rooms that were full of contraband. In quick succession I asked myself three questions. First, did the cottage at Cliffsend also have a secret hideaway? Second, had my grandfather known about them? Third, if he did, was it not on the cards that Nigel Crompton also knew? There was now even a fourth question that needed an answer. If he was aware of the contraband, I had just alerted him to the fact that I had discovered the Lydden loot. What would he do?

Suspicion is a dreadful thing. Had the solicitor's suggestion of possible injury or disappearance been an indirect warning to me? Yet, on the other hand, he was going to tell someone about my discovery. Then again, he did not want the police involved but some other person whom he knew and I did not. Faced with such a situation, one can only trust one's instincts. I found a phone box and telephoned the solicitor. He suggested I return to him at once.

Ten minutes later I was back in his office and told him about Wakefield Place. This old man, a friend of my grandfather was immediately on the phone, presumably to the same person he had spoken to earlier. He turned to me and asked, 'Can you stay down here until Wednesday?' I nodded and he merely said, 'Yes,' to the person at the other end and put the phone down.

Nigel Crompton turned to me and assured me with a smile, 'We'll need to be a little careful but I think we can resolve this with only the villains ending up in big trouble. Leave this with me, David. Don't go anywhere near the farm or the big house. Just carry on with what you intended and give me a ring about 10 o'clock tomorrow.'

86

I thanked him, feeling a little easier in my mind and a little foolish for thinking the old man might be involved – but only until I got outside his office and the nagging thoughts began again. I'd never come up against smugglers before. Up to a point I still held a somewhat glamorous picture of harmless villains able to put one over on the government. If anyone was able to get away without paying excise duty on a few items, it was fair game. I got the impression that this was big game with big stakes, and that implied big problems and bigger sentences if the villains were caught.

I appreciated that I was out of my depth. I must accept the old man's advice to stay away and let him and his associates deal with it. Or maybe I should tell my friends. How would they react? Frank would be the most useful ally to recruit. Roger might also be helpful, especially if he brought along some of his mechanics. My imagination began to run riot with little thought for the practicalities of the situation. I felt sure they would help if I was in real trouble, but it was another thing to go looking for it. Then common sense prevailed. Why did I need help when I had no idea who was behind all this? No. I must keep this to myself for the time being at least.

I suppose if I'd been 20 years younger I might have set up camp at Wakefield Place, armed myself and waited for the smugglers to arrive. Fortunately, as we grow older we usually become wiser and now, months after the events, I'm glad I left most of the action to the authorities. As it happens I did become involved, though not intentionally. Circumstances decided that I should be in the right place at the right time.

16

Exchange of News

It was later than I had intended when I finally reached my base at the Wheatsheaf. The pub was already open for its evening customers, so I went in and bought a whisky and asked the landlord if I might stay on until Wednesday, then I would definitely be going back up north. He didn't seem to mind, so I returned to my home on wheels and cooked myself cheese on toast again for quickness.

I lay down on my bunk to mull over the events of the day and promptly fell asleep. I awoke with a start and was relieved to find it was 7.30, so there was time to wash and change before meeting Helen. I was looking forward to seeing her again, though events of the day had put her out of my mind for a while. For a moment I began to speculate on who she was and what she did. It didn't really matter. In the few days I'd known her I had come to like her. We got on well together. In fact since that first meeting at the Captain Digby it was surprising how well we had got on and how many different things we'd done.

When I reached her home, the light was on in the porch. She opened the door, smiled and said, 'Good evening, David. It's good to see you again. Did you have a good day?'

'Yes, and no. I'll tell you about it later. It's been hectic. I hope your day was all right.'

'Yes, thanks. Do come in. I've eaten but if you haven't I can get you a scrambled egg or something.'

'I'm fine, thanks. It's you I've come to see. Is Joyce in?'

'No, she's gone to see a film with a friend.'

I followed Helen into the lounge, where the TV was showing what was happening in the world at large. Helen switched it off saying, 'We can catch up on news later. Tell me about your day.'

I decided not to tell her about all the contraband so I related quite truthfully most of what I'd done. 'I've seen my solicitor again, and it's just possible that I may be able to rent the farm to a cousin of Frank's. We'll try to rent the cottage at Cliffsend but the real problem is the big house along Ramsgate Road. It's a puzzle to me where the old man got the money to pay for it all.'

'Didn't you say he had sold off part of the farm some time ago? Maybe he bought it then.'

'Yes, I never thought of that. In fact, I have yet to find out who was living there and why it's empty now. By the way, I'm staying down here at least until Wednesday so maybe we can go out for a meal.'

'That would be nice, but I've got a busy week ahead so I may have to cancel. I'm a buyer for Bon Marché, so life can be a bit hectic at times – challenging too. It's vital to get the right fashions at the right price and ahead of the opposition.'

'I can see that. Do you get many trips abroad?'

'A few, usually to France but occasionally to Italy. In three months' time we'll be talking about spring fashions and six months later it will be the autumn collection. It took me a while to get used to thinking six months or a year in advance but it's almost second nature now.'

'What a busy life you lead. Are you happy?'

'Yes of course. I haven't got time to be otherwise. I may as well tell you I'm divorced, I have a good job that

I like, I can do just what I wish and I have no financial worries.'

'I don't need to know the details.'

'I'll tell you anyway and then there will be no secrets between us. The divorce was messy. He didn't like me going abroad, there were other women and I wasn't prepared to share. He's out of my life and the only good thing I got from that marriage is Joyce. She thinks she looks after me but she has her own life to lead.'

'So you've got the best of both worlds. I don't doubt you have plenty of boyfriends.'

'Well, not really. It's my own fault. After the divorce I didn't want to get involved with anyone. A few tried but I put them off. Now nobody bothers, although they are all fairly friendly.'

I didn't quite know how to respond to that. Was Helen warning me off too? She was a warm, friendly woman and it did not seem possible that she didn't have a man about somewhere. Then again, I didn't have anyone. Indeed, I had never considered another wife or partner, and I was not unhappy.

There was an awkward pause in the conversation. Whatever either of us said next would probably be wrong. The silence lengthened. I looked across at Helen and thought I could detect tears in her eyes. She got up. 'Excuse me a moment while I put the kettle on,' and left the room. Then I heard a key in the front door and Joyce called out, 'I'm home.'

She came into the lounge, and I said 'Hello. Did you enjoy the film?'

'The first part was all right. Then they had a fire in the projection room so after waiting half an hour they said we could use the tickets another day. Where's mum?'

'She's in the kitchen.'

Joyce went to see her mother and I could hear them

90

talking. I glanced through the newspaper and then Joyce came into the room with a tray, coffee and a few sandwiches. 'Mum will be down in a minute. She's gone up to change as she spilt water all down her front.'

'Anything I can do?'

'No. It's all taken care of.'

'So how did your trip to Chichester go?'

'Oh I think they approved of me. In fact they were quite charming considering I'm taking away their only child.'

'That's life. I'm sure they are relieved to know he will be in such capable hands.'

'My, my, you're a real smoothie.'

'So when is the happy day?'

'Soon I hope. No point in long engagements. The only trouble is finding somewhere to live. I don't want to go too far away from mum and John doesn't want to travel too far each day.'

'Where does he work then?'

'He's a research chemist at Frentons, just outside Sandwich. It's a big international company but of course John is only a small cog. They think quite highly of him but we don't want to buy anything until he's settled in. I'll continue to work for a while yet.'

It was small talk, filling in the time until Helen returned and yet it was pleasant enough. Quite out of the blue I wondered if I might have solved at least one of my problems.

'Did Helen tell you about our trip out to Cliffsend the other day?'

'Yes. She quite liked it. I think she remembers the lavender fields there – nothing like as big as those in Norfolk but pretty enough.'

'You know I inherited two cottages, one of which is vacant. If you'd like to have a look at it I would be glad to take you over one day. It might suit you very well for the time being.'

'That's very kind of you Mr Holden. May I think about it and tell John.'

'Of course. Don't worry if you don't want it. I just thought it might help us both. I have no need of it and you said you would be looking for somewhere to rent.'

'What would you want for it?'

'No idea, the same as the one next door, I suppose. We'll leave it to the solicitor to sort out if you really want it. Go and see it first. You may hate it, but it's only a couple of miles from Sandwich. I don't have a lot of time to take you there myself. Helen knows the way. I'll leave the key with her and you can go whenever you wish. Just drop the key back to the solicitor when you've finished'

'What a kind man you are. Mum said so the first time you met. Thanks.'

Joyce told me more about her fiancé, how they had met and his job as a research chemist at Frentons. She mentioned her father almost as an afterthought. Maybe he was not dead but he was certainly not included in their present life. Then Joyce asked about my family. In hindsight she did it quite skilfully and I had no sense of being quizzed. I didn't really mind.

In fact it was a pleasant few minutes getting to know about each other. I found myself talking more about my family than I had done in years.

17

An Understanding

Helen came into the room saying, 'Sorry about that, David. Clumsy of me. I see Joyce has been looking after you.'

'Yes thanks.'

'Mum, Mr Holden wonders whether John and I would like to rent his cottage at Cliffsend. You know, the one you saw the other day.'

Helen turned to me. 'Are you sure? That's really very kind. It's not all that far from John's work. Did Joyce tell you she's working in the Ramsgate area, so it would be ideal in many ways.'

'Mr Holden will give you the key. We can go and have a look at any time and if we don't like it he says he doesn't mind.'

I thought I'd better say something, 'That's true. No pressure at all. If you decide to take it, that will be one problem less for me to worry about. I could take Joyce sometime tomorrow but otherwise I'm busy. And on Thursday at the latest I have to see how my new house is coming along. Did I tell you I was having one built at Higham in Derbyshire?'

Helen got up. 'I'll just check my diary. I'll just see if I can manage to come tomorrow. If not Joyce and I will go later in the week.'

'No problem and no hurry. Sort it out later. Do come and sit down. Lovely sandwiches. If I make sandwiches they turn out to be doorstops.'

Joyce and her mother sat together on the settee while I stretched out in an easy chair. 'That old chalk pit was a surprise. I wonder where they managed to find all those old machines,' I began.

Helen answered, 'I think they probably got them from Dreamland or those amusement places along the seafront. I never knew that the Smugglers Retreat existed but it was very enterprising of whoever thought to put it in a hole in the ground.' Then she changed the subject. 'David, you know my story. It's your turn now. What do you do?'

I felt myself going a bit red – absurd really at my age. 'Well, at the moment I don't do anything. I am, as they say, between jobs. Mind you, with my recently acquired wealth I may never work again. But I haven't always been idle. I came out of the army about nine years ago and almost immediately landed a very good job with an electronics firm in Cambridge. Then after six years, during which time the firm did extremely well and I got rapid promotion, it was taken over by a big Dutch company. I was asked to stay on and head my own research department but it would have meant moving to Holland. I didn't want that so I resigned and they gave me a nice golden handshake. With my army pension Anne and I were quite well off. I'd been in the army since I was a lad so it was still a challenge to think for myself. Then, three years later, Anne, my mum and dad were returning from a holiday in Canada and they were all killed in an air crash. It was a tough time after that. I stayed put until Alex and June, my children, were off my hands and then I sold the family home. Too many memories.'

I stayed lost in thought for a few moments. I don't think I'd ever spoken so long about myself. I'd left out the harrowing bits about the Falklands but at least

Helen knew the bare bones of my life and I was glad she did.

'Would you like to know more about my new house?' I didn't wait for them to say yes but continued, 'Basically it's a bungalow with a large detached garage. The land at the rear slopes away sharply and faces west. My architect suggested that I add three rooms at the lower level. I agreed, and as a joke said I'd like a turret room on top, and he thought it was a good idea. It will provide a glorious view of the countryside all round and if I ever take up painting or require solitude it will be ideal. I've met a few people and made one or two friends, including the vicar and his wife. It's quite a small village but it has all the basic needs, and it's in a delightful part of the country. Once I've settled in, you must both come and visit me.'

They had both remained silent and now as I looked across at them I could see Joyce holding her mother's hand while Helen was quietly weeping. She got up suddenly and left the room.

'I'm sorry, Joyce. Did I say something to upset Helen?'

'No, it's all right. She'll be down in a minute. She's not really the hard-bitten business woman that most people see. She feels things deeply and I think it was your wife's death that upset her.'

Helen came back into the room and I rose to meet her.

She came towards me, smiling. 'Silly me.'

I held out my arms and she came into them. I held her close, really to comfort her, but it had the opposite effect. I felt her trembling in my arms and realised she was weeping again. I turned to Joyce and suggested she should take Helen upstairs to bed. I waited for 15 minutes or so, then thought I'd better leave quietly. I was scribbling a note on the back of an envelope I found in my pocket when Joyce returned.

'I'm sorry, Mr Holden. Mum asks you to excuse her.'

'That's all right. I'm sorry too. What do you think really upset her?'

'To be honest, I think it was many things. You won't ever tell her this, will you?'

'Of course not.'

'She was a bit overwhelmed with the kindness shown by your friends, and your original help with her car and then taking her over to Cliffsend. Then your wife's death and the memory of the bad time she had with my father was all a bit too much.'

Joyce hesitated for a while. Maybe she was turning over in her mind whether or not she should tell me about her father. In the end she explained.

'I was about fourteen, and although they tried to keep it from me, it was obvious the marriage was breaking up. I tried to be even-handed but in my heart I knew it wasn't mum's fault. He had a string of women, introduced to us as sisters or cousins, and in the end mum couldn't stand it any longer. Even the divorce hearing was messy and he tried to get me to support him. By then I knew the truth and was glad when he finally left. We haven't seen him since.'

'Thanks for telling me, Joyce. Say goodbye to your mother for me. I've put the key to the cottage in this envelope. I'll be in touch soon.'

'Goodnight, Mr Holden.'

'Why not make it David? We're friends now, aren't we?'

Joyce smiled and I left.

18

Plan of Action

I began to wonder how the mystery man at the other end of the phone was planning to apprehend the smugglers, so I telephoned Nigel Crompton. He merely confirmed that things were going ahead as planned, whatever that meant. 'Go and see some of your friends and we'll meet again tomorrow afternoon,' was his final word.

I didn't intend to see anyone but drove out towards Wakefield Place and parked the car well short of the entrance. The double gates at the front were wide open and parked inside I could see a couple of builders' vans and a much larger removals van. A number of workmen were scurrying about carrying planks of timber, scaffolding and bricks. It looked as if renovations were in progress, yet I owned the property and I had authorised no such work.

Could it be that the smugglers were giving the impression of legitimate operations, or was I watching 'things going ahead as planned'? As I walked slowly past, no one bothered to glance in my direction. I wished I'd had a dog so that I could let it off the leash and hope it would go inside. I could then follow in to retrieve it and possibly get a closer look at the work. I did the next best thing. I retraced my steps to the shops near the traffic lights and bought a packet of cigarettes. Back on the road once more, I walked boldly through the gates and called to one of the men, 'Got a light, mate?' He never replied but tapped his jacket pocket and pulled out a box of matches. I took them, lit a cigarette and offered one to him. He declined.

Even up close I did not get much of a chance to see exactly what was going on in my property. I did see rolls of cable being taken indoors and several boxes of electronic equipment that seemed vaguely familiar. They could be setting up listening devices and cameras. If that was the case they were in the wrong place. They should be at the back and concentrating on the summer house. In spite of Crompton's warning, I found myself wanting to get involved. I walked back to the car and drove it the long way round so that I could observe the house from the back. The broken hedge by the roadside made it quite easy for anyone wishing to unload stuff not far from the house. All they had to do was cross the old railway track, walk up the slight incline and they were at my boundary. One person could unload the contraband while another could carry it across to the back garden. Then they could join forces to get it tucked out of sight in the secret room.

No activity like that was going on at present but I could see several 'builders' on the roof of the house, and from my observation post they were not building anything but laying cables. They were definitely installing some listening device and camera set-up. I hoped the cables and cameras would be well hidden.

In my wing mirror I caught sight of a policeman on a motorcycle approaching. I quickly extinguished my cigarette and pretended to be resting with my eyes closed. A gentle tap on the side window roused me from my slumbers and I feigned surprise as I wound down the window.

'Sorry to interrupt your dreams, sir. We're having to

close this road for a day or so. I'm afraid you will have to finish your beauty sleep somewhere else.'

'What's happening?'

'Oh I think they've got a water leak and don't quite know where it is. Do you come this way often?'

'No. When are they going to start?'

'About another hour, I should think, but you'd better go now or they will have blocked the other end of the road. Go to the end of this road, turn left if you want to go to Ramsgate and then right at the traffic lights. Go right if you're going to Sandwich.'

'OK. Thanks.' I started the engine and as I went past the policeman I tooted my horn and he waved back. At the end of the road, where I turned right as though going to Sandwich I saw workmen erecting a notice board – *Road Closed*. I turned off at the next left and made my way to Ramsgate harbour. I hadn't been there for years. There were many more boats than before and a large ferry port had been constructed, the point of entry for many foreign cars now coming into Britain.

I found the harbourmaster's office, knocked and went in. 'Is there a customs office here?'

'Well yes, but not this morning. They've gone over to the hoverport, but I can get someone over if you want customs clearance.'

'I don't, thanks. I just want some information.'

'Well, go out from the harbour and follow the signs. You can't miss them.'

I thanked him and left. It had suddenly occurred to me that without asking too many questions I might discover what checks they adopted to look out for goods entering the country. I found their information office without difficulty and three customs officials were just coming on duty, two men and a woman. I was glancing at a poster when the girl left her companions, came over to me and asked, 'Anything to declare, sir?'

I turned and didn't recognise her at first. I was about to say, 'No,' when I realised it was Joyce Carlyle.

'Hello, Joyce. What's a nice girl like you doing in a place like this?'

Without batting an eyelid she replied, 'Looking out for thieves and evaders. Of course, you didn't know I worked here. Seriously, can I help you?'

'Well, I wanted to know if there's a booklet outlining the work of the customs, what one may bring in and the penalties for trying to evade duty.'

'What have you been up to? I'll have to keep an eye on you. Come this way.' Joyce had put on a stern official voice and shepherded me towards an information clerk. 'Sam, can you help this gentleman? I think he wants to bring in stuff without paying.'

Fortunately I saw the wink she gave the man.

'Sorry I've got to go. I'm on duty. See you later.'

I turned to the clerk. 'I was wondering if there's a booklet or even a book about customs and excise, how the service works and what success you've had in catching criminals. I'm writing a book and I need to get the part of it concerned with customs as accurate as possible.' The lies just tripped off my tongue.

'We don't have anything like that here, and in any case unless we deliberately want the public to know, we keep our successes to ourselves. You could try one of the bookshops in town or the library.'

I thanked the man, got back in my car and headed for my parking space at the back of the Wheatsheaf. I needed rest, peace and time to go over in my mind all the facts and emotions that crowded my thoughts. Something was definitely happening at Wakefield Place. To any casual observer it was being renovated for

100

possible new tenants and the removals van had arrived too soon. But I knew there were no new tenants and the only work that was being done was additional security measures. There was also the temporary road closure. On the other hand, if the customs and the police were setting a trap for the smugglers, what better ruse than to close the road until they had completed their work.

Today I had discovered quite by chance that Joyce Carlyle was a customs officer. True, she had been in uniform but I reckoned they had plain-clothes people too. The chances that she knew anything about Wakefield Place or Lydden were remote and I didn't see how I could broach the subject to her without raising unnecessary alarms.

And thinking of all that was going on at Wakefield Place I wondered what might be going on at Lydden. I had told the solicitor about my discovery at the farm. Perhaps covert operations were going on there as well. Had the officials already set the trap at both places, or were the people at Wakefield Place the actual smugglers getting ready to move the loot? If that were the case, who had tipped them off?

My peaceful interlude was having the opposite effect. More questions than answers were appearing. There was one factor that linked both properties. My grandfather had owned both and Mr Crompton had been his friend. Maybe they were both aware of the secret rooms and the contraband. I felt almost ashamed to think that my grandfather, such an honest man, could have been involved. Maybe it was just the solicitor who had been involved right from the start.

The one thing, that didn't really make sense was the fact that however much money the smugglers could raise from the goods I had seen, they could scarcely have made a living out of it. There must be other locations.

Indeed, it would be easy to acquire any number of storage depots around the harbour or at several farms in the neighbourhood. Numerous depots would invariably mean many people, and unless they were doing it part-time they would need to be paid. Maybe there were dozens of people involved, and if that were so my little collection of contraband was merely the tip of the iceberg.

There now came to mind another possible answer. There seemed little doubt that stuff was being brought into the country but unless there were many more secret locations the amount of money involved was hardly worth the risk – unless drugs were also being smuggled in. I'd read the papers and heard about the ingenious hiding places these people used, like false floorboards in vehicles and spare tyres. It would be easy to hide drugs in with the cartons of cigarettes or crates of booze.

Manston Airport, on the outskirts of both Margate and Ramsgate, is an old RAF station. Only a small area is now occupied by the Royal Air Force, the remainder being used as a freight terminal and passenger airport for charter firms. Yet another part of this huge war-time base is used as a civil flying club. Thinking about this, I began to appreciate how easy it would be to fly over to the Continent, pick up small quantities of drugs or booze and return almost undetected, especially if one flew low over the Channel.

My mind turned to grander ideas of customs evasion. By using freight aircraft, huge quantities could be flown in, and I felt sure that the customs could not check every consignment. Some could even be dropped on the marshes close to the airport. My imagination was going into overdrive, and I remembered Nigel Crompton's words about too much television.

19

Another Way to Skin a Cat

This affair had many ramifications, what with the hidden contraband and old army observation posts. There must surely be a way to get at the truth and find out who was responsible. One possible lead came to me quite soon. After lunch I drove down to the council offices and made enquiries about the rates of Wakefield Place and its last tenant. I thought I might have to make a formal application or even come back next week. However, the young man I spoke to seemed quite happy to answer a few questions.

He got out a huge ledger, flipped over a few pages and said, 'Here we are, owned by Charles Holden of Lydden Farm. There's also a note to the effect that he has recently died. Rates have been paid up till next March, so if there was a tenant he may have paid an inclusive rent to Charles Holden. We don't have that information but I can tell you that if the place has been unoccupied there should be a reduction in the rates and I imagine that will be taken into account when probate is proved. You could always check the electoral roll to see who resided there.'

I wasn't any wiser, but my grandfather or his solicitor must have kept records, so I would have to ask Nigel Crompton tomorrow. My next stop was the library, where there was quite an extensive reference section. The librarian was older than me, though not old enough to remember what happened locally in 1940. However, in answer to my query about local units of the Home Guard he consulted his computer terminal. One entry referred him to a couple of books and a folder that he retrieved and handed to me.

It didn't give much in the way of the location of pillboxes or hideouts – merely the name of the local commander, a certain Colonel Whitts, together with a brief note of when the unit had been formed and disbanded. One of the books was a brief history collected by members a few years after the war. The second book seemed to cover units of the Home Guard and the Auxiliary Units throughout the country. The small section covering Thanet was no help at all. However, there was a bibliography and one entry looked promising. I asked the librarian if I could see a copy. 'Sorry sir, we did have one in the lending library but it was never returned and it's now out of print. What was it you specially wanted to know?'

'Well, I think I've discovered a hideout and I wanted to know more about it.'

'I could try to borrow a copy from another library.'

'Well, I haven't got a ticket and don't live here any more.'

I thanked him and made a note of the book. I hadn't got very far with my research but I did have a few more questions to put to Nigel Crompton, and this time I would be a little more forceful in getting answers. The library also had copies of the electoral roll but no one seemed to live at Wakefield Place. Unfortunately the voters' list only covered Margate, and as Lydden was outside the boundary I thought I had wasted my time. The librarian came to my rescue. A local directory covered not only Margate but also the outlying villages. Each house was listed, and the senior member of the household, so I made a note of all my farm workers. I know I could probably have got them from the farm manager but I needed to do a little research on my own, even if it got me nowhere.

None of the names meant anything to me. Well, they wouldn't. If people had been in the habit of smuggling they would certainly not advertise the fact and their entries in the directory would not carry the designation 'smuggler'.

The war had been over a long time yet Nigel Crompton, one of those soldiers, was still alive. It was just possible that Colonel Whitts might also be around. I found a telephone box but the directory was missing so I went to the main post office in Cecil Square. There were two names of possible interest and then a little further down the page, probably the man I wanted but spelt without an H. He still retained his army rank, although I realised it might be his son.

I telephoned the number and got an answer almost at once, 'I'm sorry the Colonel is not here at present. May I help you?'

I explained part of my interest in the Colonel and was surprised when the person at the other end said, 'Yes sir. I'm sure the Colonel could spare you a few minutes. May I have your name and could you call back about three-thirty?'

I gave my name and my old army rank. Well, I could always explain when I saw him that I was no longer in the army. When I rang later he asked me to come round at once and greeted me warmly. It seemed that he had been the officer in charge of the Home Guard in the Margate area. Previously he had been a career soldier and had only retired at the beginning of 1939. He was recalled and went to France with the BEF. He had scrambled aboard one of the last transports to leave in

1940. His group and quite a few RAF personnel had escaped from Dunkirk, made their way down to La Rochelle and been brought off by the navy.

Almost immediately he had been put in charge of the Local Defence Force, subsequently the Home Guard. He recruited a band of old soldiers, officers, NCOs and other ranks and began to forge them into a useful command that covered the area from The North Foreland to Birchington. They had captured a number of German aircrews but apart from a couple of false alarms had had an uneventful war. Being close to one of the anticipated invasion areas, they had been issued with guns and ammunition almost from day one. As far as he was aware no one under his command had only a broomstick or a pitchfork as a weapon to repel the invader.

I could sense he was still aggrieved at that image of the Home Guard and I tried to steer the conversation towards his knowledge of that other army, the secret army – the Auxiliary Units.

At last it seemed he had got his own story off his chest as he turned to me. 'Holden. I know that name. No. Don't tell me. It'll come to me. Ah yes. 1940. Charlie Holden and his friend, Crompton. Couple of good blokes.'

I took the bull by the horns. 'That's what I've come to see you about, sir. Charlie was my grandfather. He died recently and I've inherited his farm at Lydden. Can you tell me anything about his involvement with the Auxiliary Units?'

'Ah. So you know about those, do you? Well, it's no secret now but at the time very few people knew of their existence. A couple of my senior officers and I were the only ones here who knew. Holden and Crompton were both patrol leaders. Over at Birchington there was

106

Holness. Stannard looked after Westgate and Solomon was at Kingsgate.'

Once started, Colonel Whitts never seemed to want to stop. As far as he recalled the men in the Auxiliary Units had special training and special weapons. He even remembered the secret arms dump that had been found at Wakefield Place. 'Funny thing, that. The war had been over for years. All the weapons were recalled in 1945. Then in 1960 someone found that one. Of course by then no one in the present army or the local police knew anything. Someone remembered that I had been in the Home Guard and I was able to verify that it had nothing whatever to do with current problems. I'm not sure the police believed me but the army sent down the Royal Engineers and they took away the stuff in three army lorries and blew it up. Most of the food was still edible, would you believe?'

I thanked the Colonel for his time. He seemed pleased that someone had been interested in his story and asked me to look in whenever I wished. I don't know that I had got very far forward but at least I knew a little more about the history of the time. I could imagine Charlie and Nigel taking their posts as patrol leaders seriously.

I went to the cinema that evening and saw a film about smugglers, *Dr Syn on the High Seas*. It was quite entertaining but didn't give me any clues as to modern day smuggling techniques.

20

A Few Answers

Nigel Crompton was just as friendly as ever. Any thoughts that I may have harboured about him being in league with the smugglers were quickly dispelled with his first few words.

'David. Things are moving quickly. I've been authorised to tell you only about the activities in your properties. However, it seems that this sort of thing is quite prevalent. The customs people have been on the lookout for ages and when I was able to tell them the location of two possible hideouts they were delighted. They've known about these people for months but have never been able to find where the loot was stored. Of course, in order to make a charge stick they have to catch the bad guys with the goods. Also they dare not move too soon or they will only catch the small fry, the carriers, not the brains behind the organisation.

'Since I spoke to the authorities on Monday it seems they have had teams installing a good deal of equipment so that when the next shipment arrives – or what is already there is moved – they will have photographic and audio evidence that is good enough for the courts. It seems that the customs, and to some extent the police, are good at playing the waiting game.'

I congratulated him and asked him about the people who had previously lived at Wakefield Place. 'Oh, that was rented out to Pierre Lareux. He was the Belgian ambassador and used it as his country retreat. He had quite a large family and his wife and children lived there for much of the time, and he often came down at weekends. He was recalled suddenly and after about a month the family went back to Belgium. Your grandfather never let it out to anyone else, hoping they would return.'

'So where did he get the money to buy the mansion in the first place?'

'Is that what has been worrying you? Well, let me tell you, everything is perfectly legitimate. Many years ago he sold off two hundred acres of the farm and two cottages. With the proceeds he bought Wakefield Place, intending to retire from the farm and live there with your gran. Your father would then have taken over the running of the farm. That plan fell through when he was killed and then your gran died. Charles didn't want to live there on his own so he stayed on at the farm. Through my contacts I found him someone to rent the place and when that person left after a couple of years it was he who recommended the ambassador.'

'Thanks for telling me. I did just wonder how he had acquired all this property. Do you mind me asking, did grandfather remember you in his will?'

'We did discuss it when he drew up the will. I thought it would have been inappropriate so he insisted on buying me some shares in an oil company. That was a few years ago. I'll tell you, he was very astute when it came to money and I have done very well with his gift. In fact there really is no need for me to go on working.'

I was glad the old man had not been forgotten and I guessed the gift must have been fairly substantial. 'Mr Crompton, I, of course, have my own solicitor. Shall I continue with him or change to you?'

'I think my advice would be to keep your own. Give me his name and I'll write to him.'

'Thanks, but could you wait until I've found one nearer Higham? My present one is in Cambridge. I know he's only a phone call away but I prefer to meet face to face whenever possible. So what do we do about the smugglers, and are the authorities checking out the farm as well?'

'Leave everything to them. As I said, they've been trying to catch them for some time, but never knew where the stuff was kept until you stumbled on two hoards. Its quite on the cards that you'll be in for a reward.'

'To them that hath it shall be given' was my comment.

'Yes I know. It was ever thus,' he replied.

'Well, if it comes to anything, why don't I leave you to do whatever is necessary. Give it to your favourite charity.'

I remembered the man with the dog I had seen on the old railway track and told the solicitor. 'He said he lived about a mile away at Westwood but I never checked and I don't know his name.' Crompton made a note on a pad and said he'd pass on the information. It seemed that all manner of small pieces of information were collated and sifted to fit into an overall picture. I got the distinct impression that the solicitor was enjoying this diversion from his normal work.

'I had intended to return to Higham tomorrow. Shall I still go?' I asked.

'Well, yes. There's nothing to keep you here. The customs people will let the farm manager know if they deem it necessary to check there. Their chief wondered if he could get a couple of his men pretending to look round on the pretence of buying it. I gather they have already checked your story about the secret room and

110

found it absolutely full. It will need to be moved before any more can be stored there, so they are hoping to follow whoever takes it.'

'In that case I'll definitely return to Higham but I'll be back in a few weeks. It's just possible that I may have found someone to rent the cottage at Pegwell Bay.'

'Ah yes. Mr Bull got in touch with me. I haven't replied yet but I think it will be in order for him to have the key to next door. He'll look after the place and continue to use the garden and its produce. He doesn't really want anything as a key holder but I'll suggest a nominal £52 a year. Is that agreeable?'

'Yes, of course. By the way, what does he pay in rent?'

The old man consulted a ledger. 'He pays the rates and water rate direct and has a standing order with his bank to pay into our account £200 a month. That's £2,400 a year. We take 10 per cent and the balance is paid into your bank. You'd better let me have the details of your bank before you leave. The rent is reviewed each year and next year will probably go up by three per cent. That is the figure I would suggest if you rent the other property.'

'The young lady's name is Joyce Carlyle and she's getting married soon to a chap who works at Frentons in Sandwich. I've met both of them. As a matter of fact she's a customs officer at Ramsgate and works at the hoverport. I've let her have my key, but if she doesn't want the house her mother will return the key to you.'

'Ah yes, and she is presumably Mrs Carlyle. Where does she figure in all this and where does she live?'

So I told him briefly how we had met and what we had done since. He wanted to know more but as I explained there was no more. I reminded him again of Frank Thompson's cousin who might be interested in renting the farm at Lydden.

111

'You know, David, I've been thinking about that. Of course probate has yet to be proved. I can see no problem there but inevitably these things take time. It's one thing to rent out a vacant cottage, and I can take care of that. But a working farm with several cottages and people to consider is another thing altogether. Ultimately it will be your decision, but if I may just suggest your grandfather would probably not have rented it out. He would not have wished to move his tenants.'

'Well, that settles it then. We'll keep everything as it is for the moment. That leaves Wakefield Place.'

'Yes, it's a lovely house. I'd be inclined to hang on to it for a while. It's been empty for almost six months. Charlie called in a couple of times to make sure everything was all right. He really liked that house. It would have been far too big for him and your gran really, but there you go. We could put out feelers in case someone of the multi-nationals or one of the big banks would like to develop it as a training centre or a holiday resort, or even a retirement home. There are at least a hundred acres of grounds and some of those could be used as a riding school. There's the potential for a couple of tennis courts and enough ground to grow its own vegetables if it was turned into a residential establishment.'

I could see the old man had already given it a lot of thought. I must get everything in perspective, I certainly did not want to upset the farm workers at Lydden, and at the same time I didn't want to be lumbered with too much responsibility. What to do with Wakefield Place was my real concern. I would have to look at all the options. But I decided to leave everything in his hands for the moment.

21

Tidying up Loose Ends

I felt a little calmer now in my mind. The solicitor had taken time to reassure me that plans were in hand to apprehend the customs evaders. Even so, and in spite of my inactivity in recent years, I found it difficult to stand aside and do nothing, especially as it was happening on my property.

My years in the army had taught me how to take care of myself. Now in civilian life I had to play by a totally different set of rules. In spite of the warnings from the old man to stay away, the more I thought about it the more I wanted to get closer to the action. Common sense told me I was only one man against – well, I didn't know how many. I had no weapons, and though I could probably acquire a shotgun, it would take some time to convince the police that I really needed one, especially as I didn't live locally. If I really needed a weapon it would have to be acquired illegally, and I didn't know the first thing about getting one.

I didn't want to involve any of my friends, and in any case none of us was young any more. I'm sure we could all give a good account of ourselves, but if we did manage to confront the villains there was always the possibility that one of us might be injured. I didn't really like to admit it, but the problem was for someone else to solve.

I wondered how Helen was, but as she was probably at

work, I decided to go over to the hoverport on the off chance of seeing Joyce. I smiled to myself as I drove there. I can be quite devious at times. Fortunately, a different chap was in the office.

'Good morning. I wonder if you could tell me if Joyce Carlyle is on duty or when she is expected.'

'I'm sorry, sir. We don't give out information about our staff but I could take a message.'

'I understand. I have a key to give her. I'll wait if I may.'

Just then Joyce and another customs officer came out, having finished their shift. She saw me and came over with a question in her eyes.

'Hello Joyce. I just wanted to know if your mother was feeling better. I didn't like to enquire directly and in any case I expect she's working. Hope you don't mind me calling over to see you.'

'No, of course not. Mum is quite resilient really and she's a bit cross with herself.'

'It's good to know that she's feeling better. I have to go back to Higham tomorrow morning so there isn't much time for me to see her. I've spoken to the solicitor about the cottage and there will be no problem if you decide to rent it even though probate has not yet been proved. The new rent would be £206.'

'Thanks very much, David. I can see why Mum likes you. You're so thoughtful.'

I didn't know what to reply so I said nothing. I walked with her to her car and watched as she drove away. Then I went to the Bull's cottage and explained that I had given the key to a friend who might be renting it and she would be calling on them soon.

I didn't think I'd have time to visit my friends before I headed back up north, so I wrote them each an almost identical note explaining that I must return to Higham to see how my new home was progressing and promised to see them again very soon. For the moment all my letters were sent to the post office in the village, so I gave them that as my current address.

It had been good to see them all, and in spite of the long absence we had all got on very well. I remembered again some of the things we had done as kids. At grammar school we always had Wednesday afternoons off, not free but for sports. During the summer months we played cricket on the school pitch, and way over on the far side there were four tennis courts. I don't think we ever played soccer at school although there was plenty of room for a couple of pitches. That whole area was devoted to our athletics where once a year we had inter-house activities.

The grass was kept short, although the only time the complete field was used was the annual sports and parents day. Then there were refreshment tents and a few discreet sideshows such as coconut shies. As soon as the races were over came the prize-giving and various speeches.

For soccer and rugby we went about two miles away to a huge sports complex. There were probably 20 pitches in use at any one time, and a number of local schools took advantage of the venue. However, not every Wednesday afternoon was given over to sport. If we managed to skive off we disappeared into Ramsgate, met the girls from their grammar school who were also playing truant and had teas or ice creams in one of the many places down by the harbour. Those who happened to be flush with funds went to one of the arcades and usually lost their money. It was pleasant to recall those memories, but there were more important things that needed attention.

My next job was to check over my motor home so that I would be ready for an early morning start.

I called in at the Wheatsheaf, had a last drink and a final meal there and got back to my camp site for an early night. All my problems faded into a dreamless sleep and I woke up refreshed. Well, I didn't really have any problems. I just needed answers to certain questions and an end to the smugglers using my premises to store their loot. I still felt aggrieved that I couldn't tackle it first hand, as it were.

Much as I regretted having to leave others to sort out the smuggling activities on my properties, the thought kept returning as to what I could actually do if I happened to be there. I don't know why my mind refused to accept that I must delegate the responsibility. I suppose deep down we all like to be masters of our own destiny.

By the time I was on my way I had settled down to the job in hand. The first few miles of the journey were uneventful, that is until I reached the AA box at the beginning of the Thanet Way. In the lay-by a mechanic was obviously trying to sort out a mechanical problem. Three people, very well dressed, stood by the telephone box and I slowed down and eased into the lay-by. An AA man came over to me and said, 'Good morning. Are you going to London?'

'Well, yes. Anything I can do?'

'Bit of a problem here. Two wedding guests and the best man have been delayed. We think we can get the car going again but not in time for the wedding. I wonder if you could take the best man? At least he will be at the wedding and the guests can be there for the reception.'

The best man needed to be in Bexleyheath at noon. That wasn't really much out of my way so with his profuse thanks we set off. This interlude had nothing whatever to do with the main story, but as other events

116

had sprung from unlikely beginnings it was always on the cards that this Good Samaritan offer might lead to something.

22

Higham, Derbyshire

The journey back to Higham was tedious. Traffic through London was unusually light but once north of the capital, it ground to a halt on the motorway, a sure sign that there was a major problem ahead. As we crawled slowly forward I resolved to take the next exit and find an alternative route.

Once in the relative peace of a minor road, I made myself a cup of tea and wrote down directions to reach Higham so that I could check my route rather than having to constantly refer to my road atlas. Three hours later I reached the village and it was just as sleepy as when I had left. This was the haven of tranquillity I needed after all I had encountered in Margate. It was almost worth the tedious journey just to be here.

I'd only been away 11 days, and in that time the walls of my bungalow had risen by about four feet, including the three rooms along the back at the lower level, which would be reached by a spiral stairway.

When I arrived on the site, three men were still hard at work. In the beginning, what the builder called his heavy gang had made short work of clearing the area where the bungalow would be built and had quickly set out the foundations. Now they had tackled the remainder of the site, clearing away all unnecessary brushwood but had left, as instructed, four rather nice trees. When finally completed it would not look as though the bungalow had just been plonked down on the site.

I said hello to the foreman, then walked the short distance to the village to collect my mail. There were letters from June and Alex, a couple of bills and a few bits of junk mail. I met the vicar on the way and he asked if the local Scout troop could collect a few logs from the building site. They were having a weekend camp in a field a few miles away and there was no wood nearby. I promised to tell the foreman to allow them to fill their trek cart. It's always a good thing to know the local vicar when new to an area, though he knew I wasn't a churchgoer.

I had also got to know the people at the local post office. As in most small villages that have managed to retain this facility, it also sold a variety of items that are often forgotten on shopping expeditions to town. They sold newspapers too, although you had to collect them. The other shop in the village stocked most other basic necessities, including bread, milk and quite a good selection of vegetables and frozen foods. The local butcher catered for everything in the meat department. It was very good quality but a bit expensive.

The pub had a small restaurant at the side that opened for lunches and evening meals. They did a special lunch on Saturdays and Sundays and could be persuaded to cater for the odd birthday or other celebration. The bar also did a variety of sandwiches, made to order, and also did lunches, a different menu each day.

Higham was a happy community of some 500 souls and so far I had come across no one who objected to a newcomer. In fact there were several properties being built and in a variety of styles to fit in with the local village plan. I suppose the more people who came to live there the more the additional rates helped to swell the county coffers and thereby the village.

119

One group of people I hadn't yet encountered were the parish councillors, who had been in office for many years. They used the village hall for their monthly meetings while someone came over from the council offices in Matlock to act as secretary. My planning application had been handled by my architect and I was happy to let him earn his money.

I started to walk back to my plot, passed the time of day with a couple of people, then a car drew alongside. The driver was Jeff Haynes, my architect.

'Want a lift? I'm just going to the site.' I accepted, and he filled me in on the progress to date and asked me to have a cheque ready in two days' time for the next stage of the building.

I said he could have it now but he replied, 'No. Pay only when asked and hang on to your interest as long as possible.'

'I'll remember that.' There seemed to be no problems with building, the next batch of supplies had already been ordered and should be delivered on Monday. He had also arranged for the hire of a much larger hut to store material on site. As the hut had not yet arrived he proposed, with my approval, to cancel it and build the garage next so it could be used for storage and so save a bit of money. It made sense, so in spite of my extra wealth I agreed.

The next few days were peaceful except that I was woken up early each morning by the builders. Why do they always start at 6.30 in the morning! I decided to explore the immediate local area. I only knew it superficially so it would be useful to see the local beauty spots, good eating places and see if there was a theatre within easy reach. A mile or so away there was a wood covering some 250 acres. The local Woodland Trust had set out a number of trails. In half an hour you could walk the short one and see a variety of plants and if lucky a few animals. A longer trail lasted an hour and a half and was much better. It meant leaving the small wood, going along a grassy path for a couple of hundred yards before entering a much larger forest area of almost a thousand acres. Here again there were a couple of trails. One was short and easy underfoot, the other much longer and involved a bit of climbing and crossing a stream. There were a few deer in there somewhere, although on my first visit I never saw them.

It certainly looked as though it would be a life of leisure for me from now on if I really wanted it. Jeff Haynes was a member of the local golf club. That was no doubt where he picked up a lot of his business. On our second meeting he had persuaded me to join as a visiting member. They had a couple of professionals at the club who promised to look after me. I wasn't at all sure that I was cut out for knocking a small ball a few miles in all sorts of weather, but I persevered. Second-hand clubs and a caddy didn't set me back very much and there were a few members who were no better than me at the game. I got to know a few more people and began to enjoy the exercise and the challenge. Even so, I didn't think I could ever go overboard like so many others who seemed to be out on the course every day.

Some months earlier I had chosen the plot of land for my new home with care. Now, seeing it again after a week or so, I began to appreciate that this part of the country has a lot to offer. Although there were large towns all around, this particular area seemed to have missed the urban spread. It was neither flat nor mountainous and had an interesting mix of small towns and villages, while the countryside seemed quite unspoilt.

I reckoned that once I'd set down my roots I should enjoy it. Mind you, the winters might be a bit colder than those at Cambridge or Margate. On the other hand, there should be no icy blasts from the north-east that the people of Thanet face during the winter. In any case, once stocked up, I should not need to move far from my fireside. I think I began to look forward to a life of ease and hoped that stagnation would not set in for many years. At heart I knew I was too active to let that happen.

23

Leisure Time

The days passed quickly and I had plenty to occupy my time. I didn't want to give the impression that I was forever watching the builders but, virtually living on the site, it was difficult not to observe the steady progress of my new home. Even so, I spent a good deal of my time visiting local towns, villages and old castles.

I knew a little about the building trade and it was easy to appreciate the occasional hold-ups with which the builders had to contend. The amount of material that goes into building even a modest house is staggering. The delivery of each item needs to be dovetailed into the actual building process and it is important not to have material lying about the site for idle hands to 'borrow'. Every so often there was a delay in delivery – the supply merchants had run out or there had been a strike somewhere along the line. Sometimes they were able to borrow from other sites but occasionally the builders were left with nothing to do.

The architect dropped in once a week and was content to leave the foreman to iron out minor difficulties. On one occasion I ran a workman into town to pick up four bags of cement. Another time I helped out by taking a chap to hospital. He was the driver of a lorry that had just delivered the roof trusses for the garage. One had slipped during the unloading, and the skin of the driver's hand had been torn away when he tried to catch it. He wasn't badly hurt but his blood flowed quite freely, and I think this was what worried him most. I waited while a doctor saw him and then a nurse dressed his wounds.

Returning to the site, we found that he couldn't drive his lorry, and since it blocked the entrance it had to be moved. In the end the foreman drove the lorry back to the depot. I followed in my car with the driver, and then brought the foreman back. I think I gained some brownie points from my builders, and they all stayed on the site to catch up with the day's work.

I paid the occasional visit to the local pub, not because I'm an habitual drinker but I'd found from long practice it is the one place to assimilate local colour and local gossip too. On moving into a new area, it is always a good idea to meet new people who may turn out to be good friends. My architect took pity on me a couple of times and invited me to his home for a meal. He and his wife, Geraldine, lived in the next village about three miles away. He had acquired an old blacksmith's forge and spent a couple of years doing it up. The result was an acceptable home, if you like that sort of thing. Maybe I'm a bit of a Philistine. I can appreciate old buildings, even old industrial ones, but I don't think I'd like to live in one. Old windmills, watermills, pump houses and barns all have their place in village life, but the moment they are turned into homes, for me, they lose some of their original charm.

The vicar and I got on quite well. He never attempted to get me to go to his church, although I did on a couple of Sunday evenings. His sermons were down to earth, amusing and well presented. After my second visit I stopped at the church door, where he was saying goodbye to his parishioners, and said how much I had enjoyed his sermon. His response was, 'Do come again, and if it's next Sunday, why not come back with me for a spot of supper.'

I thanked him, said I'd love to and couldn't resist adding, 'It must be costly if you invite all your flock into your home.'

He replied, 'Is there not something about casting bread upon the waters? However, in your case you have already helped me – remember the logs for the Scout troop.' For the moment I had forgotten, but said he was welcome to more any time.

A week later I joined the vicar after evensong for supper. I had assumed he was a bachelor and was surprised when he introduced a really beautiful woman as his wife and not his housekeeper. She was probably five or six years younger than him. She welcomed me with outstretched hand and said, 'Now you don't look like one of Richard's lost sheep. I'm delighted to meet you, Mr Holden.'

I took her outstretched hand and replied, 'I think he's taken pity on a lonely soul who doesn't know many people around here. I'm David, by the way.'

'Well, I'm glad to meet you, David. I'm Veronica. Come into the dining room. We'll have a drink while Richard gets changed.'

Richard Campion was not like any other parson I had ever met. Their home was large, comfortable and lived in. The food was beautifully cooked and the wine flowed freely. They had both travelled extensively and I soon learned that until ten years ago he had been in the army. They had met 20 years earlier when Veronica had also been in the army – a captain. Richard also held the same rank, and although they had often been sent to the same place abroad, they rarely managed to be on the same army site.

Their daughter, Fiona, an only child, was born two

years after their wedding and Veronica decided not to return to army life. When Richard retired from the army he went to a theological college and was eventually ordained a priest and came here as the vicar. He looked after two other churches in the area, so his time was fully occupied. He had a world of experience to draw on and had met many different people during his army days. This was why his sermons were out of the ordinary, entertaining, and still managed to convey the Christian ideals in such a human way.

They asked nothing of me or my circumstances. Indeed it was another week before I told them I had also been in the army. Veronica was passionately fond of cats and had a beautiful black male with bright green eyes. Richard could take them or leave them. On one of my visits to a nearby town I had come across a cat sculptured in wood. In fact there had been two, one sitting up, eyes alert and taking an interest in everything. The second was curled up fast asleep, yet the detail the sculptor had managed to convey was so lifelike the cats almost seemed to be real. I couldn't decide which one to buy so I bought both.

On my third visit to their home I gave the wide-awake one to Veronica, saying, 'It doesn't eat much and requires only a flick with a duster and an occasional polish.' At first she thought I was asking her to look after it for me until I moved into my new home. When she realised it was a gift she scarcely knew what to say.

I suppose Richard Campion was about three years younger than me. He had been in the infantry, so it was unlikely that we had ever met during our time with the colours. I didn't ask what Veronica had done in the army. There was another occasional visitor at the vicarage, a certain Vera Brentwood, who had been with Veronica in the army. I got the impression that Veronica was a shoulder for her to cry on, though as yet the womenfolk of the village were not beating a path to the vicarage door to see her. Rather they spoke to Richard, and he must have had a good filing system in his mind for instant recall of the problems of each of his flock.

The more I saw of Richard and his wife the more I liked them. I grew to appreciate all that they did for others and realised that if there really is a God, then Richard and Veronica must have been recruited to do His work.

Most of the time he wore his dog collar, 'my badge of office', as he called it. On his day off he would wear an ordinary shirt and tie or no tie at all and when they went on holiday they booked into a hotel as plain Mr and Mrs.

24

A Call from the Coast

I was settling in quite nicely, with little to do in the way of any urgent business. It was like an extended vacation in a rather nice part of the country. My time was my own. I could get up when I chose and not bother about hard and fast meal times. If I got hungry I could always nip over to the pub or a hotel or café. I listened to the radio more than usual and read a few books. The nearest library was at Matlock, some eight miles away, but they sent out a mobile library, which stopped in the pub car park for a couple of hours each Wednesday morning and contained several thousand books. It had recently added a hundred videos, although they had to be hired out. The librarian was happy to enrol me although I hadn't as yet taken up residence in the district.

After visiting the library, I would make my way into the pub, have half a pint of their local brew and sample their lunch. I wasn't the only one who got into this habit and I guessed that within a few more visits I would be on first-name terms with the other villagers. Occasionally I felt guilty about my present life of ease, and then contented myself with the knowledge that I'd done my bit for the country and it was a pleasant interlude after the concentrated problems of my few days at Margate.

I wrote a brief letter to Helen, told her how I spent my days and promised next time I was in Margate I would telephone her. My letter to Nigel Crompton, the solicitor, was even briefer. I told him how my house was progressing and asked him to let me know how things were regarding the smugglers.

I didn't really expect an early reply from either but both did so within a few days. Helen's said she was sorry for the circumstances at our previous meeting. She would definitely look forward to my phone call, and if I could tell her a few days in advance of my visit she would try to make sure she was in the country. Nigel's letter was urgent in one sense. It seemed that things, whatever they were, were definitely on the move. Moreover, I was to expect a visit from the local constabulary to see if I could shed any more light on smuggling activities in Thanet.

He suggested that if I wanted to be in at the kill, as it were, I might like to travel down to Margate the next Wednesday, so that I should be ready for Thursday, adding that I must observe from a distance and not get in the way. I was only too happy to agree. It was now Monday, so my leisure days were coming to an end.

I called in at the vicarage in the afternoon and asked Veronica if she would change my library books. Fiona was at home, asking for a loan so that she could travel down to London for an interview. Nearing the end of her final year at university and fully anticipating a good degree, she had already begun to look for a job.

I explained that if she didn't mind getting up early I'd be happy to take her to London. Veronica agreed, adding a rider – 'You will drive carefully, won't you.' Fiona was embarrassed but I said, 'Your mother's quite right and if you see the speedo at more than eighty let me know.'

Veronica looked suitably concerned while Fiona giggled and said, 'Maybe I could drive to make sure.'

'That'll be all right with me', I replied, 'I can catch up with some sleep.' Finally Veronica realised we were joking.

Tuesday was virtually a free day – or so I thought, until a man called at the building site, showed me a warrant card and introduced himself as Sergeant Warrander from the local CID. I really didn't think the customs people would send someone all the way up to Derbyshire to see me. Nor did I specially want to be involved with the local police, so initially I was a bit defensive.

This man had been very well trained, or experience had taught him when to be calm and when to be aggressive in his questions. It seemed he knew most of the story regarding the secret rooms at Margate and the efforts made by customs to apprehend the villains. He had been asked to call as a matter of urgency to see if I could shed any more light on the situation.

They had already spoken to my farm manager, who recalled a certain Rodney Leven, a farm worker who had been sacked by my grandfather for stealing. Rodney Leven had been tracked down. When he had been dismissed from the farm he had gone first to Ramsgate, then Minster and finally moved to live with an aunt in Wales. He was currently working on a hill farm there and had been there for at least three years. When first interviewed by the police he thought it was in connection with the original theft at Lydden. However, by careful questioning they had deduced he could not possibly have had anything to do with the smuggling. This negative statement seemed to me a complete waste of police time, and why should I need to know?

They had then turned their attention elsewhere – to people who had links with both properties where there were secret rooms and contraband. They could discount my grandfather as he was now dead and it seemed that some of the items found had code markings of a date later than his death. That left a few other people who needed to be interviewed. One was Nigel Crompton, who may have been aware of the smuggling even if he hadn't participated.

I asked the policeman if he knew how the interview with Nigel Crompton had panned out. He either didn't know or wouldn't tell me but muttered something about all notes taken at such interviews would be handed over to the man in charge. I was tempted to give him Eric Harding's name, merely to set the cat among the pigeons. Fortunately I refrained from such childish behaviour.

It soon became obvious that Sergeant Warrander was more interested in me as his immediate objective. I could see where his reasoning was going. He had constantly to refer to his notes, so none of his information was first hand and most of it was out of date. I didn't know whether to smile or be angry. I did neither but said quietly, 'Sergeant Warrander, I think you've been given the wrong information and in any case you are too late to do any questioning. My information is that on Thursday the trap will be sprung to catch the villains with the loot.'

For a second or two he wasn't quite sure how to answer, then he continued, 'Let me just complete what I have to ask.' I nodded and he referred to his notes once more. 'Two properties owned by you have hidden rooms in which have been found certain quantities of contraband. Can you account for any of it?'

'Certainly not. In fact I was the one who found both of them. I'm certain that neither my grandfather nor Mr Crompton had anything to do with it, and I most certainly did not.'

The policeman added a few notes to his folder. 'Can you think of anyone else with local knowledge of both places?' He was persistent if nothing else.

'No I can't, and what's more, the people who originally dug those holes are now in their eighties and nineties and too old to be involved in modern-day smuggling.'

He noted down my answers and after a while the questions ceased. He closed his notebook, smiled and said, 'Thank you, sir. I'll get this typed and send a copy to H.Q. Thank you for your time.'

I didn't answer and he took himself off. I was really irritated. I thought about making a complaint, and then realised I hadn't been grilled too hard and began to feel sorry for Sergeant Warrander. Even so, it didn't say much for cooperation between the various police authorities. Of all the people in our boyhood gang only Eric knew of the secret room at Wakefield Place, and I could not remember him mentioning it since.

He was surely too busy to get involved. On the other hand, he did spend a lot of time on the Continent – doing what? I wondered. I assumed he was in high-powered banking of some sort.

Another thought struck me. There was the odd comment by Kathleen about Eric's demeanour and the suspicion I had that Sandra seemed to be worried. No, none of it made sense, and within a couple of days it might all be over.

25

The Journey South

I knew Fiona had passed her driving test. She didn't have a car of her own, but she was occasionally allowed to borrow Richard's. Young people these days seem accomplished in so many things. I had used the M1 on the journey up here and now reckoned it might be better to travel down on the A1(M) although it was a bit longer. Also it had one big advantage if time was not important – it was easy to leave the route, drive into one of the small towns that have now been bypassed and have a break from the traffic noise. Half an hour spent in a pleasant little restaurant was preferable to most motorway eating places.

It seemed that Fiona's interview was with one of those engineering firms which sprawl out to the west of London. Her aunt lived in Uxbridge and Fiona intended to stay there overnight so that the next day she would be fresh for her interview. All this I gathered during the first half-hour of our journey south. I asked her to look for the road atlas in the door pocket and find the best way to the A1(M) and then to her aunt's. After dropping her off I would carry on to Margate, hoping to reach there in the afternoon. If I was delayed it didn't really matter. That's the big advantage of my present vehicle.

I must admit the journey passed quicker with someone in the passenger seat. Fiona and I had only exchanged a few words during my visits to her home. In fact she had only been present at one of the evening meals, although I had seen her on other occasions. Now she told me lively stories of university life and added that it wasn't all fun. The serious business of studies and exams came first and her spare time was limited. I learned she was doing an engineering course and hoped to specialise in electronics. Girls and women are into everything these days. She was surprised when I told her I also used to work in electronics. Mind you, that covers a vast array of applications. But at least it was common ground and so far since retiring I hadn't come across anyone else in my field.

We stopped at St Neots for an early lunch and I posed the question, 'Shall we cook something here or treat ourselves to a proper meal?'

'A proper meal,' was her instant reply. 'I expect you could do with a break from driving, but I'll pay.'

During our brief stay in the café Fiona did most of the talking. 'I'm glad you and dad are friends. He loves his work, and of course mum is a marvellous support, but he needs someone like yourself, down to earth.'

'Believe me, young lady, I'm glad I met your father. We have quite a bit in common, apart from our golf. We were both in the army and managed to get out in one piece while still relatively young.'

She insisted on paying for the lunch and I let her – the second female to buy me a meal recently. As we walked to the car Fiona said, 'although I passed my test a couple of years ago, mum still has kittens whenever Dad lets me drive.'

'Would you like to have a go in mine? It's a bit higher off the ground, but the gears are straightforward and its got power steering.' For a moment she didn't think I meant it and when she realised that I did she giggled her assent.

'OK, in you get. You'll need to adjust the seat and the

mirror. I'll give you a few instructions until you get the hang of it.'

We moved off easily enough, although I could sense that Fiona was tense. A few miles down the road she had settled down and was beginning to enjoy herself. I don't think I had been so composed at her age. I was then in the army and just learning to drive ten-ton trucks. With a sergeant instructor bellowing in my ear, it hadn't been the easiest of times, even though after each admonition he had added, sir.

My motor home was comfortable. To give Fiona more confidence I closed my eyes and pretended to be asleep. It was a silly thing to do, for after a few miles the purr of the engine and the gentle movement of the car did their worst and I really did go into the land of nod. It was the change in the engine note and the slight forward movement of my body as the car slowed for Fiona to negotiate a roundabout that woke me up. For a moment I didn't know where I was. 'Enjoy your shut-eye?' Fiona was asking.

Now fully awake I replied, 'Just resting my eyes.'

She smiled and said, 'We turn off at the next round-about, so maybe you'd better take over soon while I do the map-reading to my aunt's.'

'OK. Pull in at the next lay-by.'

The changeover was quick and we were soon on our way again. As we approached Mill Hill she gave me directions until at last we arrived at her aunt's house on the outskirts of Uxbridge. Her aunt seemed surprised to see us so early and explained that there had been long delays on the M1. Veronica had telephoned, so Fiona said she'd ring her mother at once.

I said, 'You'd better not tell her you drove part of the way.'

'We shall see. I might just say you fell asleep so I had to take over, ' Fiona replied.

135

I accepted the cup of tea from her aunt, almost obligatory after a long journey, and indulged in idle chatter until I felt I could decently leave. Fiona walked me to the car and said thanks for getting her to Uxbridge. I reached into my wallet and gave her a £10 note. 'I hope all goes well with your interview tomorrow. If it does, please get yourself a drink to celebrate. If you don't get the job, buy some chocolates to cheer yourself up.' I could see she was surprised and delighted but before she could say anything I'd started the engine and moved off.

Surprisingly, the traffic was fairly light and I made good progress, getting to Margate too late for tea and too early for dinner, so I thought I'd waste another half an hour in a detour to Wakefield Place.

26

In at the Deep End

With hindsight it was not the wisest thing to have done but it brought matters to a head. Approaching Wakefield Place, I changed down, intending to go slowly past the entrance. As I did so, a car overtook me and at the same time another car came hurtling out from Wakefield Place. The driver almost lost control, recovered, turned left and headed towards Margate. I can recall it now, almost in slow motion, though at the time thoughts crowded in my mind as to what might be happening inside the house.

Had the smugglers been caught trying to take away some of their loot? That seemed unlikely as no other car emerged in pursuit, or possibly the villains had disabled the police car. The small car that had overtaken me was forced to mount the pavement in order to avoid a collision and I was almost involved. I stopped and noticed yet another car that had previously been parked in the road facing towards Margate. It set off, obviously in pursuit of the first car, and as it did so those in the fugitive vehicle sent a volley of shots into the windscreen and forced the driver to stop.

I turned my car round, raced to the stricken car and screeched to a halt. Fortunately both occupants were unhurt and I could now see that both were policemen. I wound down the window on the passenger side and shouted, 'Jump in and we'll catch them.' They needed no second bidding.

It takes a few minutes to retell the incident although it all happened in the space of a few seconds. I introduced myself, and asked, 'Do you want to catch these people or just see where they go?'

'If you could follow at a safe distance, we'll try to get someone to stop them further along the road when we know where they're heading.'

So that's what we did. The villains, probably thinking they were safe, travelled at a steady pace and I even allowed a car to overtake me so that we were not immediately behind. We went out towards Birchington along the back way, so they obviously knew the district, but so did I. Once past Birchington and on to the road to Canterbury, they took the third exit at the round-about. One of the policemen smiled and got on the phone to his colleagues at headquarters. 'We're following the target vehicle and it has just entered the Thanet Way, possibly heading for London. Could you arrange for support and a road block at junction six.'

He then turned to me and asked how much petrol I had. 'Enough to get to London and back twice. Are you going to tell me what's happening?'

'Sorry, can't go into details, though we're grateful. Our colleagues will stop these people at junction six and you'll be allowed to continue on your way. Where were you going, sir?'

'Oh, I've just come down from Derbyshire to see some friends and hopefully conclude some business.'

'We're very grateful and hope you won't be too late for your appointment.'

As we approached the junction I could see on the far side of the roundabout, dead ahead, that three police cars were in position to stop any vehicle, while the traffic from London was already building up. The villains could also see the road block and did a complete circuit at the roundabout and then made off to the left, going towards Ashford. Without further instructions from the police, I followed. The officer sitting next to me got on the phone again and asked for instructions. Whatever was said he didn't like very much and said to the man at the other end, 'Stand by. I'll ask.'

He turned to me. 'Would you allow me to drive your vehicle, sir? We need to stop those people.'

'No. I'll overtake them. I'll ram them if necessary but I'm doing the driving.'

'We could commandeer your vehicle,' was his reply, but he said it with little conviction.

'You could, but it wouldn't do you much good.'

He looked at me and smiled, so I explained that I was an electronics expert and had coded the engine to respond only to me. By now we had just passed through the village of Sheldwick, the proverbial one-horse town but I knew there were a number of side roads where the culprits could turn off, so I told the policemen that I thought we should stop the other car soon and certainly before we reached Ashford.

Another phone call and this time we were given permission to halt the target car if possible. In the meantime they would try to set up another roadblock just outside Ashford.

I began to enjoy the chase. 'Right, here we go then.' I gradually increased speed, overtook the two cars ahead of us and then our quarry was fully in view. It was a four-door saloon, a Ford, and I reckoned that if we couldn't persuade it to stop I could just ease it off the road. I tooted my horn, indicating I was about to overtake, but the Ford just stayed in the middle of the road. I flashed my headlamps but his only answer was to switch on his rear lights. So I tooted again and got up really close.

I realised that the chap in the back of the target car could be getting ready to fire at us through his side window, so I hit the accelerator. The slight bump as my car touched the Ford caused his shot to go off target and only succeeded in shattering his rear window. A car coming in the opposite direction forced the villains to pull over a bit, and as soon as it had passed I drew level. The policeman lowered his window and indicated for them to stop. The driver's only reply was a toot on the horn and two fingers in the air.

I didn't wait for further instructions from the policemen. I just turned my wheel slightly, hoping that the sheer weight and size of my vehicle would be enough to force the lighter car into the gutter.

He wasn't giving up so easily and tried to escape by going on to the grass verge. Unfortunately he hit one of those old-fashioned stone mileage indicators. The driver was forced forward by the impact and the man in the rear was hurled forward into the front of the car. I stopped my car a few yards further on and switched on the hazard lights. The villains, now in shock, scarcely knew what had happened. The policemen were out of my car in a flash. They opened the door of the target car and relieved the men of their weapons.

This happened so quickly it was difficult to take it all in. Later, rather like looking at still photographs, it was imprinted on my memory and I was able to recall precisely what happened. Fortunately I sustained no damage to the side of my car and even the bump at the front was scarcely noticeable.

By the time I had walked back to the other car the police had both men handcuffed and were on the phone. As I approached I heard the end of the conversation, 'Both suspects have been apprehended. Send an ambulance and a tow truck. We are about eight miles from Ashford on the A251. I know because their car has just hit a stone mileage post.'

While we waited for the tow truck and the ambulance I put the kettle on and made some tea. The officers drank theirs quickly and asked if I'd mind giving the prisoners a cup. Neither of the villains seemed badly hurt and both accepted a cup of tea. The younger one had the cheek to ask for a biscuit. They sat on the rear seat of my car and drank their tea.

No one spoke. I stood outside near the open rear door of my car while the prisoners drank their tea as best they could, being handcuffed. The younger one eased himself forward and came towards, me holding out his cup. I took it and he lunged at me with his two hands. The metal handcuffs caught me a glancing blow on the side of my head. The quickness of the attack was enough to knock me over. It was a mad attempt to escape but I suppose captured felons try anything. Possibly he saw me as the man who had stopped them getting clean away. I was soon on my feet but one policeman was quick off the mark. He merely put out a foot and tripped the fleeing man. It was all over in 30 seconds and the poor chap was in a worse state than me for his face grazed along the road and tore the skin off in several places.

The ambulance arrived next and one of the policemen travelled back in it with the prisoners. The other came back to Margate with me. It was only later when I had dropped him off at the police station and was preparing to go on my way that he said, 'Would you mind coming in and making a statement, sir.' What he really meant was that I couldn't go away at once. It was another half an hour before I was allowed to leave and of course there was a problem when I couldn't give them my address either in Margate or back in Derbyshire.

I explained the situation and finally they agreed that

141

the solicitor's address would be acceptable. They phoned Nigel Crompton at once to check that he knew me and fortunately he was in his office even at this late hour for him. The older of the policemen came to say goodbye. 'That was a nice piece of driving, Mr Holden.' He handed me a form and said, 'This is to claim for the petrol used and any damage to your car. You'll probably get a letter of thanks from the Super, too.'

What had started out as a pleasant trip with a young woman had ended up with me in a police station giving a statement about my part in capturing armed villains. More to the point, they had come away from Wakefield Place, and so far I had no idea what they had been doing there.

For the moment, at least, the police did not know of my connection with Wakefield Place. Perhaps stupidly, I had not mentioned it either. It certainly didn't figure in my statement, although eventually the connection would be made. When that time came would be soon enough to give them the complete picture. My only concern now was to leave.

I owed it to Nigel Crompton to call and explain things, so that's what I did. His secretary explained that he was still with a client, so I began to run over in my mind the events of the day and in particular the recent few hours. In the end I gave up, and flipped through old copies of *Country Life* until the man himself popped his head in and said, 'OK, David. Do come through.'

27

Picking up the Threads

Nigel Crompton was pleased to see me although concern showed on his face when I recounted the full story of the chase and capture. I anticipated a reprimand for getting involved and I wasn't disappointed, although it was quite a mild rebuke.

'Of course this couldn't have come at a worse time. I realise there was little you could do, but the really big names will have realised something has gone wrong. They will certainly suspend operations until they think it's safe to start up again. I'll ring my contact, though the chances are that he already knows.'

I told him of Sergeant Warrander's visit at Higham. He had apparently known about that possibility. Although he assured me the police had to cover all options, I still consider that interrogation was a complete waste of time and resources.

He seemed concerned for my safety but even more so for the fact that the plan to capture the villains had not been successful. While he was speaking I began to think that all might not have been lost and said, 'How well does your contact get on with the police and the press?'

'What's on your mind?'

'Well, if the press were told about the chase and the fact that the "car thieves" had both died in the crash or afterwards in the ambulance maybe Mr Big would swallow it. He might lie low for a while and then start operations again sooner than he might otherwise have done. Alternatively, their injuries might have been so severe that they had to be transferred to a specialist hospital.'

'David, you've been reading the wrong sort of books or watching too much TV,' was his comment. However, I could tell he thought my suggestion had some merit and that it might just be plausible. He reached for the phone and dialled his mystery contact once more. After a few minutes' conversation he smiled and replaced the phone. 'They quite like the idea and have come up with a few twists of their own – even to the extent of setting fire to the car, once the police have inspected the vehicle. The car has already been removed from the crash site but they will take it back and later this evening set it alight.'

Now this was something I thought the police would not do – interfere with evidence – but I suppose it is sometimes necessary. I got up to go, and he asked where I was staying. I wasn't sure, so I promised to call him at home later to let him know.

I stopped at the nearest phone box and telephoned Helen Carlyle. 'Sorry I couldn't phone earlier. May I call to see you tomorrow, early?'

'Yes of course. Where are you staying tonight?'

'Not yet sure...'

'Well, why not come and have a meal here first and we can sort out something.'

I hadn't realised how much I wanted to see her. Maybe I just needed to be with someone in a normal situation. The last few hours had been anything but normal. While the chase had been on I was excited, keyed up and prepared for almost anything. Having been out of the army for several years, I was surprised how easy it had been to be in action again, even to the extent of being fired at, although that hadn't caused any problems this time. I was keenly aware that part of me had actually enjoyed it. Now that it was over I felt different just imagining what might have happened.

Helen opened her front door and I must have looked awful as the bruise began to show, for I could see in her eyes that she was concerned at my dishevelled appearance.

'Come in quickly, David, and sit down. Are you all right? You look as though you've been in an accident, or had a nasty shock. I'll make some tea.'

I made a poor attempt at a joke, 'You should see the other fellow,' but I made my way to the sitting room and flopped down on to the settee and began to relax. The tea helped in the revival and I began to tell her a bit about my adventure. It was surprisingly easy to unburden myself, even though I related only the fact that I had helped the police to catch a couple of criminals. She listened without interrupting and when I'd finished I asked her not to repeat any of it as there might be further developments. She agreed and then said, 'You are not sleeping in your car tonight. You can stay here but first you're going to have a long soak in the bath.'

To be honest I was too weary to raise much objection but managed a quick comment, 'I'm too tired. You'll have to scrub my back.'

'Not this time, my lad. You've had enough excitement for one day. Once you're in the bath you can manage well enough. I'll get you a meal and then we can watch television.'

Just as I was getting into the bath the phone rang. I was glad it couldn't be for me and I heard Helen answering it. I'd forgotten how good it was to have a soak in a bath. Then I realised it must be months since I had enjoyed such luxury, relying on the small shower in my motor home to keep me clean. I kept willing myself to stay awake. The last thing Helen wanted was a corpse in her bath. It occurred to me yet again that I was getting too old for the activity of this afternoon.

It seemed only a few minutes later that there was a knock on the door and Helen called out, 'Something to eat in five minutes so don't be too long.'

I felt like a new man as I made it to the dining room and sat down to eat the meal Helen had prepared. It was obviously a makeshift one, but it tasted freshly cooked – though it could have been produced via a microwave.

Afterwards she insisted that I sit down while she did the washing up. I gave in to her and it felt great to let someone else do the chores, though when she returned I felt a bit guilty. Her first words made me realise that the phone call had been about me after all.

'So are you going to tell me exactly what happened this afternoon, or shall I tell you?' Helen asked, and then explained, 'Your solicitor has been on the phone. He thought you might have called in to see me so he phoned here on the off chance. He was very concerned about you but I was able to reassure him that on the outside you seemed to be all right.'

I felt a bit sheepish. 'Sorry, I thought I had explained. The police who were trying to stop some thieves had their car wrecked. I offered to drive them in mine and we eventually caught up with them.'

She probably realised that I was sticking to my story, and simply said, 'Well, come and watch television, catch up on the news of the day and then we'll have an early night...'

It was such an innocent and ordinary remark. Helen stopped in mid sentence, blushing as she appreciated what she had just said. I looked directly at her and said nothing as she completed the sentence '... you in

Joyce's bed and me in mine.' With that she turned on the TV.

There were the usual stories of violence in many parts of the world, a report on the latest progress at cricket. Then followed a bit about politics and the state of the pound. Suddenly the newscaster switched to a late item just in. 'We have just received a report of an accident just outside Ashford. A car speeding towards Kennington lost control and hit a bollard on the pavement. It burst into flames. A passing motorist gave what assistance he could, managed to get the driver and his passenger out and called an ambulance. The police are anxious to interview that driver and anyone who witnessed the accident. They think someone coming in the opposite direction may have been responsible. The police have already identified the car as one that had been stolen two days ago in Herne Bay. The weather for the next few days...'

Helen looked at me. 'You never said the car caught fire and nor did your solicitor.'

'Well, maybe it was another accident.' As soon as I'd uttered the words I could appreciate how stupid they sounded. Helen didn't pursue the matter, for which I was grateful. I'd done enough explaining for one day.

28

A Bed for the Night

The programme that followed was a repeat of a quiz game. 'Are you interested in this,' Helen wanted to know and when I shook my head she turned off the set and said, 'I promised your solicitor that you would phone him, so why don't you do that now.'

I duly obliged. It was a one-sided conversation, once he knew where I was and that I was all right. 'I don't think you'll hear any more from the police. My contact was pleased with your contribution and in the papers tomorrow you'll see quite an acceptable version of events.'

I interrupted him to tell him I had already seen the news on TV. At the other end of the phone line I heard him chuckle and could almost see the twinkle in his eye.

'That just proves what I've thought for a long time – you can't always believe what you read in the papers or see on the television. By the way, you'll be pleased to know that before they set fire to the car the police got all the fingerprints they needed. They only found two bottles of brandy and two cartons of cigarettes. However, in one of the bottles instead of brandy they found cocaine. And one of the cartons contained cigarettes while the other was full of cocaine. Each individual pack had been repacked with the stuff and even the cellophane wrappers had been carefully replaced.'

I felt I should say something. 'So do they think the

operation will continue? And what will happen to the two men already caught, because I and several police know there was no fire and that the men were alive when I saw them last.'

'It's in the hands of the authorities. Let them deal with it.' I was too tired to argue. No doubt all would be revealed sometime and in any case I consoled myself with the thought that it wasn't my affair. Yet deep down I knew that I was still involved. One other thing had been worrying me. If only two packs of cigarettes and two bottles had been discovered in the car, why had the two men taken such a small quantity from the stock hidden in the house? Nigel Crompton must have read my thoughts for his next words answered my unspoken question.

'You will be pleased to know that the hidden cameras provided absolute proof of what was going on. Unfortunately the camera was not as quiet as expected and the smugglers realised they were being photographed. They hoped to get away with just a small amount but hadn't realised the police were waiting outside.'

I thanked him for letting me know and rang off. I realised I must stop myself thinking about it and get on with my own life. Hopefully, part of that was sitting in the lounge right now.

I went in to sit next to Helen. 'I'm sorry to cause you this extra work. I'll sort myself out tomorrow, but I am grateful.' And I certainly was glad to be there. My recent experience didn't really warrant the attention I was receiving. I reckoned a good night's sleep was all I needed.

I wanted to show Helen how grateful I was. Shaking her hand was not enough yet I thought if I kissed her it might be misconstrued as somewhat forward. In the end I took her hand and rather like an old-fashioned courtier

149

drew it to my lips and kissed it. She didn't draw away. Instead she lightly kissed my cheek saying, 'That's enough excitement for one day. Sleep well.'

Smiling my thanks, I went to bed. I thought I wouldn't sleep and for a few moments was content to lie down quietly going over the events of the day. The sharp images of the chase, the accident and the interview with the police all gradually faded and I slept. The next thing I knew was a voice that I vaguely recognised. 'And who's been sleeping in my bed?'

Joyce had returned from a three-day stint at Dover. Apparently she had knocked on my door, well her door really, and receiving no answer assumed it was all right to enter. Now completely awake, I thanked her for the use of her bed and remarked how comfortable it was.

'You're welcome. Mum isn't here but she left me a note, so it wasn't too much of a surprise. How are you? I'm getting myself a late breakfast. Would you like something? By the way, it's half past ten.'

'God! I must have been really tired last night. I only came to let your mother know I was in town. Give me ten minutes and I'll be down. If you've been on duty all night, would you like me to cook breakfast?'

'No, it's all right. I have this duty once every three months so I've got used to it. I'll go to bed tonight and my body clock will gradually adjust.'

Joyce was a dab hand with the old frying pan. She asked no questions as to why I had suddenly turned up, apparently exhausted. When we had finished and washed up, I couldn't resist asking, 'So what's for lunch?'

'A quick run round the block, down to the beach and back. Then we'll think about a bowl of soup and a ham salad, maybe.'

Then Joyce handed me Helen's letter. It wasn't very long:

150

Dear David

I'm sorry I have to leave you today. I must go to Paris for three days. It's a viewing that I really must attend. However, all being well I should be back on Sunday evening. In the meantime Joyce will sleep in my bed so you may continue to use hers. She is home for at least two days and then she goes to Ramsgate. John is in America for a couple of months. Don't forget to telephone Mr Crompton again, sometime today. I had another phone call from him.

Do take care. I'll see you soon.

Helen

I'd never received a letter like that before. It covered all the points of interest, a reminder about the phone call, information about herself and Joyce yet nothing about the reason that brought me here in the first place. There was nothing about my encounter with the smugglers, nothing about my superficial facial injuries and nothing about hoping I'd soon be my old self again. It didn't tally with the concern I had seen on her face only yesterday. I sat puzzling over it and then showed Joyce the letter.

After she'd read it she remarked, 'Yes. That could only have been written by my mother – very businesslike. You have to know her like I do to be able to read between the lines. I do know my mother was concerned about you. She realised it must have been something of an ordeal but she's learned not to get too emotional.'

29

Joyce

To change the subject I asked if she'd like to go out anywhere. I felt it would be better to do almost anything than stay in the house. She thought for a moment and then said, 'If you aren't fed up with driving we could go over to Pegwell Bay. John and I have decided to rent your cottage and it would be nice to go over while he's away and do some measuring.'

'That's fine with me. Your car or mine?'

'We'll take mine and I promise to drive carefully. Mum would never forgive me if I crashed with you on board.'

I just had to put in a quick call to the solicitor. He had nothing new to report. Maybe he was just keeping tabs on me. Then I was off to see my cottage. I guessed that Mrs Bull would be surprised to see me with a different woman. I was wrong again for she recognised Joyce immediately, having seen her when she and Helen went to see the property while I was in Derbyshire.

Joyce was quite methodical in her approach. She had one of those new-fangled machines that estate agents use to measure rooms. By simply pointing it at a wall and pressing a button it records the actual measurements in feet or metres. She handed me a notepad and biro. 'David, if I call out the measurements would you mind noting them down?'

Well, it kept my mind off other things. With the rooms completed, she started on the windows, ceiling heights and doors. She offered as explanation for the door measurements, 'Mrs Bull says that in winter when the wind blows from the north she fixes heavy curtains against the doors. I thought I'd take the measurements just in case.'

'Why don't you ask the landlord to put in double glazing and a storm porch? Then you would not need to worry about curtains at the doors.'

She turned to me and smiled. 'Do you think he'd do it? I don't know him very well and I haven't paid any rent yet.'

'It's worth a try. Would you like me to speak to him? I know him quite well.'

And so the banter went on. We called at Mrs Bull's to say goodbye and I told her of the possible solution to the winter draughts. 'I'm going to ask the landlord to fit double glazing next door, and a storm porch. While they're doing it, would you like yours done at the same time?'

'Oh that would be nice. Would it put up the rent?'

'Hadn't thought about that. Why don't I try to persuade him it will increase the value of his property. Would you like it done if the rent remains the same?'

Joyce, by this time, could hardly suppress her laughter. Mrs Bull suddenly exclaimed, 'But Mr Holden, I thought you were the landlord.'

'I'm sorry. I was joking. Shall I ask a builder to get it done? I don't expect it will take more than a week to get both cottages completed.'

'Shall I ask John? He's only down the garden.'

So we waited while she went to fetch her husband and I suppose she convinced him on the way back. He shook hands with both of us and then said, 'Nice to see you again, miss. I think you should bring Mr Holden over more often. We'll probably end up with a new roof.'

I was immediately concerned, just as he had intended, and he laughed as he realised I had fallen into his trap.

'Nice to see you too, Mr Bull. I'll be down here for the next few days. I'll try to get someone over tomorrow to give an estimate. Will you be in?'

It seemed that they would be and he suggested I should get at least three quotes. We said goodbye, but left Joyce's car outside as she wanted to show me something at the end of the lane. As we walked she suddenly put her arm through mine, rather like my daughter and my wife had done years ago. We stopped after about 50 yards and there nuzzling up to his mother was a young colt which couldn't have been more than a couple of weeks old.

'Isn't he adorable?' Joyce wanted to know, and I had to agree.

'You know, this field also belongs to me but I rent it out.'

'Is there nothing around here that you don't have a finger in?'

'Oh lots. But let's face it, I didn't know anything about it until a couple of weeks ago.'

We stayed watching the mare and her foal for a few minutes until the mare decided to investigate the strangers looking over her fence. The foal followed but unfortunately we had nothing to offer them. However, they seemed quite content to hear our voices. After a while they lost interest in us so we retraced our steps and drove to the hotel where I'd had lunch with her mother.

'What time do you have to go on duty?'

'Oh, not until eight o'clock this evening. We've got time for lunch, if that was your intention,' Joyce replied, as she brought the car to a stop in the hotel car park.

As we went in a few couples were finishing their meals. A man said hello to Joyce so we stopped at his table.

154

'Hello, Mike. May I introduce Mr Holden? I've just been to see a house he has to rent. Mr Holden, this is Mike Jevons, one of my many supervisors.'

Formalities and pleasantries completed we moved to an empty table. Joyce was giggling. 'Hope you don't mind, David. It's near enough the truth but you know what gossips some workmates can be.'

'I don't mind. I wondered if you were going to introduce me as a long-lost uncle or even a sugar daddy.'

'I would never do that. You're much too nice.'

I turned to Joyce and said, 'I hope that after all this wining and dining you will definitely take my cottage.'

'Yes of course, Mr Holden. Where do I sign?'

We finished lunch and Joyce drove back to her home. I felt more relaxed but couldn't summon up the energy to visit any of my friends so I asked if there was anything I could do around the house. Joyce wasn't aware of anything that needed repairing so I volunteered to cut the grass in the back garden. It was quite pleasant, and having done that I sat down on a bench beneath a tree, closed my eyes and thought of pleasant things.

Joyce came looking for me to ask what I'd like for tea. It was a light snack. I volunteered to do the washing up and after Joyce had left I watched television until it was time for bed.

Before that, although it was dark outside, I went out with a torch to check over the car. I really couldn't detect much in the way of damage. The slight dent on the front bumper where it had hit the Ford was no worse than what happens almost every day in car parks. I wouldn't lose any sleep over it.

30

Sandra

The following day as I was washing up after breakfast the phone rang. It was Joyce to say she was going back with a friend to Broadstairs and would I mind being on my own. No, I didn't mind being left to my own devices. I pottered around the garden and then decided to go down to the shops to replenish the larder. I glanced through the papers that had been delivered earlier and could find nothing of interest regarding the car crash. However on page seven a small paragraph said that two witnesses had come forward in answer to the police appeal. I wondered who they could be or whether the police had decided to tell a few more white lies. As far as I could remember there had been no witnesses to the accident.

I felt like being lazy so I took the car to the shops. Northdown Way is a secluded area with detached houses kept private from each other by fairly high hedges. The roads are narrow, with sharp right-angled turns but no cross roads. On both sides of the road there are narrow footpaths and trees have been planted at intervals. It is a delightful enclave between two main roads. It's almost impossible to speed through this estate, and because of the high hedges it is necessary to slow down and check carefully in both directions before driving out into either main road.

As I emerged, to go to Margate, a car being driven

slowly but rather erratically was attempting to enter Arlington Gardens. I sensed that the driver was having trouble with the steering, so I stopped as soon as I could. By this time the other car had mounted the pavement and also stopped. I ran over and was surprised to find Sandra quite distressed at the wheel.

I don't think she recognised me at first and when she did burst into tears – most unlike her. I opened the door and persuaded her to get out while I moved her car back on to the road and locked it. Then I walked with her over to my car and sat her in the passenger seat. She had recovered a little and said she was going to see her mother-in-law. I needed to know what had caused her distress for she was normally such a level-headed person. I guessed before she blurted it out that Eric was at the root of her trouble. In between spells of silence and quiet weeping she told me what her life had been like over the past few months.

It seemed that Eric, without telling her, had changed jobs from the fairly well paid one with IT Finance to another that paid more and had better prospects of advancement. However, it involved a lot of travel on the Continent, but to all intents their life continued as before. His trips abroad increased and became longer in duration, so eventually Sandra was convinced another woman was involved. Not wanting to ask him outright, Sandra joked about a rival. Eric didn't rise to the bait and when finally she asked him outright he denied completely any affair.

The truth only emerged some few weeks later when Sandra needed to contact him urgently as their daughter had been taken to hospital following an accident. His firm could tell her nothing. Even his old department chief was reluctant to say anything but finally relented when Sandra explained about her daughter. As gently as possible, he told her that Eric had virtually been given the choice of facing a charge of embezzlement or leaving of his own accord.

Sandra, normally a self-reliant woman, had hardly taken it in but realised she no longer knew her husband. Two days later Eric had turned up and explained how he had certainly left his old firm but of his own accord after a blazing row and got a better position with a rival firm. It also partly explained why Eric had sold his car and rented one as required. Sandra had accepted his explanation and life in the Harding household had returned to normal. Their daughter had recovered and left hospital. Eric was at home most weekends, although the rest of his time was spent abroad, and sometimes Sandra did not see him for a couple of weeks. These absences usually led to rows and subsequent reconciliation.

Yesterday he had failed to return after he had expressly promised he would do so, and Sandra decided that was enough. She imagined he had gone off with another woman or, worse, had left her altogether. She was on her way to see his mother and ask if she knew where her son was and if she could shed any light on his recent behaviour. She had worked herself into a frenzy and, nearing Arlington Gardens and fearful of what she might be told, had simply lost it.

I took Sandra to a little café, and over tea and cream cakes she gradually recovered her composure. We stayed there chatting for half an hour and then she accompanied me round a small supermarket while I got a few groceries. She thought I was staying in my car until I explained the situation and told her part of my adventure and the chase with the police. She had seen the item on the news. I warned her not to tell anyone of my involvement. I didn't really think that Mr Big would come after me, but I should never have told Sandra. Now I sought to employ a damage limitation exercise. She assured me she'd say nothing and I believed her.

We returned to Arlington Gardens and as she was now completely recovered Sandra decided to see Eric's mum. She promised to call me at Helen's number if she needed me.

I was still in two minds regarding Eric and his possible involvement with the smugglers. I had no real grounds for believing that. The thought just popped into my head. I suppose it may have been his absences abroad and the fact that he knew about the summer house and had never mentioned it to me. There was also his treatment of Sandra. In addition there was the question posed by Kathleen. Did it all begin to make sense now? I'm sure that if Sandra had suspected anything like that she would have told me. She seemed to accept that he had another job but was still concerned that there might be another woman somewhere. Whatever job he now had, it seemed to pay well, for as far as I could judge their life style had not changed. I was wrong.

Later that day I decided to call on Alice Harding, merely to let her know I was in town. Mr Harding, looking old, opened the door. He explained that his wife was not well and had gone to lie down but asked if I would like to come in. 'Yes I would, although I can't stay long.' I wondered if he might broach the subject of his son's disappearance and he did so immediately.

'I'm glad you've come, David. I don't know all the details but Eric seems to be in a bit of a jam.'

'I thought when I was down a few weeks ago he wasn't his usual cheery self, although he seemed all right physically.'

'Yes. Well, if you can spare a few minutes I'd like to tell you what I know. You were his best friend but I think he's let us all down, especially Sandra.'

I waited, and soon the story of Eric's downfall emerged. It was worse than I had imagined and far worse than Sandra had told me. Perhaps she only knew what Eric chose to tell her. It seemed that an important deal that Eric was negotiating had fallen through, apparently through no fault of his. However, his boss and the board of directors were convinced he had messed up. They wanted to retain his services but at a lower level and lower salary. Knowing it was not his fault, Eric would have none of it so he had left after a row and joined another firm.

Initially all had been well, but when that firm was taken over, Eric, as one of the newest staff, had been made redundant. His severance pay had not lasted long. He had re-mortgaged his house without telling Sandra and helped to maintain the pretence of still being in work by spending more time abroad. He began by bringing in more than his quota of cigarettes and alcohol and had found a ready market, apparently having been shown the ropes by fellow travellers doing the same thing.

He had told his father he was with a big firm of importers but the old man had put two and two together and arrived at a very good answer and as near to the truth as possible. He didn't want to fall out with his son and had tried to dissuade him from these activities but had told no one else. Now, following Sandra's visit, he was relieved that he could share his secret. He had earlier offered his son all his spare cash, some £3,000, but Eric finally told his father the truth and said he needed nearer £30,000 to clear his debts. As a consequence he would have to continue with his present way of life, implying that it would be difficult to leave with the knowledge he had acquired.

All I could do was sympathise. 'Leave it with me, Mr

Harding. I'll go over and see Sandra. I'm sure we can sort something out. I can't believe that Eric's a bad lad. Its just a bad patch, and circumstances have caught up with him.'

I wasn't sure that I really believed my words, although the old man seemed to take comfort from the fact that someone else knew about it. After lunch I rang Nigel Crompton. He asked me to call in as he had a document for me to sign. It was the agreement between John Matthews and me for renting the cottage at Pegwell Bay. That completed, Nigel Crompton, astute old man that he was, saw that I had something on my mind. Seeking to reassure me, he told me there was nothing to worry about regarding the car chase.

'It's not that, Mr Crompton. I've been concerned for some time about Eric Harding and now I've discovered he's left his job. His wife is also worried and thinks there's another woman.' I went on to explain that other friends had also noticed a change in Eric and told him that he was the only one of our youthful gang who knew the secret of Wakefield Place.

'Well David, I don't think Eric put any of the loot into the secret rooms at Wakefield Place or Lydden, at least not recently. The police now have photographic evidence and have identified three men. I can't reveal who they are and the only reason they told me is because of the help we have been able to give the authorities.'

He could see the relief on my face and couldn't resist adding, 'That's not to say he didn't bring in stuff from across the Channel. Although very much concerned with the loss of revenue from non-payment of duty, the police and customs are much more concerned with the drugs that are coming in. It's not unknown for anonymous tip-offs to alert customs about stuff being smuggled in.'

There was no answer to this. I don't know whether he

161

expected me to accuse Eric. I certainly needed more proof before I would even consider that option and even then I must warn Eric first. Friendship must still count for something and so far I had no real proof that Eric had done anything illegal. I certainly didn't know all the details of his move from one job to his present line of work, whatever that was.

31

Options

I thought back to our childhood, now many years ago. We'd all done well enough to get to grammar school. Then I had gone into the army and Frank had gone three days a week to an agricultural college in Ashford before joining his father on their farm. Roger did two days a week at a technical college as well as serving an apprenticeship at a local garage for a pittance. Bob Simmonds, another member of our youthful gang had left the area. Eric had been the only one to go to university.

As for the girls, Sandra and Kathleen had both gone to university after grammar school. Mary, whose father was a wealthy landowner, had gone to a private school and then to university. When she left she got a job as a teacher, then married Roger and had two children. Now she was a school governor. Anne, my wife, was the only one who had not lived locally. I had met her soon after joining the army when I was stationed at Chelmsford. We had moved from place to place but when she became pregnant we bought a house in Margate, so for a few years we all lived quite close to each other.

We had all met occasionally and when I was not around the others looked after Anne and the children. It was only after I left the army that we moved to Cambridge. I searched back through my memory and knowledge of them, especially Eric. There had never been any hint that he was anything other than an honest and trustworthy friend. Now I wanted to believe he was still just that, although maybe he needed a bit of help. It was going to be difficult even to suggest it, especially if he wasn't around.

I left it another day before going over to see Sandra and during that time Joyce came and went. We chatted, shared meals and got on with our lives. After lunch on Saturday I bought a small bunch of flowers and drove over to St Peters to see Sandra. She looked as I always remembered her – composed, well dressed and friendly. She smiled when she saw it was me and invited me in. 'Are these for me? How thoughtful. They're lovely.' She took the flowers and kissed me. 'Come on in. I'm just having a cup of tea. Thanks for the other day. I'm glad it was you who found me.'

I smiled in return and followed her into the kitchen, muttering something like, 'What are friends for?' She busied herself with putting the flowers in a couple of vases, made a fresh pot of tea and took it into the living room. As we sat down I could detect nothing of the distraught woman of two days ago. She was putting on a good act. I knew it and so did she, for after a while she said, 'This is no good, David. I don't have to pretend with you. I feel awful. I wish I'd never married Eric.'

It's surprising how much ground the mind can cover in a few seconds. Years ago when we were both at grammar school we had played tennis after school and later had travelled home on the bus from Ramsgate to Margate. I remember one time at the end of term Sandra and I had become quite close, even holding hands on the way home. We'd lingered outside her front door until her mother had come looking for her. I'd forgotten that incident until now.

I finished my tea and went over to sit with her, merely

to reassure her. 'Try not to worry too much, Sandra. Until we know for certain it may not be as bad as you think. I saw Eric's dad the other day and he reckons the bust-up with Eric's firm was not his fault. I'm prepared to believe it, so we must wait until we get the true story from Eric. In the meantime, I can let you have a few thousand pounds to tide you over.'

Maybe I should have handled it better but Sandra realised I was prepared to help in a tangible way and was relieved. Without warning she turned, threw her arms around me and was kissing me. It was quite a pleasant experience and I didn't turn away. Maybe I was in need of a bit of companionship too.

'David, that's most generous of you. I wish I'd married you instead of Eric. He's been awful these past few years.'

'Yes well. Circumstances sometimes change us. I'm sure he still loves you. Let's deal with practical things first.'

The spell had been broken but I think we both realised how deep our friendship was. We looked at each other and smiled. Sandra said quietly, 'Thanks,' and we laughed, gave each other a hug and a kiss.

'Sandra, I've a suggestion. Don't say no straight away. Think about it but for the moment its just between the two of us.'

She was obviously puzzled. 'Go ahead. What's your bright idea?'

I hadn't really worked out the details myself but I might have a possible, if only temporary, solution to the financial problems. 'If, say on Monday, we saw your solicitor and got the true picture of the mortgage on this house, and if the sum involved is not too much, I might be able to redeem it. You would then just need to find the rates and living expenses. If that is not possible I might be able to buy your house. It would be relatively easy for me to get a mortgage. Then when your finances are in better shape you could buy your house back.'

As I finished uttering my thoughts I realised it was over the top but on the spur of the moment I couldn't think of anything else. Possibly her solicitor might come up with a better plan. If not, I felt sure Nigel Crompton would suggest something. Either way, my new inheritance would be put to good use. Sandra was overwhelmed. 'That would be marvellous, David. If it works out I could never repay you enough. The house is in our joint names so I must discuss it first with Eric when he turns up. He'll be cross that other people know about our problems but that can't be helped. Even if nothing ever comes of it I feel better already. Thanks.'

I must admit for the moment that Eric was not uppermost in my thoughts but of course he must be told of this possible way out. 'Let me talk to him first. I can explain that his father told me about some of the problems. As I'm an old friend who is now in a position to help, he might just go along with the idea.' I was speaking my thoughts out loud. On the face of it the whole idea was crazy. I consoled myself with the thought that if Sandra had wanted to borrow a fiver I would have said yes without hesitation. This was in a different league but the principle was the same.

Sandra agreed to let me know the moment Eric arrived and I explained that Joyce and I would probably go to the hoverport on Sunday evening to meet Helen, who was returning on the last sailing of the day.

I needed to see Nigel Crompton before meeting Sandra's solicitor on Monday. I hoped he wouldn't mind me calling his home number, and I was right.

'Nice to hear from you, David. I hope you're having a restful time.'

'Yes thanks. But I have another problem. I know it's

short notice but could I see you first thing on Monday morning?'

'Why not come over now? If you're quick you'll be in time for tea and cucumber sandwiches.'

I thanked him and agreed to go over at once. Do people still have cucumber sandwiches at four o'clock? I'd never been to his home before, though I knew roughly where it was. I thought it would be a Victorian mansion but I was wrong. It was a fairly new and quite large detached house not far from the ruins of Salmestone Grange, and incidentally not much more than a stone's throw from the rear of Wakefield Place.

He opened the front door and welcomed me in as a friend rather than a client and introduced me to his wife. She must have been about his age and had aged well, as he had. 'Do come in, Mr Holden. Do you take sugar and milk?'

'Yes. Both please.' I turned to Nigel Crompton and said, 'Very good of you to see me at such short notice. This is nothing to do with the problem at Wakefield Place.' Then I told him what had happened to Sandra and that I'd like to help.

He listened without interruption and then asked just one question.

'David. Answer me this honestly. Are you emotionally involved with Mrs Harding?'

I didn't answer quickly. After what seemed ages I heard myself saying, 'No. We're just friends and have been for years, in fact since we were about fourteen. I didn't expect that question.'

He smiled. 'I've heard it said that I'm a cunning old sod, though never to my face.'

'Well, Mr Crompton, I would never say it to your face either, though I might think it – and with admiration.'

That answer sent him into one of his rare chuckles and

he gave me the answer I had been hoping for. 'Find out the amount of the mortgage. Up to £35,000, pay it off with the money from your inheritance. If it's more than that, still pay it off, but take out a loan that can be financed from your interest together with the rents from the two cottages. Don't touch any money from the farm. If you don't want to do either of those you could sell a bit of land at Wakefield Place or, better still, the field at Pegwell Bay. The Hardings can repay you from whatever assets they have. They may prefer to sell the house and buy a smaller property so that they would be solvent once again. My advice would be to tell Mr Harding what you propose.'

I said goodbye to the two of them and left. I wasn't exactly singing on the way back to Helen's but I was certainly relieved. I thought grandad would approve of his money being put to such good use.

As I got into the hall the telephone rang. I thought it might be Sandra but it was Joyce to say she would be home about seven with some fish and chips and would I put the oven on and a couple of plates to warm. I just had time to make a trifle and nip down to get a small tub of ice cream as a surprise.

32

Detained

Joyce arrived with our fish supper and appreciated the trifle. Some time later we glanced through the papers and then watched television until it was time for bed. I quite enjoyed living in a house once more. Next morning, being the proverbial day of rest, I intended to be lazy. Joyce had other ideas and asked if I'd accompany her to church, and I was happy to do so. St Mary's, a small chapel that had once stood in the private grounds of a wealthy landowner, had been enlarged out of all recognition. It was only a few minutes' walk away and Joyce intended to be married there, so she thought she should start putting in an appearance. We also attended evensong there that night before going on to meet Helen at the hoverport.

After the service we took my car and headed off towards Pegwell Bay. With half an hour to spare, we waited in the restaurant at the port and Joyce spoke to a few off-duty customs people. A low rumble increased in volume to a deafening roar as the hovercraft approached, then reduced and finally stopped as the vessel berthed. We watched from outside as a few cars drove off and then went inside to wait for Helen. When she failed to appear after half an hour Joyce assumed her mother had missed the ferry on the other side. She went off to enquire if there was a later one.

There wasn't, but the man she asked told her he had

seen Helen and that she had been detained. Joyce's first reaction was that there must be a mistake and said that her mother always declared what she brought in.

She decided to see one of the senior customs officers. 'Stay here David, just in case she comes out.' A few minutes later Joyce returned, obviously worried. 'Mum has definitely been detained. She hasn't been searched although she's been there nearly half an hour.'

'Do they know she's your mother?'

'Oh yes. They know her quite well. In fact it's because she brought in cigarettes that are not her usual brand that set alarm bells ringing. Well that's what they told me.'

'Can't she just pay the duty and leave?'

'It's not as simple as that. It seems she has also brought in some brandy, except that it's not brandy.'

I knew instinctively that it contained cocaine and told Joyce as much, adding, 'Can you get me in to see the senior customs man?'

'I don't think you can do anything. It's obviously a mistake and they'll sort it out soon.'

'I'll be back in a minute, Joyce.' I went to my car and retrieved a piece of writing paper and an envelope. I wrote quickly – about half a page – put it into the envelope and addressed it to the Senior Customs Officer, URGENT. 'Joyce, please give that to the senior man and insist he reads it at once.'

'I'll try,' replied Joyce, and off she went.

I appreciated just how little influence I carried in trying to persuade the customs man to let Helen go, but the name of Nigel Crompton and the police chief at Margate might do the trick. For good measure I had added a brief account of the car chase and capture of the smugglers in which I had been involved. It might just make the customs man interested enough to talk to me.

Joyce returned after a few minutes. 'I'm impressed. Whatever you wrote has opened a door – just a bit. On the other hand, he may want to nab you as well, so be careful. I'll just wait here. He wants to see you.'

I knocked on his door. 'Come in, Mr Holden. I'm intrigued, so I'm prepared to listen to what you have to say.'

'Thank you very much, sir. First of all, may I assure you that Helen Carlyle is completely honest and would never seek to evade paying duty.'

'No doubt, Mr Holden. She's only helping us with our enquiries, but do go on.'

So I told him a little of my involvement with the car chase and the cache of contraband at Lydden Farm, as well as the cigarettes and brandy the police had recovered after the car chase. I also told him it was probably the same gang that had managed to plant the stuff on Helen.

'Your concern does you credit, Mr Holden. You're absolutely correct. That much we have established. Mrs Carlyle often comes through here and always declares what she brings in. It was only a chance remark by one of our officers who noticed that Mrs Carlyle had changed her brand of cigarettes that alerted us. Now we actually know where she got the different cigarettes and the brandy, when she got them and from whom. As I said, she is helping us. She obviously knew the person who gave them to her and initially was reluctant to tell us his name. Perhaps you know it?'

As soon as he posed the question that somehow sounded more like a threat, I did indeed know. It suddenly came to me in a flash. 'I've no idea. It can't be the people we caught the other day – I think they're still in custody.'

'Are you sure, Mr Holden?'

171

'Sorry, I've no idea.'

'Well, shall I tell you?'

'Please do, and if you know who planted the stuff on Mrs Carlyle, please release her and detain him.'

'Oh we have. He's a friend of yours.'

'Well, you've got me. I've only recently returned here so I don't know many people. So please tell me so that we can all go home.'

'OK. Do you know Eric Harding?'

'Yes. Of course. He's an old friend. You surely don't expect me to believe he's part of this.'

'Well, if he is it's only a very small part. We're actually discussing whether to charge him or let him go in the hope that he may lead us to bigger fish.'

I suddenly had a crazy idea. 'Does he realise he's a suspect?'

'No. Not yet. So far we have not found a thing on him. If we charge him it will be his word against Mrs Carlyle's. We're going to let her go, so we shall probably release Mr Harding as well. He admits handing over the stuff to Mrs Carlyle because she didn't have any duty-frees with her and he wanted to get some more. Later he admitted he was bringing them in for someone else, apparently as he had done on previous occasions. However, he strenuously denies they were anything other than brandy and cigarettes, although the bottles were full of cocaine. I think I'm prepared to believe him.'

I felt sure this was the same trick that had been done with the bottles found at Wakefield Place. Surely there must be a connection. I let my crazy idea take shape as I voiced my thoughts out loud. 'I know this is asking a lot. You know who I am. Let Eric go. Release Mrs Carlyle, together with the stuff, and I will keep an eye on him and let you know everything that happens. Tell Mrs Carlyle this is my plan and I think she will go along with

172

it. Better still, keep the drugs and give her other bottles of brandy and packs of cigarettes – I'm sure you can find identical ones from your store of confiscated loot – and we'll see what happens.' I don't think I sounded too convincing but I was making it up as I went along.

The customs chief thought it over. 'Give me a couple of minutes, Mr Holden.'

He came back with a smile on his face and something akin to relief. 'We can't recruit you as a temporary customs officer but we have decided to let Mr Harding go, together with his cigarettes and brandy. At the moment we don't intend to charge him, so there's no bail involved, but I shall want to talk to him again. We shall, of course, be keeping an eye on him to see what he does with them. We've given Mrs Carlyle the same brandies and cigarettes that she will pass on to Mr Harding as arranged. I suggest you take Mrs Carlyle home and leave the rest to us. Goodnight, Mr Holden, and don't dream about smugglers.' We shook hands and I went outside to the main concourse, where Joyce was waiting.

'Well?' Joyce demanded. 'Have you waved your magic wand?'

I know I had a smug look on my face as I answered. 'Of course. What did you expect?' But inside I was quaking, fuming, angry with Eric and fearful that I might let the cat out of the bag when I saw him.

Helen emerged soon afterwards, pushing a trolley with her samples and the contraband. Joyce ran over to her mother while I hung back for a few minutes. Then I, too, greeted Helen. We kissed and I knew she was pleased to see me as she asked, 'I hope you've been rehearsing your lines. David, I can't believe I was taken in by Eric. He was such a charmer.'

Joyce looked puzzled so I said, 'Say nothing. We're

173

acting out a scene and I'm just waiting for an old friend who came over on the ferry with your mum.' And there he was, smiling, relieved or arrogant that he had got away with it. I don't know. He greeted Joyce and said thanks as Helen handed over his extra brandy and cigarettes.

'Hello, David. You're surely not waiting for me?'

'No. Didn't know you were arriving, but do you need a lift home?'

'Thanks. Helen and I met on board and as she hadn't got any cigs or booze she took mine through and I got an extra supply. Sorry I took so long. Going through the green door is usually quick. I think they're looking for something. They kept me ages. I didn't realise Helen needed to declare her stuff or I could have gone through with her.'

Helen interrupted. 'Yes. I do every time. These are only samples but each article has to check out with my list. Here you are, Eric. You'd better take your stuff.' With that she handed over the bottles and cigarettes. I looked around but could see no likely passengers waiting to take the goods from Eric.

We hurried out through the concourse and made for the car park. Eric stopped to talk to someone and then caught up with us. Ten minutes later we drew up outside Eric's home in St Peters and I realised I must warn Sandra.

'Stay here a minute, Eric, and keep out of sight while I go and surprise Sandra.'

Sandra had probably seen the car draw up and opened the door almost at once. 'I've got Eric with me. Look surprised and for God's sake don't tell him that I saw you earlier or that we've made plans. Just be cross with him for being late and take it from there. Ring me tomorrow and we'll see your solicitor.'

174

I returned to the car and explained, 'Sandra says you're not at home and she doesn't know when to expect you but I reckon you're in for a rough time. She's on the warpath.'

He had the grace to look a bit sheepish and agreed he was several days late in returning. 'Don't worry. It's happened before. I'll make it up to her.'

I was really angry and for the proverbial two pins I could have knocked him down then and there in spite of his extra weight. However, I merely said, 'Well, see that you do. Goodnight. See you soon.'

At the time none of us noticed that Eric didn't have the extra cigarettes and brandy with him. It was much later that I found out what had happened to them.

I started the car and in a few minutes we were back in the peace and tranquillity of Helen's home though inwardly I was still seething.

33

Explanations

We were all keyed up and on edge following the revelations at the hoverport. Quite unaccountably, I felt responsible as Eric was my friend. However, after a second cup of tea, when I tried to apologise to Joyce and Helen, they would have none of it. I was grateful for their forbearance yet all the same I did feel guilty. As part of the smuggling story had already been let out of the bag, in fairness to the two women, I thought I should tell them a little more regarding my solicitor's involvement. Even so, security demanded that I withheld most of the story.

They listened and made no comment, though as I brought them up to date it suddenly occurred to me that old man Crompton may have had a hand in Eric's arrest. I appreciate that customs people and the police must occasionally have lucky breaks, but the more I thought of it the more I became convinced I was right, especially when I remembered what he had said to me about possible tip-offs.

I also explained about Sandra's money problems and that I had offered to help once we'd discussed it with Eric. That might not now be possible, but I was determined to help Sandra. After all, nothing had actually been proved against Eric.

It was Joyce who asked, 'David, do you see good in everyone?'

'Well, I'm not a fool but I reckon we all need a second chance sometime. The trouble is we don't always get one.'

Helen chipped in, 'Why don't we all go to bed, try to get a good night's rest and see what tomorrow brings? In any case, I've got work tomorrow and so has Joyce.'

We went upstairs, me to sleep again in Joyce's bed while she shared her mother's. I had just got settled, preparing for a restless night while thoughts churned through my mind in the hope of finding a solution to all the problems, when there came a knock on the door and Helen asked, 'Are you decent?'

'Yes thanks, but I don't need to be. Come in.' I don't know if she heard my remark but she gave no indication as she came towards me and sat on the edge of my bed. I waited while she gathered her thoughts.

'David, I'm not in the habit of entering men's bedrooms but I just wanted to say something and if I don't I'll fret about it all night.'

'Well, we can't allow that. Would you like me to leave in the morning?'

'Oh no. It's nothing like that. I wanted you to be absolutely sure that I do understand your position. You mustn't blame yourself for the actions of others. I'll be more careful in future and in any case we don't know the circumstances that made Eric do what he did.'

I was at a loss to know quite what to say. I took both her hands in mine and in doing so she fell towards me. We laughed and I let one hand go but pulled her towards me and kissed her. She didn't pull back. In fact she responded and we both laughed again. There was no need to say anything else. I think I might have pressed home the advantage that now seemed within my grasp, but there was another knock on the door and Joyce appeared.

If she was embarrassed at seeing her mother on my bed she didn't show it. 'Sorry. Have you finished, mum, because I want to ask David something just to show we trust him.'

'You'd better come and sit on the other side. I don't think I've ever had two lovely women on my bed before.' I wondered if they'd discussed this two-pronged attack.

Joyce said, 'In your dreams. I know mum wanted you to know she realises none of this is your fault. I wanted to say much the same and to ask if you'd give me away when John and I get married.'

That was the last thing I expected. 'I'd be honoured. That is, if none of your other friends or colleagues would be available.'

'They may be, but mum and I have discussed this. I would like it and so would she.'

'Then I will. Just let me know when and where.'

Joyce kissed me. Then Helen kissed me and said, 'This time we really ought to get some sleep.' They left, closing the door behind them and I lay in my bed trying hard to believe it was not all a dream.

I know I went to sleep quickly. Well, it had been a tiring day. The first thing I knew was that the light of a new day was streaming in though the windows, the birds were singing and there was a sound of crockery being laid out on a table. Then Helen's voice from downstairs, 'David, breakfast in fifteen minutes.'

Breakfast that morning, following the unusual events of the previous day, was totally normal. Everyone chatted as though it was an ordinary day and I suppose, in one sense it was. Joyce was on duty at the hoverport while Helen needed to take her samples to head office and discuss what orders should be placed with the manufacturers.

After the girls had gone to work I got busy with the

178

washing up and then the phone rang. It was Sandra. She had asked Eric to get in the week's shopping and had then made an appointment with her solicitor. She arranged to collect me. The meeting went surprisingly well and quickly. Their mortgage was for £30,000, including a small charge for redeeming it too soon. I decided to pay at once and arranged for a banker's draft to be drawn against my funds still held with Nigel Crompton. Sandra's solicitor agreed to handle this and said it would be completed tomorrow.

We would tell Eric later but now it was time for us to return home. On the way back I asked Sandra to stop at an electronics shop, where I bought a small state-of-the-art tape recorder. The microphone was minute and could be worn behind a buttonhole and activated by a switch in a pocket. It was a most compact system and I was surprised that such a small shop had one.

Sandra then took me back to Northdown Way, where I got into my car and followed her back to St Peters to await Eric's return. He wasn't really surprised to see me. They invited me to stay for lunch and afterwards I managed to get Eric to tell his side of the story. It didn't take that long, and as we sat down in the lounge I switched on the tape recorder and felt a bit of a heel.

Sandra butted in occasionally and I hoped her comments would be picked up as she was sitting on the other side of Eric. I deliberately asked some questions to which I already knew the answers and some which Eric had already covered. By this ploy I hoped to emphasise important aspects. Eric seemed not to notice the repetition. I tried to judge the time and hoped the tape would not run out before we had completed the session. In the end I drew it to a close by suggesting that Sandra made us a cup of tea. She agreed, and as she went to the kitchen I coughed and switched off the machine. The recording might prove helpful later on when Eric had to answer much more searching questions from the police and the customs officials.

Eric had not realised that I had been recording our conversation. Sandra hadn't noticed either, so her comments and questions would add a certain authenticity. My plan was to get the customs official to listen to the tape although it was unlikely he would take any notice of me. I was a civilian he did not know. Still, it was worth a try.

Over tea there was, inevitably, some comment on the story we had just heard. Eric assured us that last night had been the first time he had brought in drugs and vowed it was in total ignorance. He reiterated that he had merely brought in the cigarettes and brandy for a fellow traveller, someone he had met on several trips abroad. Then, seeing Helen, he had asked her to carry them through so that he could get the brands he preferred. Now he was extremely angry at how easily he had been duped and wanted nothing more to do with his fellow couriers, that is, apart from sorting them out.

We both tried to dissuade him from going down that route and told him to forget about retaliation. We reminded him that he was not completely in the clear and that he still had to convince the authorities that he was innocent but probably very stupid.

I made my excuses and left, anxious to get back to Northdown Way before Helen and Joyce returned from work. I played back the tape and was surprised how much ground we had covered. Then I played it through again, with several interruptions while I made notes of the more important points.

His explanation was simplicity itself and no one hearing it for the first time could doubt its honesty. It had the ring of truth and the actions of a man who foolishly had got into financial difficulties. It had never happened before. He had always been in work and to be sacked for something that was not his fault had hit him hard. He felt aggrieved, anxious about the future and not being able to look after his wife. The opportunity to make a little money on the side, purely as a temporary measure, had kept him busy. He was adamant that the rules made it perfectly clear there really was no limit to what he could bring in, so long as it was for his own consumption, but admitted the tobacco and alcohol were far in excess of anything he could use himself.

To save on expenses he had already sold his car, telling Sandra it was cheaper to hire one on the Continent. Only occasionally did he bring it over on the ferry, so he couldn't really bring in much in the way of cigarettes and spirits.

He assured us his customers in this country paid only a little more than he did. His profit paid for his fare with a little left over. That plus dipping into his savings helped to keep up the appearance of still being at work. He reasoned that the only thing he was guilty of was depriving the customs of some excise duty. He went on to explain that he had seen many others doing exactly the same and that he now realised how easily he accomplished his duty-free exploits.

I toyed with the idea of dropping the tape off at the customs office but then realised that such a gesture would almost certainly be misinterpreted. Fortunately the matter was taken out of my hands. Mr Bushell, the chief customs man, rang me. He had already spoken to Eric and asked him to attend at the Ramsgate office at ten o'clock tomorrow, and Eric had asked if he could bring me.

It all seemed very informal, being summoned by telephone, instead of an official letter. I was a bit suspicious, wondering whether this soft approach was merely a ploy to lead him into a false sense of security. However, I agreed to accompany Eric and asked Mr Bushell if I might see him first. He wanted to know what it was about but I said I didn't want to discuss it over the phone. He accepted this and asked me to be there five minutes ahead of the appointed time.

Helen and Joyce returned from work within a few minutes of each other. Over the evening meal they discussed the events of their day and nothing was said about Eric. I told Helen I was seeing the customs people tomorrow. Then we watched something on the box and retired early.

34

Testament of Truth

Tuesday turned out to be a successful day for all concerned. Even the weather was kind – a beautifully bright day with not a cloud in the sky and a light breeze so that it was not too hot. Helen and Joyce had already gone to work when I drove to St Peters to pick up Eric. I wanted to be a little early for my session with the customs man. If I couldn't persuade him that Eric was not really a smuggler, then he would have to extricate himself as best he might. Sandra assumed she would be coming with us and I could see no valid reason for her not to accompany us, even if it meant waiting in the car or the lounge at the port while we dealt as best we could with the customs officials.

I managed to get some time alone with Mr Bushell and then handed over the tape recording. 'Please listen to this before you see Mr Harding, but don't let him know I recorded the conversation. Take a copy if you wish. It seems to me it is a truthful admission of his part in this unpleasant affair.'

He took the tape. 'I'll certainly listen to it, but not until I have heard what Mr Harding has to say. As to the legality of it, I'm afraid it cannot be used.'

'Yes, but it does give a clear indication that Mr Harding ...'

He stopped me before I could finish the sentence. 'I know you want to help your friend but I cannot be influenced in any way. The best I am prepared to do is to allow you to be present at the interview and to speak if asked.'

'Thanks. I'm happy to do that.'

'Then let's ask him to come in. This will be as friendly as possible, so we'll have a cup of coffee.' He turned to a younger man. 'Tom. Ask Mr Harding to come in.'

Eric entered the room. 'Thank you for seeing me, sir.' He had an air of righteous indignation, of someone who had been unjustly accused and was prepared to forgive his accusers, and who wished to set the record straight and get on with his life. Gone was the arrogance of yesterday yet he was by no means grovelling. I felt his whole attitude was completely wrong.

The chief had risen from his chair and I got the impression that he was so surprised by Eric's attitude he actually extended his hand in greeting. Eric had a slight advantage in height but it was enough, and I felt for Mr Bushell. In all honesty I don't think it was Eric's intention to be intimidating.

'Do sit down, Mr Harding. We will go through the events leading up to your arrival yesterday and you will answer my questions. These proceedings will be recorded and later I will ask you to sign a written statement.' Mr Bushell had recovered his position and was once again in charge.

'Yes sir. I'm prepared to answer any questions. At the end I hope you'll agree I've been a bit foolish but little else.' Eric was still trying to gain the high moral ground but I knew this was the wrong approach and glared at him.

The questions and indeed the answers were quite straightforward. I had expected trick questions but none came. I was relieved, for it began to look as though the customs man might accept the answers he was getting.

They were virtually identical to those I had received when I questioned Eric yesterday. However, Mr Bushell was trained to look beyond the immediate answers for any shift in Eric's stance. He seemed to be pleased with what he was hearing and I began to feel uncomfortable that I had ever doubted Eric.

The interview continued and I wished now that I'd brought my own tape recorder with me. Eric went on to explain that following last night's arrival in England he had handed over the cigarettes and brandy to his usual contact and was certainly not aware that they contained drugs. He was adamant that he knew nothing about drugs. He was either a good actor or he was telling the truth. I was prepared to believe him. I only hoped Mr Bushell could be convinced. Eric didn't know the man's name but had seen him many times on the ferry.

Eric more or less repeated what he had revealed in our heart-to-heart yesterday afternoon. He went on to explain that when he was made redundant he had been extremely angry at being blamed for the failed contract with his original company. However, due to his earlier contacts in France, Belgium and a few in England, he was able to set up as a freelance consultant. His fees and commission had been good although it was not a steady income. Then he had resorted to selling tobacco and alcohol that he had acquired. These had been small amounts at first but gradually increased as there was a ready market.

Later, as a favour to someone he knew casually, he was asked to bring in a few cigarettes and bottles of alcohol. These were usually collected by people as he came off the ferry at Dover or the hovercraft. He never asked for payment, although after a while these people insisted on paying for his tickets and that had helped with his general expenses. He realised he wasn't the only one providing this service and got on quite well with the other couriers. In fact they often played cards together to pass the time. He never checked what he brought in and merely reckoned that someone was making a few pounds with each consignment. He appreciated this might be illegal but thought the amount too insignificant to worry about.

Then the questions went off on a different tack. The customs man leaned across and said in a most disarming manner, 'Now, Mr Harding. I'm quite prepared to believe most of what you've told me. You must surely be aware that we already knew the answers to many of the questions.' Mr Bushell had not finished yet. I sensed that the customs chief enjoyed every word as he told Eric, 'Mr Harding, you have admitted bringing into this country certain goods for which you have not paid duty. I'm afraid we have to formally charge you with that offence. For the moment we will leave aside the possible offence of trying to implicate Mrs Carlyle.'

Eric was really angry at this suggestion and bristled with rage. Fortunately he said nothing. I looked across at him and I'm sure he felt as crestfallen as I did. Mr Bushell spoke again, 'I want you to answer this next question as accurately as you can.' We both waited for it and then Bushell continued, 'As I understand it, you have been bringing in goods in excess of your allowance for some time. Could you tell me exactly when this started and what quantities in total you have brought in?'

I think Eric was really shaken by this question but he answered quickly enough. Maybe his financial training had taught him to be careful with accounts. He replied, 'I don't have the figures with me, although it was necessary to keep a record of my expenditure and receipts. I could let you have it tomorrow.'

'Then tomorrow will be soon enough. I must warn you

186

now that this admission may not help you in the long term, although it will be taken into consideration. I don't suppose you know the names of the people you handed the stuff over to?'

'No. I'm afraid not.'

Mr Bushell stood up to make his final statement. 'I am prepared to allow you to leave without imposing bail. This is a formality to adhere to the rules and to cover ourselves. You're a very lucky man. Return here tomorrow at the same time, when we shall have some documents for you to sign.'

We got out of his office as quickly as possible. I reckon that Bushell was having a real belly laugh at our expense. He must have known all along what he intended. Maybe that was how he got his kicks. He was probably good at his job but I didn't take to him very much.

Eric on the other hand thought he was marvellous. 'What a good sport. I thought I'd had it then. Do you think I'll go to prison? Maybe it will be a fine, especially if I'm prepared to help them.'

I didn't share Eric's optimism but kept silent except to say, 'Well, keep your nose clean from now on. Do what he wants and you'll probably get off with a fine.'

35

Off the Hook

We weren't out of the woods yet but life was beginning to look good again. Sandra came running over to us and she could tell at once that things had gone well. She threw her arms around Eric and hugged him. Finally when she broke away she came to me, 'Thanks, David. We can never repay you. Thanks for sticking by Eric.'

'There's no need to say anything. I'm glad I was able to help but I don't think I did much in there. It was down to Eric. Why don't I treat you to a celebration lunch and then we can all go home and relax.'

They agreed, so for the third time I drove the car out to The Viking Hotel at Pegwell Bay and ordered lunch. This time I paid, and we shared a bottle of wine, more for the occasion than because we really needed it. I only had one glass as I was driving and the last thing we wanted now was for me to be breathalysed.

We sat chatting over lunch. It was a pleasant meal. The wine and the good news from the customs helped so we were quite relaxed. I felt this as good a time as any to tell Eric about his mortgage.

'All being well, this time tomorrow you will be totally in the clear. I have to tell you something else. Please hear me out before you make any comment, Eric.'

'The other day your father told me that you had financial problems and that you had re-mortgaged your house. You weren't around at the time and Sandra was worried but reluctant to go behind your back. The result is that your mortgage has been redeemed and the house is now yours again. You can pay me back whenever you can and if that's not possible, it will be my gift to you now, rather than when I peg out. My grandfather left me more than enough, so I really won't miss it, and you'll be helping me – otherwise I'll have to pay more tax. So there.'

Eric looked across at me and smiled, then began to laugh and then cry. I said nothing for a while and as he gradually recovered I realised all would be well. He held out his hand and quietly said, 'Thanks. I most certainly will pay you back. It may take some time but I'll do it. I promise.'

I said, 'You do appreciate that we were in an awkward position not knowing the full story and not even knowing where you were. Sandra was at her wits' end.'

'Yes, I know. I've been a bloody fool. You're a crafty old sod. I'm sure you wheedled the story out from my old man. Thanks again.'

'There's just one more thing, and Sandra doesn't know about this because I've only just thought of it. If you need a bit more cash to keep you going, let me know. I could let you have a few thousand.'

'May I think about it? It will take some time to get another position but I'm determined to get back on my feet. Let's wait till tomorrow to see what Mr Bushell has in store for me. I think I've still got to persuade him I'm not really a bad boy.'

On the way back to St Peters he asked me to stop at a florist's. Sandra called to me from the rear seat and as I turned to look at her she kissed me full on the lips. 'At the time I meant what I said the other day. Now I think Eric and I will be all right.'

'I'm sure you will, but if not come and see me any

time.' I tried to make light of it but she realised that I was very fond of her and would help if she needed it.

Eric returned with two bouquets of flowers. One he gave to his wife saying, 'I hope these will go a little way towards a better life for us. Please forgive me.' The other, he explained, was for Helen. Would I take them for her, together with a note he would write? This he did a few minutes later at home, and then I was on my way back to Northdown Way. I was relieved but I suppose the tension had also got to me. I sat in the car for several minutes before I went into the house. A quick shower did wonders and I had an hour before Helen was expected back from work.

I prepared a mixed grill for when the girls came in for the evening meal. I had put Eric's bouquet in a bowl of water in the sink and his letter on the draining board. Helen arrived first and I quickly explained that the flowers were not from me. She read the note and passed it to me without comment. As I handed it back she said, 'I'm only doing this for you. I still can't believe he didn't know but I'll give him another chance.'

Joyce arrived home a little late and explained that they had had more successes during the afternoon in stopping smugglers. This time there had been no excuses and no let-off. They had not only been caught red-handed but had actually confessed and given a few important names of people a bit higher up the ladder. This information was now being followed up by the police.

Over dinner Helen showed her daughter the letter. Joyce seemed glad that she had decided to give Eric another chance, 'If he really had been one of the gang, I think Mr Bushell would have found out. I've not seen him at work but I'm told he's absolutely marvellous at interviewing suspects.' She then went on to explain that

190

certain safeguards would have been set in motion. She reckoned that Eric would be watched for some time, followed by spot checks at irregular intervals.

Joyce had another piece of news that we all relished. The man who took the stuff that Eric had brought in on Sunday had been followed to a block of flats high up on the cliffs at Ramsgate. As he went in, two customs men followed quickly before the door had time to close and asked if Mr Billingham lived there. The man didn't know but was most surprised when they asked what he'd got in the bag. They accompanied him to his flat and found an enormous quantity of stuff inside. His subsequent arrest led to more people being taken into custody.

The following morning we arrived promptly at ten o'clock and were ushered into Mr Bushell's office. Eric handed over his list of expenses and receipts. He had shown me the figures that covered some 15 months, and in view of the length of time they didn't amount to very much. Bushell took the list and made no comment.

'I have one important question and, depending on your answer, there may be supplementary ones,' he began. He gave Eric no chance to say yea or nay but continued, 'We are anxious to get our hands on the controllers of these smuggling operations. You have been caught out, though at present you are only on the fringes of the organisation. Would you be prepared to continue whatever role you are playing and report back to me whatever you think may lead us a little closer to the leader? I must advise you that we shall be pressing the courts to make an example of your involvement and suggest that you pay a hefty fine but receive no prison sentence.'

It was like something out of a TV drama and I think I might have dismissed it. Eric saw his chance at possible redemption and agreed at once. 'Yes, I most certainly would be glad to help whenever I can. I do assure you I'm not part of any gang. I must emphasise I really was only helping a casual colleague and trying to keep myself afloat financially.'

If we thought that was the end, both he and I were mistaken. Then followed the supplementary questions, all of which Eric answered to Mr Bushell's apparent satisfaction. It all seemed to be going too easily, and then I thought Eric had really upset the apple cart as he asked, 'May I ask a question?'

'Yes, of course.'

'Well I really need to make a living to support myself and my wife. Is there any way I could claim expenses?'

Without hesitation Mr Bushell replied, 'Yes. I'm coming to that. You must sign this document, and I'm prepared to offer you a small retainer and reasonable expenses. They will have to be approved, and any over and above the limit will be down to you.'

He opened a drawer and took out a document that I recognised as the Official Secrets Act or at least a short version of it. 'I'll get one of my officers to witness your signature.' He pressed a bell on his desk. Eric also had to sign the transcript of the confession given yesterday. He was so relieved to be getting off he did not bother to read the statement. I was sure he had no idea of the significance of this sudden change in his future.

On the face of it, Eric had gained little enough for the risk he was prepared to run. We were about to leave the office but the other customs man said, 'Please come with me, Mr Harding. We can't let you go into the lion's den completely alone. Memorise these numbers and destroy them. Use them only if your life is threatened, not that we think that is likely. You may not always see us, but one of us will be watching over you for a while, so try to act normally. All very mysterious, I know, but we try to look after our own – and for the time being you are on our team, so don't let us down.'

He continued, 'We've looked at your list and have calculated that your fine is likely to be £2,500. Unfortunately, this will be multiplied by three, so the total amount is likely to be £7,500. This is a very low amount as far as we are concerned, so the court may not agree. We will review the situation after six months.'

This was something neither of us had anticipated but I suppose it was comforting to know that he might not go to prison. Also in his temporary role he would not be alone. That arrangement could mean they didn't really trust him. However, I didn't share that thought with Eric.

As for me, I tried not to analyse my feelings for long. The incidents were best forgotten. Part of me was thankful that I could trust Eric once more, although that feeling was tinged with regret that I had ever doubted him. Yet I couldn't ignore the fact that he had been tempted and succumbed even though, in his opinion, he may have had valid reasons for his temporary lapse.

On a more charitable note, I wondered if I might not have done the same. On balance, I don't think I would have had the nerve. But my recent association with the police – and Joyce – had demonstrated just how few criminals were really brought to justice.

36

Down to Earth

With all this immediate activity I'd momentarily lost sight of the big picture and the major players. What I regarded as the real smuggling operation was, in one sense, much closer to home because those involved were using two of my properties to store their loot. As yet, nobody seemed to know who they were. The two who had actually been caught had probably given false names.

I had been dying to ask Eric if he knew anything about the booty at Wakefield Place and Lydden Farm. In fact I was a bit surprised that the customs man had not mentioned them during the interrogation. I supposed he might have been hoping that Eric would volunteer the information. He might still ask, for I was convinced they had not yet finished with my friend.

I wrote what I considered to be an adequate report on recent events and intended to drop it off at Nigel Crompton's chambers in Cecil Square. However, he was returning from lunch as I entered the building and he asked me to go in with him. He explained that the big-time operators were now using Sheerness on the Isle of Sheppey and also Harwich on the east coast. The police and customs at both ports were pleased with themselves, having completed a lengthy surveillance operation during which they had recovered goods and drugs to the value of half a million pounds. They had also arrested four couriers and were in the process of following others.

They hoped to collar the second group after they had hidden their booty. By comparison the contraband at Wakefield Place and Lydden was small fry.

Helen was already there when I got back to Northdown Way, and she asked me to telephone Eric.

When I returned the call Eric said he was making a trip abroad and wondered if I'd like to go with him. He explained, 'I've got to meet a couple of my clients tomorrow. Can you come too and keep an eye on Sandra for me? She could do with a break and she'll see that I really am working. Take your car and do a bit of sightseeing while I'm at work.'

My instinct was to refuse and my excuse was that although I had my passport with me, I didn't have the necessary documents for my car. Eric had already thought of that. 'No problem. It's not what you know, it's who you know, especially if they want a favour from you.'

He then explained that he had told Mr Bushell the situation and the customs man had agreed to provide the documents at very short notice. All I had to do was to turn up at Dover, report to the authorities, pick them up and we would be on our way. We would be away for two nights and I could stay at the hotel that Eric used on these occasions. I said I'd think about it and promised to ring him back.

I discussed the idea with Helen and Joyce. Joyce was all for me going but her mother was concerned. 'You've already had one scrape with these people. Are you sure you can trust Eric?'

'Oh yes. I'm sure. And it's a measure of his trust in me that he wants me there at all. I'll know what to look out for. Why don't you come along as well?'

'Thanks, David, but I have work to do, and in any case I've only just got back from France. You go. Treat it as a mini-break, but be careful.'

I rang Eric and agreed to call for him on Friday at 7.30 and with luck we would catch the 9 a.m. ferry. I was happy with this arrangement as I didn't like rushing into things. Eric said he didn't mind going a day late. He could telephone his clients and it would give Mr Bushell more time to get things organised for the car.

At the Carlyle household the conversation after the evening meal drifted on to other matters and Joyce wanted to know more about my new home being built at Higham. I imagined it was progressing. I seemed to have been in Margate for ages and to be honest hadn't given it or my friends in Higham a single thought. I needed to get back but it would be comforting to know that the current problems in Margate had been resolved.

I wrote a couple of letters, one to my architect and one to Richard Campion, explaining to both that I had been delayed but would be returning soon. I gave Helen's address in case they needed to contact me and remembered to ask how Fiona had got on at her interview. Helen said it was all right to remain in her house but I thought I had deprived Joyce of her bed long enough. I considered staying at a hotel, and I guess any of my friends would have taken me in for a night. In the end I compromised by sleeping in my motor home parked in the drive and having my meals in the house with Joyce and Helen.

Thursday was a nothing day – no telephone calls, no letters and nothing much in the papers or on television. I checked over the car, including filling the tank with expensive British petrol and stocked up my provisions cupboard. I even began to look forward to my mini-break. It had been some years since I'd been to France and it would give Eric and me a chance to get to know each other again in our new-found friendship. Helen gave me a few francs to keep me going until I could exchange some money.

During the evening, for the first time for many years I played a board game. I joined Helen and Joyce in a game of Trivial Pursuit. They had played it before but there are so many questions in a variety of categories it's impossible to remember all the answers. You either know them or you don't.

As I went out to my car to sleep Joyce said, 'I'll set the alarm for six thirty and there'll be a cup of tea for you. I'll also get breakfast as I have an early shift.' A few minutes later she came to the car. Eric had phoned to advise me not to have breakfast as we could get it on the ferry and it would help to pass the time.

Joyce said, 'I'll still get you an early morning cup of tea.'

I thanked her and said, 'Come here a minute, Joyce.' She looked puzzled and then surprised as I kissed her. 'Give that to your mother on the way in.'

In the morning it was Helen who woke me up with a cup of tea. I couldn't resist asking if she'd received my present. 'Yes, thanks. It kept me awake for some time.' She then kissed me and added, 'Look after yourself in foreign parts and you might have another when you return.'

I didn't really have any qualms about the trip to France. Following the remarkable change in Eric's future, I knew he felt obliged to continue with his few financial clients there and in Belgium. With the blessings of the customs people he had agreed to continue his activities in the courier service, albeit now without fear of prosecution. I felt sure he only wanted me with him as extra surety. Maybe I was wrong in that assumption, but with his recent confession of smuggling I knew I would be watching my back as well as his.

The documentation for my car was ready at Dover. We queued with the other passengers to get vouchers

197

enabling us to obtain duty-free items on the way over. Then we queued at the Bureau de Change to buy enough francs for three days. The duty-free shop on board was thronging with eager passengers, and when I saw the prices I could appreciate why they bought as much as possible. Most passengers would have to carry their purchases around with them. We took ours down to the car and then went up a couple of decks to join Eric in the restaurant.

Breakfast on the ferry was really something. The cooking was done along one side of a huge restaurant, with plenty of tables in the remaining area. As we moved along the serving counter with our trays, the people dishing out the meal seemed to be in automatic mode. Two rashers of bacon, two fried eggs, tomatoes and two sausages arrived on the plate. For those who were really hungry a spoonful of beans and a couple of slices of black pudding were also available in the inclusive price. Tea or coffee, toast, marmalade and butter completed the meal.

As we were leaving the restaurant a young man approached me and asked if I'd got any duty-frees. I looked puzzled for a moment and then shrugged my shoulders. Now I don't know why I said it but I replied in French, 'I don't understand what you are saying.'

Without batting an eyelid he said in much better French, 'I've got a couple of vouchers but I haven't got enough money to buy anything. Can I sell them to you for a few francs?'

I gave him ten francs and received a voucher which would enable me to purchase another lot of duty-free goods. I looked round but as far as I could see no one had witnessed the transaction and when I turned back my benefactor had vanished. I caught up with Eric and Sandra and told them what had happened.

Eric said, 'Sorry. I should have warned you. It happens all the time. Don't worry, the voucher is genuine. If you don't believe me, exchange it at the shop and get me some cigarettes.'

So Sandra came with me and got cigarettes for Eric, and wine. We felt a bit guilty as we now had more than our entitlement. By this time we had reached Calais and were approaching the quay. We went down to the car and waited until it was our turn to drive off.

Nobody bothered us as we disembarked. No one stopped us to check the car and no one asked to see our passports. Once on the quayside, I drew over to one side and stopped to watch other passengers, cars and buses as they arrived on French soil. Not one was checked. It was as though we had just arrived on the Isle of Wight from England.

For the most part their luggage consisted of a few sandwiches and flasks of tea or coffee. The huge bags they carried would be filled for the return journey with French produce and as many bottles of spirits and packs of cigarettes as they could get past customs without having to pay duty.

37

Continental Break

Eric knew his way around Calais and although I had been there years ago, so much had changed I was glad to have someone to do the navigating. The roads in the town were busy with tourists, but once clear of the built-up area around the docks Eric directed me to a newly built business complex at Coulogne, some four miles inland.

Eric asked us to wait while he went into one of the buildings. He returned a few minutes later with a useful map of the whole of the Pas de Calais and a sheaf of leaflets of places to visit. We promised to pick him up about 6.30 in the evening and the rest of the day was for us to join the other tourists if we wished. Mind you, if we saw all the places in the brochures it would take us months.

We spent a few minutes looking through them, and decided for this morning at least, we would not venture too far. So we went to one of the hypermarkets, mainly because Sandra had heard so much about them. Well, we were on our holidays, so we joined the many British, Dutch and German day trippers who descended from dozens of coaches and made our way into the hanger-like building.

Like so many hypermarkets it was made up of dozens of different shops. What was different here was that the goods on display were stacked from the floor to the ceiling, which was about 20 feet high. Instead of just bottles, the wines and spirits were stacked in crates and boxes, although it was possible to purchase individual items. So this place or one like it was where all the booze and fags originally came from. Of course we saw no evidence of drugs, but I imagined that a similar warehouse, possibly on a smaller scale, took care of that side of the smuggling. Prices here were only marginally higher than the duty-free stuff on the ferries. Here one could purchase as much as one could carry away. It was up to you how you managed to pass through customs without paying anything further.

The store was a veritable treasure house, not only of wines, spirits and tobacco but every other commodity you could possibly need. Shelves were stacked with razor blades, toiletries, tinned stuff, biscuits, cakes and other good things, while the price of well-known brands was considerably less than similar goods in England. Meat, fish, poultry and vegetables were also much cheaper than at home and they all looked beautifully fresh. Possibly the only items that seemed expensive were cheeses, and there were so many varieties I had never seen half of them before.

Sandra did a quick calculation of her shopping needs for a month and reckoned it would be cheaper to shop here, including the fare for her and the car. Along one side of this vast emporium were several small shops selling chic clothes, while along the back wall there was a huge furniture warehouse. We wondered about the transport costs of a three-piece suite – the furniture was a fraction of the price in British shops. A small bistro or café was sited almost every 50 metres so there were plenty of eating places.

After wandering around for an hour we slumped down at one of the tables, happy to rest our weary bodies. We thought we should definitely return here before we caught the ferry home. Once refreshed, we were on the open road again and two miles further on we came across an equally large store, this one selling everything required to build a house, while strategically placed on the opposite side of the road we saw everything you might possibly need for the garden, from plants, trees and shrubs to garden furniture, statues and sheds.

We decided to do a bit of sightseeing so headed for the coast a few miles south of Calais. We stopped off at a small café for a light lunch. Most restaurants we passed seemed to be closed, and then I remembered that the French enjoy their main meal in the evening. We continued our journey south, took in the scenery and admired the blue sea along this part, known as the Pearl Coast. On the landward side of the road most of the fields were pock-marked with shell holes left over from the war. I suppose they left them as a tourist attraction. Much of this part of France had been devastated during the D-Day landings of 1944. We left the car and wandered down to the beach but it was chilly, so we retraced our steps and were glad of the shelter provided by my home on wheels.

We chatted about old times and more recent events and then it was time to make our way back towards Coulogne and meet Eric. He was waiting outside the complex and once inside the car gave me directions to the hotel. His room was available, unfortunately there was no room for me. They were all for leaving and trying somewhere else but I said I'd sleep in my car if the proprietor didn't object. It seemed that he did not especially when he realised we would be having dinner there.

After the meal we walked just round the corner and spent an hour trying our skills with skittles. We were not the only visitors, and once we'd mastered the art of bowling we had a friendly competition with two other groups of holiday makers. Mind you, if we'd abstained from drinking our aim might have improved considerably but it did us all good to let our hair down.

The following morning Eric needed to catch an early train to see clients in Belgium. He thought he could fit them in although he might be very late back. Sandra and I decided to take advantage of a long day and motor down to Rheims. It would be an all-day trip. There wasn't a cloud in the sky and the sun was already warming up the earth as we headed south-west. In this region there are numerous villages and small towns, all having historic associations with both world wars. Most had war memorials and quite a few had turned large houses into museums.

We strayed off our route for a few miles to visit Arras, and while there we bought stuff for a picnic later on. Then we were on our way once more, stopping for coffee at St Quentin. A few miles further on the landscape began to change and we were among the hills north-west of Rheims. By this time it was really warm so we came off the road and drove a short distance into the wooded countryside for our picnic.

There's nothing quite like French bread, although it doesn't stay fresh for long. This, with plenty of butter, cheese and a mixed salad, went down a treat. Sandra had also bought two bottles of *vin ordinaire* that tasted really rough at first. A few more gulps of the plonk and we had acquired the taste so much so that the first bottle was consumed before we had finished our first course. For sweet we had fresh peaches. We finished the second bottle and then lay down on the blanket.

Blue sky above the tree tops was speckled with high cirrus clouds. Birds chirruped intermittently while the canopy of trees reduced the heat of the day to a lazy and comfortable warmth. I know I slept and had pleasant dreams – that is, until the ache in my arm became uncomfortable. I was suddenly aware that reality had invaded my dream though in my waking moments I couldn't be sure. We are told that dreams that seem to encompass hours are in fact split seconds in time when our mind is on a different plane.

I have no idea how it happened but I woke to find Sandra's head resting on my arm. For a moment she looked totally relaxed and with a slight smile on her lips. I blew gently on her face. Her arm came up to whisk away the imaginary fly and she returned to her slumbers.

I called out, 'Hello Eric. I didn't expect to find you here.'

Sandra was awake instantly. She realised what had happened and said, 'You horrible pig,' and hit me playfully on the chest. I bent down and kissed her. Though wide awake it was still pleasant and comforting. I wondered if Sandra felt the same.

'It's time to make a move.'

Sandra's reply was a sleepy, 'Just a few more minutes. I like being here with you.' She reached out, put her arms round my neck, pulled me towards her and kissed me with a passion I had not experienced for many years.

I liked being there, too, even if she was Eric's wife, but I was worried. She and Eric seemed settled with each other again. I thought of Anne and our happy years together. This present idyllic moment would pass. We still had a few miles to go if we really wanted to see the shops in the big city, so I reminded her, 'We really should go if you want to do some shopping in Rheims.'

Sandra said nothing and I momentarily wondered if she had been playing games. We scrambled the picnic things together and started out for the city. Once there we did a bit of sightseeing like any other tourists and then decided it was silly to come all this way and not buy anything. Sandra made two purchases. One was a pretty dress and the other a two-piece of jacket and slacks. She didn't have enough francs for both and neither did I. In my best French I managed to persuade them to take English pounds. I hadn't used French for years yet it came tripping off my tongue with the greatest of ease. It must have been quite good, for the salesgirl understood perfectly and even complimented me on my command of her language. Sandra was also impressed and when we got outside praised me. 'I didn't realise you were that good. Of course we all did French and one other language at school but most of us have forgotten it.'

'That's nothing. You should hear me when I get going in Spanish. Actually I always liked languages and they came in useful on more than one occasion. When the fighting was over in the Falklands we had hundreds of enemy soldiers to deal with. Sheer numbers just swamped our intelligence units so I helped out. It was really a case of finding out who the soldiers were, what they did, which unit they came from and where they lived so that we could send them home. There was a hard core of about five hundred diehards, and it was the proper interrogators who dealt with them. Most of the soldiers were conscripts, only in the army for a short time. We didn't know what to do with them so we were glad to repatriate them and I think they were grateful.'

'There's more to you than meets the eye.' Sandra smiled then turned to me and suggested we should go back to the coast, so that's what we did.

We drove all the way back to the hotel. Eric was already there and had drinks waiting for us at the bar. Sandra wore her new dress for dinner and explained that it was such a bargain she could not resist it. I said nothing but wondered how she'd explain the other purchase later on. After dinner we sat in the lounge chatting, had a few more drinks and then went to bed – Sandra and Eric to their room and me back to my car. It was really quite comfortable and in a way I was glad to be on my own.

Eric was free the next morning so he joined us as we drove to see the British cemetery just outside Boulogne and later wandered around the shops in town. We had a midday snack in one of the bistros, and while Eric made a last call on a client Sandra and I drove to a hyper-market to buy a few things.

38

Smugglers en Masse

All went well and we caught the early evening ferry. As on the outward voyage, we passed the time by having a meal on board. After dinner we made our way from the restaurant and did a constitutional around the deck and passed close to the shop. As we watched it was obvious that a few people were going in more than once and I drew Eric's attention to this. His only comment was, 'Money talks. How many vouchers do you want?'

Before we could reply he had walked over to a small group of people. We saw him hand over a few coins and he received in exchange three vouchers entitling him to purchase duty-free items from the on-board shop. Sandra and Eric joined the queue, intending to buy a few more bottles and cigarettes. While I waited for the others I recognised the chap who had approached me on the outward trip. He obviously didn't recognise me for he sidled up and asked if I'd be prepared to carry a couple of bottles ashore for him as he had too many.

It seemed, at face value, such an innocent request. He could see I didn't have any purchases with me but I hesitated and he said, 'Go on. It's my mother's twentieth wedding anniversary and we want to give her a good party.' In the end I agreed and took the bottles. He said he'd be waiting for me after we'd cleared the customs at Dover.

Now this may have been all fair and above board and

in ordinary circumstances I would have thought nothing more of it. Except that I knew something similar had happened to Eric just a few days ago. I told the lad I'd just go to the shop and get some cigarettes and I'd see him later. Off he went and I bought my cigarettes – well, cigarettes for Helen. I couldn't see the others so I returned to my car and put the cigarettes in a side pocket and then went in search of a crew member and asked him to direct me to the purser's office. He didn't question my reasons. Once with the purser, I explained what I thought might be a problem. He listened and then passed me on to the second officer. I could tell he was definitely interested even though they were busy as the ship was approaching Dover.

I explained that a friend of mine had recently been arrested for a similar offence and I didn't want to end up in prison. He took down a few details. 'Don't worry, sir. Thank you for bringing it to our attention. I will contact Dover and the police will be on the lookout for you. Go through the green exit and then hand over the bottles to the chap and walk away.'

I remembered that I would be driving my car off and he asked if I had anyone with me who could do that, so that to all intents I was a foot passenger. I agreed and set off in search of Eric and Sandra to explain the change in plans. We looked round but couldn't see my contact, so we returned to the car to deposit all our goodies. I cancelled the code on the ignition so that Eric could drive it and went up on deck again with my cigarettes and the two suspect bottles, although they both looked like the genuine article.

Only time would tell, and that time was fast approaching, for the ferry was being manoeuvred into position for docking. In a few minutes my car would be driven off and I would walk ashore with my duty-free goods. I spotted my contact a few yards ahead. He seemed to be on his own and I wondered how often he did this trip and whether his mother had really been married for 20 years. It crossed my mind that unless I was carrying something much more than wine, such an enterprise could never provide a living, not even if it happened several times a day.

I did exactly as I had been instructed, passed through the customs and then handed the bottles over to the young man and walked on without a backward look.

Glancing through the outer doors of the building, I could see that Eric had already disembarked and was waiting with Sandra in the car. I hurried forward and inadvertently bumped into someone. I apologised and vaguely recognised him as having been on the ferry.

He smiled. 'That's all right. Can I give you a lift? My brother's outside.'

'No thanks. I also have transport.' With that we parted company.

I joined Eric and Sandra and thought no more about the incident. We sorted ourselves out and I got into the driving seat, but we waited a little while until most of the traffic had left the concourse before starting out on the journey to Margate. It was getting dark as we left the docks so I switched on the lights and headed up the long incline on the A2. Near Barham I left the motorway to go cross-country to Wingham, a bit of a winding route but very pleasant in daytime and quiet. Now we were the only vehicle on the road, and made good time.

We had to wait at the 'T' junction before getting into Wingham. It was then that I first noticed the other car. As I moved forward, it did too, although when I increased my speed it stayed back. The long street in the village was deserted so I pulled into the side on the pretext of checking my front offside tyre. As I got back into the driver's seat I saw the other car just starting to move forward again. Did it also have a tyre problem? Well, there was nothing really sinister in that. It meant only that another car was on the same road and going in the same direction.

Twenty minutes later we were in St Peters and I said goodbye to my friends. They asked me to go in but I wanted to get back to Northdown Way and to Helen. I think my near involvement with Sandra had decided for me where my future might be. I glanced in my rear view mirror and there it was again, the black car. It might still have been innocently going along the same route but some inner voice told me this was no coincidence. I decided to stop off at the Wheatsheaf.

I parked, walked in through the public lounge entrance, ordered a whisky and waited by the door. Nobody came in for a full five minutes and then three teenagers burst in, giggling. One headed for the bar while the other two looked for a table. It couldn't be they who were following me but took I the opportunity while they were getting their drinks to go to the toilets and out through a side door round the back.

From there I could see my car and another that hadn't been there when I arrived. It was black. There were no lights showing and I could see no one inside until I realised it had darkened windows – a bit suspicious in itself. Even my mobile home didn't have darkened glass although it did have curtains. I returned to the pub and made three phone calls. The first was to Helen to let her know I was on my way home. The second was to Nigel Crompton to advise him of my suspicions that someone might be following me. The third was to the customs people at Ramsgate. Mr Bushell wasn't on duty but his deputy was there and appreciated the significance of my call.

Nigel Crompton had promised to call the local police to put them in the picture. I don't doubt that he also phoned his mysterious contact. It had now been 15 minutes since I'd arrived at the pub and I reckoned I should make a move. Just then another car drove into the car park – actually a van – and four workmen emerged. Two went directly into the pub while the other two said cheerio to their mates in loud voices and disappeared.

At least that is what I imagined, and what was obviously intended for me and anyone else who might be watching. It vaguely crossed my mind that it was a bit late for workmen to be going home. I was about to return to my car when I saw the two workmen come back to the car park.

They took full advantage of the shadows and used bushes and other cars as they crept closer to the car with the darkened windows. I watched fascinated. Just as quickly as they had arrived they disappeared, and soon the other workmen emerged from the pub and got into their van. I walked quickly to my car, started the engine and moved out from the car park.

Glancing in my mirror, I caught the lights of headlamps and although I couldn't be sure, I guessed I was being followed by my original trackers. Just to make certain, I deliberately went past Northdown Way, and entered it from the other end. The other car followed at what they thought was a safe distance, and now I caught sight of a larger vehicle behind them. Fifty yards behind them under the lights from the street lamps I made out the workmen's van. I wondered whether I should stop and confront my followers but decided to get back to Helen. I drove slowly up the drive, got out the various bottles and cigarettes and rang the bell.

39

Confrontation

Helen was obviously pleased that I had arrived back. Instead of a handshake I received a full-bodied kiss on my lips. It was a kiss that told me I was welcome and that she was relieved to see me in one piece. I detected concern in her eyes.

'Come in and tell me all about your trip. But before that, will you ring Nigel Crompton? He rang a few moments ago and I gather it's important to ring him back.'

'Can I take my coat off first?' It was a rhetorical question. Helen smiled, took my coat and hung it up while I went to the phone. The solicitor's message was brief. The police had told him that my suspicions were correct. Two men had been following me, probably since I got off the ferry. After my earlier phone calls the authorities had swung into action.

A police team, posing as workmen, had followed the suspect vehicle from the Wheatsheaf, while customs people from Ramsgate had been alerted and were sending over two of their people. His final words were comforting, 'Nothing for you to worry about now, David. You really can leave this one to the authorities. Thanks for letting us know in the first instance.'

I went into the sitting room to join Helen. Joyce had apparently been trying on a new uniform, and as she came downstairs to show her mother there was a ring at

212

the front door. She opened it and later described the look of horror on the faces of the two men outside. However, they quickly recovered and asked to see the gentleman who had just returned from France. They added, 'We don't know his name but we think he may have inadvertently taken the wrong bottles of wine.' Joyce told the men to wait in the porch while she came inside to tell me.

My first reaction was to confront the men. This was quickly replaced by a more cautious approach. I knew I didn't have any bottles that I had not bought. I also knew that the only other bottles I had brought into the country had probably been confiscated and their owner would now be helping the police with their inquiries. Alarm bells were ringing, but I couldn't keep the men waiting outside too long or they might force their way in. On the other hand, I didn't want to alarm Joyce or her mother. Maybe the cavalry was just round the corner, but I must be prepared.

I called to Helen, 'I suspect the men in the porch are bogus but I need to find out. Will you pick up the phone and dial 999 if I call out to you?'

I opened the inner door just as there came another ring at the front door. I closed the door behind me and opened the front door. One of the workmen from the pub car park said, 'Good evening, sir. Mind if I come in?' and at the same time showed me his police warrant card.

'Please do.' He followed me into the hall, and as he did so there was a slight scuffle behind as the two visitors sought to escape, only to be forcibly prevented by the policeman's colleagues, who turned out to be the other workmen I had seen at the Wheatsheaf. With the minimum of fuss the undercover plan had gone remarkably well, except that I was still very much in the dark.

Thinking back, the authorities had mounted a smooth operation in a remarkably short time if they had acted only since my phone calls. On the other hand, they may have been watching me all along. Talk about Big Brother, though at present it was reassuring.

The two men were bundled off into the waiting police van that had been parked in the driveway to prevent the escape of the villains. The policeman came into the sitting room and introduced himself as Sergeant Hornby. I later found out that he was known as Puffer to his friends. He apologised for the disturbance and said how relieved he was to have captured the men, adding that although they could have turned violent, once they realised the game was up they had accepted the inevitable. Sergeant Hornby reckoned the customs people and the government were getting fed up with the smugglers and might make an example of the latest prisoners. 'Oh yes, Mr Holden. The bottles you brought back for that young man at Dover contained drugs. The wine was in a cleverly constructed bottle within a bottle. The larger, outer one did contain wine but the inner one was sealed and contained a useful amount of heroin.'

Joyce offered the man a cup of tea but he declined, saying he'd better get off with his prisoners as there was a lot of paperwork to complete. Then speaking directly to Joyce he said, 'I'd like to have seen their faces when you appeared in the uniform of the very people they were trying to avoid.'

'Yes. It was like alarm, fright, indecision all rolled into one and they didn't know whether to stay or flee,' was Joyce's comment.

The sergeant edged towards the front door. 'We'll probably need a statement from you, sir, but I'll let Mr Bushell or my inspector contact you sometime tomorrow. Take care and don't go talking to any strange men.' We

214

heard the van drive off, breathed a sigh of relief, and then the car was taken away by one of the 'workmen'. We returned to the sitting room and Joyce made a pot of tea.

Then followed a silence that seemed to last for ever, all of us wrapped up in our own thoughts, until Helen asked if anyone would like another cup. No one did but it had the desired effect and we all started talking at once. Joyce smiled. So did I, while Helen said, 'What a night! We don't want many more like that. David, before you tell us how you enjoyed your break, you'd better tell us about those men who followed you to my house.'

So that's what I did. As I finished, Joyce remarked, 'A likely story, Mr Holden. I'm arresting you for telling a plausible but unlikely tale.'

It lightened the mood and I handed Helen the cigarettes I'd bought for her. 'You'd better check them carefully. They haven't been out of my hands but for all I know they may contain drugs.'

Joyce said she was on duty at 11.30 so she went upstairs to get ready. Helen and I sat close together on the sofa, holding hands like shy school kids. We said nothing, yet in those few minutes I knew that Helen was the woman I wanted to spend the rest of my life with. Joyce returned, dressed in civvies and carrying a suitcase.

'I'm off. Take care of each other. I'll see you in three days' time and I shall want a full report about the smugglers – and anything else of importance. I've put clean sheets on my bed, David, just in case you are staying.'

I got up, kissed her and said I'd look after her mother. Joyce answered quietly so that her mother couldn't hear, 'I'm glad. Don't let her down.' She said goodbye to Helen while I went outside to move my car so that she could get hers out and waited while she started the engine.

'If you manage to find out more about those villains, we'll compare notes when you get back,' I said.

I returned to the house and told Helen, 'I've had instructions to look after you, so just tell me what you want me to do.'

Helen's reply was enigmatic to say the least. 'If you don't know, there's little point in me telling you.' I must have looked puzzled, possibly hurt, for she added quickly, 'I'm sorry. That didn't come out as I'd intended. Come here, Mr Holden.'

I did just that. We kissed gently at first as friends. Then as the kisses became more passionate I guessed for that night at least I would not need Joyce's clean sheets or her single bed.

We had a final nightcap, then I said, 'You go up. I'll just make sure everything down here is locked up.'

40

Romantic Interlude

We woke quite early the following morning with no guilt or awkwardness between us and did what many couples do. After a leisurely breakfast Helen suggested I should telephone the police rather than wait for them to call us. That way we'd at least be able to plan the remainder of the day as Helen did not have to go to work. The police were pleased to get my call. It seemed that a customs officer from Dover would be coming over and they would appreciate both of us attending at 11.30 at the Margate police station.

We had plenty of time to get ready yet neither of us mentioned the smugglers or even other events of the previous day. It was almost as though we didn't want anything sharing our new-found intimacy, and our mood was so in keeping with our present happiness as to need no comment.

Once at the police station and settled into the interview room, it was obvious they were all pleased with the outcome so far. I hadn't seen the customs officer before, though he seemed to know Helen. 'Come in, Mrs Carlyle and Mr Holden. Before we begin the formal statement we thought you'd like to know that after leaving your house the police had a most successful few hours. The young man pointed out by Mr Holden had been in trouble with customs before. He was a lot older than he looked and had been operating a similar scam for the past two years. He used Dover, Folkestone, Ramsgate and even New Haven. On two previous occasions when they had searched him they had come away empty-handed. This time there was no escape.'

The policeman continued the story. 'Your telephone call from the Wheatsheaf enabled us to put in a four-man team of plain clothes officers. They were able to check the licence plates of the car with the darkened windows. This time the villains had really slipped up. For once their vehicle had not been stolen and we were able to identify the owner and where he lived. So while we followed the car and eventually arrested them at your home, other officers raided a house in Deal.

'I can't tell you all the details as we haven't finished yet. That car had more hiding places than we've ever seen before. Not only that, but their house in Deal has revealed cigarettes, tobacco, alcohol, beer and drugs in such quantities we can't believe our luck. There's one other piece of information, and I'm sure you'll be interested in this, Mr Holden. We found another ex-army hideout in the woods at Nonnington. That's not far from Deal.

'We were actually taken there by the girlfriend of one of the smugglers. Like the one at Lydden, it was full of contraband. It was quite late last night when we got there so we're continuing our search this morning. We can't believe our luck. Actually, the girlfriend had been worried for some time about her involvement in the smuggling operation. Once arrested she turned Queen's evidence, and so far we've got a good haul. Mind you, it might not help her much but I suppose her sentence will be less than the others.'

He had come to the end and was smiling, obviously relieved at the success that had been achieved. 'Congratulations to both the police and the customs,' I said. 'I can tell you we were very relieved when your men arrived last night. Does that wrap up the gang?'

'Well, hardly. The amount of paperwork we now have to complete is enormous and I daresay we are only scratching the surface, but it's a good result by any standard. Sadly, within a week everything will be back to normal. We continue to watch while the villains continue to bring the stuff in. Are you both ready to add your statements to the paper mountain?'

'Yes, of course. We'll keep it as brief as possible.' We did just that then we were free to leave, with smiles and handshakes all round.

As we walked towards the car Helen turned to me and said, 'David, do you know where I'd like to go for lunch?'

'Yes, of course. Captain Digby, here we come.' We drove towards Margate sea front and kept to the coast road all the way to Kingsgate and the public house where we had first met.

We lingered over lunch and then walked down the road to the gap in the cliffs and down to the beach below Kingsgate Castle. The tide was out and we walked along the sands holding hands. We made no plans for the future but told each other little snippets of our lives before we'd met. Even this late in the year the sun was warm and there was no wind. We lost track of time and even how far we'd ambled along the sands. After a mile or so the beach gave way to rocks though only for a short distance, and then it was sand again for the next mile.

No mention was made of our night spent together. Nor did the police, customs or anything else intrude upon our thoughts or the peaceful scene as we approached Broadstairs. At this point the tall chalk cliffs meant we had a long climb up man-made steps to reach the top. We both felt tired. Although we had travelled no great distance it was the furthest I had walked since my army days. We gratefully slumped into chairs at the first teashop we came across.

Tea and a selection of cream cakes arrived. They weren't particularly good but it was worth it just to rest. We sat there almost in silence – happy in each other's company. At five o'clock we caught the bus and sat on the top deck until we reached the Wheatsheaf, then remembered we'd left the car at Kingsgate. I really couldn't believe we'd done that.

We walked the short distance to Helen's home and she drove me out to the Captain Digby to collect my car. Five minutes later we were back in Northdown Way and slumped in the comfortable chairs in her sitting room to ease our tired limbs.

After a meal we sat in the sitting room and turned on the TV. I scarcely took in what I saw but continued to mull over in my mind the events of the past 24 hours. When Helen got up to make some tea I turned off the box and offered to help. 'No thanks. You put your feet up and rest while you can. Tomorrow may be a busy day.'

She couldn't possibly have known, but her prediction was remarkably accurate. Today had been marvellous, not only in our personal relationship, but the weather had been remarkably warm and the smugglers had been apprehended. All that was about to change. In the early hours the storm broke. Helen's house, a mile or so inland from the coast and protected by other houses and the high hedge, suffered no damage. We lay in bed listening to the storm as it raged overhead. The slight gaps between each onslaught only served to emphasise its ferocity. By five o'clock, with the storm still venting its rage, we had got up to make the inevitable cup of tea.

Just before the kettle boiled the power was cut. Helen's only comment was, 'It'll be cold milk and cereals for breakfast. Would you like it now or later?'

'I'll have a cup of tea now and we'll think of something for breakfast. I'll just nip out to my car and finish making the tea.' So I took out the kettle with the warm water, poured it into my kettle in the car and lit the gas. I returned to the house with my teapot and more hot water in Helen's kettle.

Helen smiled her thanks. 'I bet you were a Boy Scout.'

'I was for a short time, but remember I joined the army when I was quite young. That's where I learned my survival skills. I'll see if there's any damage in the garden and then if the power is still off I'll cook breakfast in the car.'

After breakfast we walked down to the coast. A few houses near the cliffs had borne the brunt of the storm, evidenced by the broken windows and tiles littered all over the pavements. Several chimney pots had been torn away by the wind and were now broken on the ground. As Helen and I leaned over the railings on the promenade above the cliffs, the sight some 70 feet below was one of utter devastation. Mother Nature can be awesome and sometimes wilful. The debris thrown on to the beach was bad enough, though higher up the beach and closer to the cliffs, huts that had been there for years had been shattered beyond recognition. There was no way they could be repaired but they would make a glorious bonfire on Guy Fawkes' night.

The wind was still quite strong, and though we were both well wrapped up it was cold. I was a bit surprised that no one else had come out to view the damage. Accidents like the storm last night usually brought out huge numbers of people. Maybe they were concerned with their own problems. The tide had turned but the sea was still rough and appeared quite unfit for the small boats that were braving the waves. Then we saw three small motor boats smashed beyond help high up on the beach where they had been left by the receding tide. Close to the water's edge was a much larger boat – a motor cruiser, flopped over and showing a large hole on its port side. Floating close to the cruiser, heads facing downwards were two bodies.

41

Boys' Own Adventure Story

Looking towards the motor cruiser and the bodies nearby, I thought I could detect some movement, although the distance was too great for me to be certain. It may just have been the motion of the waves gently moving the bodies.

I turned to Helen. 'I'm going down just to make sure. Could you find a phone box, get hold of the coastguards and tell them what's happened? They may already know but I don't expect they'll mind being told again. Tell them roughly where the boat is and they will pass on the message to the police.'

She agreed. 'You take care, David. If there's not a phone box within a hundred yards I'll knock on one of the houses.'

I needed to find a way down to the beach while Helen went in search of a phone. I thought I remembered a gap in the cliffs nearby, came across concrete steps and started to run down. After the second right-angled turn I slowed, remembering Helen's words. If I tripped I could easily have knocked myself out on the concrete sides. Even so, I was breathless by the time I reached the bottom – and then came the difficult bit. Walking across the dry sand was hard going until after 50 yards or so it became firmer underfoot and slightly wet from the receding tide.

As I neared the boat it seemed to be more damaged

223

than it had appeared from the cliff top. The bodies looked lifeless. Down at sea level the wind had dropped, although it was still quite cold. I reached the first body and with a good deal of effort turned it over to face me. There was no doubt this one was very definitely dead. A bullet wound to the temple had made sure of that, and there wasn't much left of the face for identification.

The second also looked beyond help. I'd seen enough dead bodies in my time. However, I thought I could detect a faint pulse and though there couldn't be much life remaining I struggled to move the body higher up the beach and completely out of the water. It's amazing how heavy an inert body can be, or possibly I was finding out just how unfit I really was. The clothing on the man was heavy with sea water.

I needed something to roll the body on to in order to drag it from the water's edge, so I scrambled on to the boat in search of a blanket or something similar. It was then that I realised that wherever the boat had come from, it had recently been to France, or maybe that had been its destination before tragedy struck. Several bundles of French francs in various denominations from 50 upwards had spilled out on to the sodden seats. I had never seen so much money.

Then I noticed the cans of beer and bottles of spirits, some of which were still in large cartons. They had mostly survived the shipwreck. The same could not be said about the cartons of cigarettes that were floating about all over the inside of the cruiser.

I made my way to the inner cabin, pulled off a couple of blankets from a bunk and went outside to help the man on the beach. Once I had spread the blanket on the sand and rolled him on to it, I thought it would be easy to drag him. At first, in spite of my best efforts, nothing happened. Then slowly my burden began to slide. In no time I was sweating but at least the body was clear of the water and I could see no visible wounds.

He still looked deathly pale and I wondered, for a moment, if it might not be kinder to let him die. I knew only a little about life-saving and it seemed that every few years the authorities changed the recommended survival techniques. However, I managed to get him to open his eyes. He groaned, then relapsed into his comatose state. I turned him on his side and went on board once more to look for something dry to cover the poor wretch.

Just as I entered the boat I saw a blue Land Rover coming along the sands from the Margate direction. Even at that distance I recognised it as a coastguard vehicle. Maybe the police would come from the other direction. They didn't, but more or less following the route I had taken I could see one policeman hurrying across the sands.

My search for a blanket was put on hold as I watched the two services coming towards me and wondered idly which would arrive first. To be honest, I think I was taking a breather, relieved that the experts were on their way and would soon take over.

I looked up to the cliff top to see if Helen was there. She wasn't, and as I ranged along the cliffs I caught a movement out of the corner of my eyes to the left. Another vehicle was travelling quickly along the wet sand. It didn't appear to belong to any of the emergency services, and as it got closer I could see it was a pick-up truck. There were two people in the cab and one standing up in the back.

I continued my search for something dry. There were several storage cupboards in the cabin, but instead of a blanket when I opened one, half a dozen packets fell out. They were drugs and this probably meant that the dead

225

man and his almost lifeless companion were smugglers. There had been no attempt to hide the drugs or other contraband.

Looking through the porthole, I saw that the coast-guards were the first to arrive. They could now see for themselves what Helen had told them on the phone. The next to arrive was the pick-up truck, and as it slithered to a halt the man in the back jumped down and moved towards the coastguards. The two others took their time and walked towards the boat.

I sensed that there was likely to be a confrontation – three against two although the policeman was approaching fast. So far no one had seen me and to this day I don't know why I didn't show myself. As luck would have it, I turned out to be the surprise that the good guys needed. The coastguards and the policeman took one look at the dead man and then concentrated on the other until the policeman noticed the newcomers were edging towards the boat and seemed to have no intention of offering assistance.

'Where do you think you're going?' asked the man in blue.

The answer he got was not encouraging, 'You carry on with your job and we'll try to salvage our boat.'

At that point one of the coastguards said, 'Afraid you can't do that, sir. We need to look at it before anyone else goes aboard, but first we have to help this poor fellow.'

Again the answer was not helpful. 'That's what you think. Stand back and don't do anything stupid,' where-upon he drew out a revolver.

One of the coastguards took a step forward. The man with the gun said, 'That's far enough. One more step and I fire.'

Then the policeman intervened. 'You can't get away

with it, and if you discharge that weapon it will only make matters worse for you.'

The policeman may have been following laid-down procedures, but it wasn't going to help the present situation. The men were determined to get into the boat and I knew why.

Then three things happened all at once. The coast-guard took another step forward. The man fired, although I think it was only intended as a warning and it hit the ground. The policeman drew his truncheon and in one action brought it down heavily on the man's gun arm. He quickly followed this up with a tackle and had handcuffs on the man before anyone realised.

But all was not over yet. One of the other men produced a gun and from a safe distance threatened them all. I looked around for a weapon and all I could see, nestling in its place in the open cockpit, was a Very pistol used for sending up a distress flare. I moved cautiously forward into the cockpit and released the retaining catch.

I was still surprised that no one had realised I was there on the boat. The policeman tried again to quieten things down and to reason with the gunman, who now appeared to have the upper hand. The policeman said something like, 'You can't take all of us. One of us will get you, so why not give yourself up.'

His words fell on deaf ears for the man merely replied, 'Anyone who stops me getting on that boat is dead.' To emphasise his intentions he fired a warning shot, and at the same time I fired the flare directly at him. I intended my intervention to be merely a distraction so that the policeman could wade in with his truncheon again. However, it was a better shot with the cumbersome weapon than I thought. The flare hit the man full in the chest, and in the confusion that followed, the policeman

227

lashed out – and this time I heard the gunman's forearm break.

Now there were two villains down and only one remaining. That one saw his chance, and as the coast-guards helped the policeman to restrain his companion he ran towards his truck. I quickly reloaded the Very pistol and fired at the retreating man. At 50 yards or more my aim was not so good, although the flare, designed to shoot high into the air, still had enormous momentum. It hit the man on the backs of his legs and he fell down. I leapt from the boat and held on to him while a coastguard went to get some rope to secure the prisoners.

42

Day of Reckoning

They had recovered from my surprise appearance and were mightily relieved that the only ones hurt were the villains. The policeman came over and said, 'Nice to have you on our side. Who are you?' I told him, and explained that it was my partner who had raised the alarm while I had gone down to see if anyone was alive, not realising they were smugglers.

One of the coastguards offered some advice. 'If anyone asks, you'd better say you were sending off distress flares and the prisoners got in the way. You're pretty handy with that weapon. Lucky the cartridges weren't wet.'

The policeman introduced himself as PC Williams. 'Thanks, Mr Holden. Please thank your wife for telling the coastguards about the boat. They passed the message on to us. I wonder how the others knew about it.'

Helen had heard the shots and come down the steps and was now walking across the sands. I waved to her as the others turned their attention to the lifeless man.

By this time the coastguards had called their base on the radio and asked for an ambulance. The policeman also contacted his superiors. He explained the situation, and asked for transport for his prisoners and a crane or tractor to drag the boat out of the water. He also asked for a metal detector. I suppose this was to try to locate any gun that may have been ditched, or spent bullets. Finally he asked for several lengths of police blue and white tape and some stakes to cordon off the boat. He was certainly on the ball.

Helen arrived and spoke first to the policeman. I moved towards them and caught the end of her comments: 'Yes. If I let him out of my sight for more than two minutes there's trouble. He was only supposed to come and see if anyone was alive.'

She smiled at me and we kissed while I assured her that everything was all right as far as I was concerned. I then told PC Williams about the money, drugs and other items I'd seen on board. I knew what would happen now. We'd all have to go off to the police station and make statements. I could certainly do without another trip there and was relieved when he said he'd get in touch with us later. I reckoned he had more than enough on his plate. 'By the way, sir, thank you for your timely intervention. I'll just wait for my colleagues to arrive and then I'll go and collect my motor cycle. Hope no one's pinched it.'

Just as Helen and I were making our way towards the steps, a police van came along the beach, having come down the slope near the old jetty and driven along the sands. Then a helicopter flew overhead and landed close by on the hard sand. By this time the railings along the top of the promenade were crowded with sightseers, all anxious to see what was going on. For the moment, windows broken by the storm, missing slates and chimney pots took second place. I wondered why no one had attempted to come down the steps. As we reached the top I could see why. Two policemen were preventing them.

We declined their offer to take us home and walked slowly back to Northdown Way. We had left the house just before eight o'clock. It was now gone ten and it felt like we'd done a day's work. As we went through the hall

Helen said, 'I hope it's not always like this wherever you go.'

'Of course not, unless there happens to be an R in the month.'

Helen had just started to get an early lunch when the phone rang. 'Can you answer that please, David.'

It was Mr Bushell, and his first words were not encouraging, though on reflection I think he was trying to make light of a difficult situation. 'Ah, Mr Holden. I'm glad I've caught up with you. I've just said to my colleagues we ought to have recruited you when you were in my office.' I didn't reply and my silence may have put him off a bit. After a moment he spoke again. 'Are you still there, Mr Holden?'

'Yes. I'm still here. What can I do for you?'

'The police have just been on to me, asking if someone from this office could come over to Margate to take charge of a motor cruiser and its contents that I gather include some drugs. I understand that you were in at the kill, so to speak, so perhaps if I could have your version of events.'

I wondered what the police had already told him. 'Oh I just happened to be out for a walk, saw the boat and went down to see if any of the bodies floating nearby were still alive. While I did that, Mrs Carlyle phoned the coastguard. They can tell you more than I can.'

There was a distinct pause before he replied. No doubt he was wondering why I was not telling the complete truth. In the end he merely said, 'Well. Thank you, Mr Holden. I'm sure the emergency services are grateful for your help.'

'Oh. That's all right, Mr Bushell. I'm only down here for another day or so and then I'm back to Derbyshire. Life's a lot quieter up there. I'll send you a Christmas card.'

I told Helen the gist of the conversation and she said in a kind of motherly way, 'What am I going to do with you?'

It was too good an opportunity to miss so I took the plunge, 'Well, you could come back to Higham with me and we'll take it from there.'

She didn't answer straight away and I wondered at first if she'd actually heard me and was waiting for me to repeat it. She came into the hall drying her hands on a towel. She had heard. 'Yes. I'd quite like to come up and visit when your house is finished. When is that likely to be?'

Helen looked directly at me, rather like I had done when I had first stayed at her house. Her expression didn't change, and I realised I was being paid back in kind. I lowered my gaze and said with a smile, 'You win. Would you really come to Higham? I'll be going back in a few days, so I can at least get a provisional completion date.'

After lunch we considered what to do for the rest of the day. As Helen hadn't been to the farm at Lydden I thought she might like to see it, and on the way back we could call in at Wakefield Place. I first got in touch with Nigel Crompton to find out if the police operations there had finished. It was a slight inconvenience having to go through a third party but it couldn't be for much longer.

He seemed to think it would be all right for me just to turn up. The secret room had been cleared out and customs men were taking an inventory before loading the stuff into vans for ultimate destruction. Three men had been arrested and were behind bars awaiting trial. This had happened as a result of the arrest of the men at Northdown Way. They were only carriers and small fry but fear of a long prison sentence and hefty fines had induced them to give the names of people higher up in the organisation.

One other piece of information had come to hand. The second man on the beach had regained consciousness, though it was still too early to know if he would make a full recovery. The paramedics in the helicopter had worked on him all the way to hospital and by the time they had landed he was able to tell them his name.

He had even more news. The two men caught on the way to Ashford had also revealed the name of their boss. Three others had been apprehended and the police were confident of getting the top man soon. It all seemed a bit of an anticlimax, but it could mean that I could get on with my life.

Yet another piece of the jigsaw fitted into place. I don't know how the police found out but the men who had followed me to Northdown Way had really intended to recruit me to their ranks. They knew I had brought in the bogus brandy and hoped I might be persuaded to join their band of couriers. Apparently they were then unaware that the man I had given the bottles to had been arrested.

All this information I gleaned from a single phone call to Nigel Crompton. There was still more to him than he was letting on.

Helen was interested in all she saw at the farm. I introduced her to Roy Sneddon, and then to Mrs Baldwin, who looked more motherly than ever. She was full of the news regarding the secret room. Roy was more concerned with his position as farm manager, so I assured him he was in the clear. Although I'd seen it all before, I was also impressed with the farm. It was not so much the size, because compared to some it was a small farm but here in miniature was a homestead that was self-sufficient, not only paying its way and employing many people, but actually making money against the time when things might not be so rosy.

43

Newspaper Story

Ever since that first shot outside Wakefield Place and the car chase, I had kept a brief diary of events in a small notebook. I'd left a few pages at the beginning blank and subsequently filled in the background story as far as I knew it. Now, following the night of the storm and the capture of the men on the beach, I had made no entries for two days. It was a pleasant and relaxing time. The storm had left much debris to be cleared away, broken windows and roof tiles to be replaced and this work continued. Helen and I remained happy in each other's company. The change in our personal relationship was not recorded in my book. That was for no one but us.

Life returned almost to normal. I pottered about the garden, prepared the meals for when Helen returned from work and wondered how long this idyllic situation could continue.

I had another talk with Colonel Witts and asked him more about his time with the army and later as colonel of the local Home Guard during World War II. It wasn't long before I was able to steer him round to talk about the Auxiliary Units. It was a fascinating story. The more I heard about it the more surprised I became that so little had filtered through to the general public.

As for the Colonel, once started it was as though the floodgates of his memory had been opened. Although not actually part of that secret army he certainly knew

234

many local people who had been members. I asked if he had ever considered writing a history of the time. He smiled. 'Too old now. I'm happy to keep my memories alive but I don't have the patience to write it down. There is one thing you might like to know. Colonel Gubbins was the brains behind it all and was in overall command. He gradually rose through the ranks and retired as a major general. He tried to get a medal for the men of the Auxiliary Units but the powers that be would have none of it. They argued that as it was a secret army it could not be recognised. To be honest, I doubt whether any member cared about medals. However, a few years later the War Department relented and ex-members were allowed to write in for a gong. Personally I doubt if many bothered.'

I thanked him for his time, gave my address at Higham and Helen's telephone number, and promised to keep in touch. I was more determined than ever to look into the history of the secret army.

At the weekend the local paper carried the story of the storm, accompanied by vivid pictures and personal accounts of local residents whose homes and cars had been damaged. It also included the story of the motor cruiser washed up on the beach, the capture of three smugglers and the plight of the two men who had been on the boat. No mention was made of the drugs, money or contraband found on board. Maybe the press hadn't been allowed that close.

There was a dramatic picture of the helicopter landing on the beach. No names were mentioned but there were also two photographs of the people on the sands. The pictures were hardly clear enough for individuals to be identified, although I recognised at least one of them. I bought an extra copy of the paper and put it in my suitcase. At the time I had not seen any newspaper people. Possibly an amateur photographer had got close enough although I hadn't noticed at the time.

Joyce came home at the weekend, so to preserve the proprieties I returned to the loneliness of my car. I had the distinct impression that Joyce knew about our situation although she said nothing to me. Helen would no doubt tell her daughter when she was ready.

So far the police had not bothered us for statements about the excitement on the beach and I was happy not to remind them. In fact it was Colonel Witts who made the first move. He'd seen the story in the paper and somehow realised I might be involved. When he phoned he merely said he had something to discuss and would I call to see him. I was happy to go.

The colonel opened the door himself and ushered me into his study. He came straight to the point, 'This is not about the secret army – well, not directly – but it does concern one man and his grandson. At least it may do. I read in the local paper about the smugglers on the beach. No names were mentioned but I recognised one of the men taken away by the police. The editor should never have allowed that to be published. I also recognised one of the other men, not from his face but from his clothes – in fact from the very jacket you are wearing today.'

There was no way I could deny it as I admired the astuteness of the old army man. There were probably dozens of jackets similar to mine but not many had a hood that had been repaired with black tape. Although my face was hidden, the hood had photographed extremely well. He seemed satisfied when I acknowledged that I was indeed involved and went on to explain that this was not my first encounter with the smugglers. He didn't probe any further though his next words were quite startling.

'Major Holden, I'm going to tell you a story and then ask your advice.' He began his tale. It was quite brief yet it covered all the important pieces of a jigsaw.

'That man in the picture, the smuggler, is a grandson of someone I have known for a long time. In fact he was the patrol leader of the Auxiliary Unit at Kingsgate. Remember, I told you about him when you first came to see me. His name was Solomon. Your grandfather was not the owner of Wakefield Place when the armaments were found in the 1960s. I mentioned the hideout to Solomon and he accompanied me when we showed the army engineers where it was. I thought nothing about that connection until I saw the photograph in the paper yesterday. Let's have a cup of tea while you look through this list. They're the Auxiliary Units I told you about the other day.'

He got up and went to the kitchen where I could hear him pottering about while I glanced through the lists he had drawn up.

Five patrols were listed, giving the patrol leaders and as many men in each as he could remember. In some cases only the surname was given while a few in each patrol had only a number. For someone not directly involved in that secret army it was an impressive attempt, now many years after the event. My grandfather's name was there as well as Nigel Crompton's. Colonel Witts returned with tea things on a silver tray, bourbon biscuits and silver teapot. He set the tray down on the table and said, 'Will you do the honours, Holden?'

'Certainly, sir. I'm impressed with the lists and your memory. May I keep them?'

'Yes. Always had a good memory. At one time I knew all the chaps in my regiment and a good deal about their families. They like that, you know – makes them feel more like a family.'

He continued with his story. 'Now this chap Solomon was very fond of his grandson, especially after the father died. I know for a fact that he had told him about Wakefield Place, and when I learned of this I tore him off a strip. Poor fellow was proud of the fact that he had been part of that force. He may have known of other bolt-holes or searched until he found them and I don't doubt that he told his grandson. Still, nothing I could do really. We weren't in the army any longer. Some years later the grandson got into trouble with the police and the old man asked me to intercede. Well, there wasn't much I could do but in the end they let him off with a caution and a hefty fine. I lent old man Solomon part of the money. It was eventually repaid and I thought no more about it until yesterday. 'I'm convinced that man in the photograph is his grandson, name of Samuel Solomon. My problem is what to do. I've helped the man once. His grandfather is now dead so I reckon I've done my duty to an old comrade. Now I don't really want to get involved.'

I realised why he had asked me, a comparative stranger, to help him decide. 'Leave it with me, Colonel. I'll see a friend in the local police and they can take it from there. You're absolutely sure it is Solomon?'

'No doubt whatever. It's a few years since I saw him but I'm good with faces. That's him all right.'

I promised to let him know the outcome. Somehow things had a habit of sorting themselves out. Maybe this time luck would be on the side of the good guys.

44

To Catch a Thief

After my visit to the Colonel, I had intended to discuss with Helen what I should do next. When I realised she would still be at work I chose the alternative – and went directly to the police.

For the first time in ages I thought of Anne. In the past whenever there had been a problem I had come to rely on her judgement; not that I had always taken her advice. She had often brought a new slant to the situation and invariably saw through to a better answer.

Also, for the first time since I'd met Helen I began to compare her with Anne. That would never do – although similar in many ways and initially that's probably why I liked Helen, they were two totally different women.

I parked my car and walked through to the enquiries desk and asked if PC Williams was on duty. 'Yes, sir. May I enquire what it's about?' The constable on duty was polite, efficient and a female. She looked so young. 'I'm David Holden. I met PC Williams recently on the beach when he arrested some villains. I haven't yet made a formal statement and I wondered if he is free.'

'Just wait there a moment please, Mr Holden.' She disappeared behind a partition and I heard her call out, 'Can someone find Taffy and tell him a Mr Holden wants to see him.' I didn't hear any reply but she returned to the desk and told me he would be a few minutes. She lifted the receiver to answer an incoming call and I waited.

This was a fairly new police station and the room I was in was quite large. A desk ran the whole length of one wall although only the solitary policewoman was on duty. Along the side walls were several doors leading to offices. The main room had almost two dozen chairs, a few tables and a sprinkling of magazines. Maybe they sometimes handled a lot of enquiries.

PC Willims came out of one of the rooms and asked me to go in. I came straight to the point. 'How are you getting on with those people we caught on the beach?'

'I'm afraid it's a slow process. One man is still in hospital in Canterbury nursing a broken arm. The dead man is still in the mortuary and his friend is recovering gradually in a hospital in Ashford. The other two are also recovering from bruises caused by someone firing a distress signal at them. They have all been charged except one man. He's a Sydney Short and claims he knows nothing. He says he cadged a lift in the back of the pick-up and had never seen the men before. He gave an address in Broadstairs but there's no one there who can verify it. We'll have to let him go soon.'

I brought out my copy of the newspaper and showed it to the policeman. 'Is this the man?'

'Yes. That's him. You were lucky to have got that copy. They had to recall that edition because the villains could have been recognised.'

'You'll never know how lucky. I have reason to believe that man's name is Samuel Solomon. At the moment I can't tell you how I know, but if you throw the name at him it may just startle him enough. His father is dead. His grandfather was in the army but he's also dead.' I waited while this information sank in.

'I'd like to see someone in CID and run this past them.

Do you mind waiting a few minutes?' PC Williams asked.

'No, of course not. Shall I come with you?'

'No, sir. Just wait here. I'll not be long.' I appreciated that he needed to see the CID man without me being present so that he could fill in the background of our earlier meeting. Five minutes later he returned with another officer and introduced him as Detective Constable Price.

'Good afternoon, Mr Holden. I understand you've already helped us and now you've got some information. If it's true it could be really helpful. Please take your time and tell us what you know.'

'First, I have no reason to doubt the truth of what I've been told. The man who told me knew the man you have in custody and his grandfather. He's getting on in years but his mind and his memory are still sharp. He has only seen me once yet he recognised me from the photograph in the paper, not from my face, which you can see is obscured, but from a patched repair to the hood of my jacket. The face of the other man in the picture is clearer. My informant recognised him at once. Apparently he was in trouble with the police some time ago but was let off with a caution and a fine. My informant is very sure it's Solomon because he paid part of that fine on behalf of the man's grandfather.'

I could see that the CID man was impressed, though when I had begun his body language showed me he was only mildly interested. I could almost hear him thinking. What could a total stranger possibly know? Now he was eager to hear more.

'Thank you very much, Mr Holden. I may need to know the address of your informant, but first we'll check our files and then the information you've just given us. I heard from Sergeant Jackson that you helped the police earlier – a car chase as I understand it.'

So he had done his homework. 'Yes, I just happened to be in the right place at the right time, the same as on the beach with PC Williams.'

'This could be just the opening we need. We have to interview Short or Solomon again.'

He got up to go but I needed to know if I could go back up north. 'Just before you disappear, do you know if I need stay down here to give a statement about the incident on the beach.'

'I'm not sure, Mr Holden. Someone else is dealing with that and it will probably be PC Williams who will call on you when necessary.'

'If it's all the same to you, I'd prefer to do it now or not at all. I don't live down here and I need to return to Derbyshire within the next two days.'

The two policemen looked at each other and then PC Williams said, 'We'd prefer it to be done now, sir, and one from Mrs Carlyle.'

I rang Helen and explained, and she agreed to come down at once. That's the trouble with helping the police. You have to tell it all again and again.

'OK, Mr Holden, we can do yours now, but before you actually begin could I suggest that the first time you fired the pistol you hadn't realised it was loaded. You merely intended to help the police as best you could.'

'Yes I could do that, but it doesn't explain the second shot. There's no way that could be an accident.'

'That's true, but I'll say I shouted to you to fire again and that you were only obeying my orders.'

'Do you think anyone is going to believe that?'

'Oh, I think they will, especially as the coastguard will corroborate the statement. We can't have you up before the court for illegally discharging a pistol in public and actually causing bodily harm.'

Well, I'd told a few white lies so I suppose one more

would not make much difference. At least this time I did so with police approval, although I was not happy. I made my statement as suggested and waited for Helen to arrive. At least hers should be a true statement. While I waited I did wonder how often statements were manipulated to fit the circumstances. Hopefully, not too often.

Helen arrived and gave her statement. PC Williams actually saw me to my car and thanked me while Helen got into hers and drove off. It had been a strange interview but then I didn't know how the police really worked. In detective stories or dramas on the telly it's often the odd snippet of information that solves the crime. Maybe in real life it's a different story. We had told them all we knew and, for the time being at least, we were free.

If I could have overheard the conversation between them later I would have been pleased. I subsequently found out that they interviewed Samuel Solomon again and that was indeed his true name. He was arrested and then, having been rumbled, was happy to give vital names and information regarding the smuggling operations. One name in particular they could scarcely believe and had to move forward cautiously in their enquiries. It was several days later when I learned the name of Mr Big, although I had already met him briefly in the dining room of the hotel at Pegwell Bay – Mike Jevons, one of Joyce's many supervisors.

When this news broke there were some embarrassed faces, particularly in the customs and excise service. The lower echelons, and they included people like Joyce, were not badly affected as they had only occasionally come into contact with the man. It was the more senior officers like Bushell who felt the betrayal most.

I found out later that Bushell was quite put out. He saw things in black and white, the villains in black and the good guys in white. There could be no shades in between if they were to do their job effectively. He had been completely taken in and blamed himself in some small degree. However, from then on, once he had put it behind him, I felt sure he would become a most diligent customs man.

Those in the lower ranks who had experienced Jevons' sarcasm were only too happy to condemn the man and felt he deserved all he got. Like most tragedies in life, this whole incident would soon be forgotten and only those directly involved would remember Mr Jevons. It's best that way, for on balance there are more good things in life than bad.

45

Return to Derbyshire

We returned to Northdown Way, and I told Helen about my recent visit to Colonel Witts. It really was surprising how snippets of information, of little significance in themselves, now began to reveal important bits of the jigsaw.

Helen was travelling down to Worthing to discuss fashion trends with a department store there and then to another in Brighton, but we spent the next day together before she set off for the south coast, while I took the longer trip to Higham. This was a journey that I needed to make. Staying with Helen had been exciting and I felt sure we would be happy together although little had been said about the future. If that came about we would need to decide where that might be – Margate or Higham. The toss of a coin could decide the issue if it came down on the side I really wanted. If not, it would have to be the best of three.

For me, once the decision had been made I would have no regrets. Both places had attractions. At Margate I had many old friends, at least two places where we could live, or I could build another dream home. Higham was equally attractive, perhaps more so as I had already found it, built a house there and made more friends.

Against living at Higham was the fact that Helen might not wish to give up her work and move away from her friends. In any case, that was not yet an option as I had not even asked her. That decision did not need an immediate answer but completing my new home did.

There was one more thing I needed to do before I got back to Higham. I took a fairly wide detour to Cambridge. Anne had never been far from my thoughts but I needed to visit her grave. I knew she wasn't really there and in the past I had made only occasional visits. But this occasion was important, and after I'd put a bunch of her favourite flowers on the grave I stood for a while in silence.

Nothing magical happened. I didn't hear her voice but I did come away more content and happy in my mind that she approved of my relationship with Helen. Then I resumed my journey northwards.

Derbyshire had not experienced the storm and the fact that the weather had been mild meant that building my new house had gone on apace. The garage was finished and they had started again on the house. All the roof trusses were in place, the felt laid, battens fixed and when I arrived they had just begun to lay the roof tiles.

One more day should see the completion of the chimney-stack and then, as tradition demands, would come the topping-out ceremony. This merely consists of drinks all round for the builders and lighting the fire to see if the smoke is carried away correctly. They had done a good job and I was happy to provide the drinks the next day. We dispensed with glasses and I joined the builders in drinking from cans of beer. I made a mental note to get in a few bottles of whisky when they had finished the job.

There was still quite a lot of work remaining but when I spoke to the foreman he reckoned that another month should see the completion, even allowing for snags and bad weather. They had already finished the drive and he suggested I should get the lawns laid and any flower beds and shrubs planted before the winter set in.

The following day I got the architect to give me a couple of plans of the site so that I could pencil in a few ideas for planting out the garden. He said he could do better and invited me over to his office to look at his latest toy – a computer programme that showed not only where trees and shrubs should be planted for best effect but also what they would look like when fully grown.

He showed me what to do, and although I produced a blank screen twice, I persevered and ended up with a credible garden design. The programme was comprehensive for it not only gave all the varieties of each plant I had selected but indicated those most suitable for varying soils and in different parts of the country. I decided to look more closely into the computer age. Maybe it was time I acquired one.

Away from the dramatic events in Margate I was enjoying myself, but there was a lot to do before I could actually move into my new home. The first thing was to have the telephone connected. That proved easier than on previous occasions, and the telephone was connected on Saturday. My first call was to Helen.

We chatted for a long time and she promised to call me once a week. My next call was to Veronica to ask if she and Richard would like to come over and see the empty house. She seemed pleased at the prospect and promised to call round on Wednesday afternoon. That left me plenty of time to buy a few bits of crockery and cutlery. At least I could offer them a cup of tea.

With the central heating going full blast and the fire alight in the living room it began to look inviting even without the furniture. I began to plan where everything should go. The days were full and I was happy just pottering about. Only in quiet moments did I remember

247

the events in Margate and with hindsight realised it could all have gone horribly wrong.

I gave myself two weeks to clean the house from top to bottom. As builders go, mine had not made too much mess. Even so, it was surprising how much dust and mud I removed. Veronica came over a couple of times and on the second occasion brought a vacuum cleaner. I couldn't remember what condition my own was in so bought a new one.

There were no carpets in storage as I had sold them with the house so I asked Veronica if she'd like to help me choose new ones at least for the living room, dining room and study. The next day she turned up with two books of swatches. We spent some time rejecting most until we found one, the same plain colour for all three rooms. She phoned the shop and they sent someone over to check our measurements and promised delivery and fitting within seven days.

I was very glad to have the vicar's wife on my side. She actually negotiated a handsome discount and then managed to knock off the odd pounds on the bill. 'Silly to have odd bits of money. A nice round figure is so cosy,' was her comment to the man. I couldn't see the logic of her argument but was happy to accept while he, poor man, agreed and seemed pleased to get the order.

When the man had departed I congratulated Veronica on her business sense. She replied, 'If you don't ask you don't get. They will make a nice profit even at the reduced rate. What you've saved can go towards curtains or carpets for the lower level rooms.'

The carpets arrived and were fitted on time. I still felt a bit guilty about the discount and asked him to measure the lower rooms and give me a price. He did this and showed me some samples he had in the van. I chose a neutral beige. Veronica was not around so I asked, 'Do I

248

get the same discount as before?' He agreed without a murmur. I was so pleased with myself I went out and bought an expensive malt whisky.

I hesitated about putting my old furniture in my new house but in the end decided to have it all delivered so that I could gradually replace it if necessary. It would be good to have my books with me again.

Before then, I had time for another trip to Margate and back. Helen had phoned a couple of times and on the third occasion I told her I was hoping to come down to see her. She immediately offered to put me up, and I asked whether she meant in her bed or the bed in Joyce's room.

'You may decide,' was her reply to my awkward question and I immediately felt guilty. Did she or did she not want me with her? There was still a niggling thought that she could take me or leave me. This interlude at Higham had been restful but now I looked forward to returning to Margate and made arrangements to go down in a few days' time. Before that, however, I needed to tell Richard and Veronica about Helen.

I'd forgotten to collect my mail for several days so there was quite a pile waiting for me at the post office. An official-looking one was from the Margate police. It was a fairly formal statement thanking me for my initial help in catching the smugglers during the car chase. They also appreciated my initiative in phoning the police from the Wheatsheaf, which resulted in the arrest of several people. Finally they acknowledged my assistance in apprehending the villains on the beach at Margate.

It seemed that the trials for all these people would be in different places, Ashford, Margate and Ramsgate, more or less at the same time. The important bit for me came at the end of the letter. 'It is anticipated that the defence lawyers will accept our suggestion that you need not be called to give evidence. However, please hold yourself in readiness.' The letter also told me that others who had been caught in connection with the smuggling activities at Deal, Sheerness, Dover and Herne Bay would face trials in those towns.

I was surprised that so many people had been involved and with so much paperwork, all because of a few greedy people. I hoped they would throw the book at them. The trials would begin in 21 days' time and I was hopeful I would not be required.

The next important letter was from Nigel Crompton. It was hand-written in beautiful copperplate. Maybe he didn't want his secretary to know. He covered the news in minute detail. I suppose his training had taught him to be concise and accurate. The gist of it was how pleased he was that the smuggling had stopped, at least for the time being. He'd found out that in addition to the old army hideouts that had been used new bolt-holes had been constructed in the woods at Nonnington when the mines had been abandoned.

His was a factual report though his personal feelings and greatest condemnation were reserved for Mike Jevons. 'That vile man', he called him, who had betrayed the trust of his calling. I think what worried him most was the fact that he had done the conveyancing when Jevons had bought a large house in the Palm Bay area of Margate. His letter also revealed that in total six hideouts at Margate and four at Ramsgate had been discovered.

Apparently the smugglers used lorries and vans to move the stuff although occasionally it went by rail. A few loads went by sea on coastal steamers and sometimes by motor cruiser. The one I had seen on the beach at Margate did in fact belong to Jevons and had just returned from France. It was sheltering in Margate harbour and had broken away from its moorings. Initially Jevons had denied all knowledge of the boat and then, in hoping for a much shorter prison sentence, had pleaded guilty.

So, in a nutshell, I knew a good deal of the smuggling story and was glad that Eric was not really part of the gang. Although only on the fringes, I had been more involved than him. It would be a relief to put it all behind me and get on with my life up here in the relative calm of my new home. I began to take stock and make plans for the future.

While I had quite enjoyed meeting up with my old friends in Margate and for a time had been tempted to return there, I decided that Higham should be given a chance. I had never been really idle and now with no financial worries I could do anything I wished. I wrote lengthy letters to both my children and put them in the picture regarding my brush with the smugglers. Once the trials began they might worry. I also told them about Helen. Replies came quickly, the one from Canada actually arrived before the one from Scotland. Both seemed happy for me that I might have found someone to share my life. While I was not actively seeking their approval, it was good to know they didn't object and that I was doing the right thing – that is, if Helen also agreed.

46

Future Assured

The other letters were a mixed bag. One was from my old firm, inviting me to a farewell party for the Managing Director. It had been redirected three times before finally reaching its destination. The date for replying had passed. So had the actual date of the party, but I sent off a quick reply wishing him a happy retirement.

There were no begging letters so no one had yet heard of my inheritance. A few were from local firms touting for business – garden maintenance, replacement windows, insurance options for cars, house and contents, and several urging me to make financial provision for my retirement.

The envelope that next drew my attention was written in Joyce's bold hand. Inside was an official invitation to her forthcoming wedding and a long letter reminding me that I had promised to give her away. She apologised for the suddenness and no, it was not for the usual reason. She and John had decided there was no need to wait any longer. He had now returned from America and been promoted on to the next rung of the ladder. She briefly mentioned Mike Jevons and the smugglers and was pleased it was all over.

I looked at the wedding date. It was eight weeks ahead so I really had plenty of time to go down to Margate as planned for a week or so, return to Derbyshire and then go down again for the wedding. I replied at once to Joyce, walked down to the village and managed to catch the afternoon post. That evening I rang Helen and we spoke for some time about the forthcoming nuptials. It seemed that the young people hadn't yet got a list of possible wedding presents. In fact they had only sent out one invitation so far – mine.

The following morning I rang Richard to ask if he'd like a game of golf. He invited me over to spend Wednesday with them. This was their day off as far as possible and they hoped to keep it free to catch up on things and have a little time to themselves. Fiona was there, looking relaxed and mature. She was having the last few days at home before joining the London firm.

They asked about the house, so I told them I would definitely be moving in on my return from Margate.

I told Veronica and Richard about the smugglers. At first they were much concerned, then intrigued by all I was able to tell them. When I mentioned the ex-army hideouts, Richard said he'd heard rumours but thought that was all it was. I assured him the Auxiliary Units were definitely flesh and blood, even if they hadn't been called upon to put their training to the test. We managed a part round of golf in the afternoon and I stayed there until quite late.

The following Wednesday I called over on my way to Margate to drop off my spare key for Veronica in case the carpet people delivered, and it was lucky that I had forgotten it earlier. They were taking Fiona down to stay with her aunt at Uxbridge when they found the car wouldn't start. I offered to try, and did all the checks they had already carried out, without success. I had an inkling it might be the timing belt – a vital piece of equipment on most modern cars that needs to be changed after seven years or so. If it fails while the engine is running it could cause thousands of pounds of damage. This had simply seized up, so in a way Richard was fortunate. He rang the garage and explained their situation.

The garage were sending a truck round at once but the car would be out of use for two days. I offered to take Fiona to her aunt's but in the end we waited for the tow truck to collect the car, and then Richard and Veronica came along too, although they would now have to return by train.

We took the same route as before and stopped off at the same restaurant. The journey to Uxbridge was uneventful and this time I declined the aunt's cup of tea. There were no hold-ups, although traffic in the opposite direction was heavy, and I was soon through London and on the road to Margate. This time I made no diversion, although I did stop off at Birchington to buy some flowers. I'd forgotten that Wednesday was early closing but this place actually grew flowers, mostly under glass. They were very helpful and I selected two bunches from those that would be distributed to local florists the next day.

Helen was in the garden as I arrived and came over to greet me most affectionately – a kiss on each cheek and then one on the mouth.

By the time I had taken the flowers in and unpacked my stuff from the car Helen had finished her chores in the garden. She noticed the flowers and asked, 'Are these for me?'

'Yes. With my love. I couldn't decide which you'd prefer so I bought two bunches.'

We sat together on the settee, drank tea and then held hands in companionable silence until I made a move. 'I'd better go and have a quick wash.'

My bag was still in the hall where I had left it, so I

254

took out my washing things and headed upstairs to the bathroom. When I came down a few minutes later, Helen had finished arranging the flowers and I tentatively posed the question, 'Where am I sleeping tonight? I'll just go and unpack.'

'Where would you like to sleep?'

'Well I don't want to pressure you or push my luck but I rather liked it when I slept in your bed especially when you were there too.' I'm sure Helen actually blushed but she answered quickly enough, 'Yes, I'd like that too – and we can probably make a habit of it.'

Now was not the time to pursue the question uppermost on my mind so I took my bag upstairs and opened one of the wardrobe doors. Helen's clothes had been moved into the next compartment so I had a lot of space to hang my few belongings. When I returned downstairs we spoke about Joyce's forthcoming wedding and it seemed that as yet no thought had been given to wedding presents. However, Joyce and John would be coming over this evening so we might know then. We had our meal, washed up and returned to the lounge to watch TV. It all seemed so natural I wondered if this might be the right time.

I hadn't really rehearsed what I'd say although I'd turned over a few things in my mind. Now the words came easily and more or less spontaneously. 'Helen, would you like to get married again, and if so could it be to me? It's wonderful being here with you and I'd like it to continue. Since we met I've come to love you very much. I think we could be very happy together. Will you marry me?' It all came out in a bit of a rush.

There was no surprise on her face as she answered, 'I had a feeling you would ask me, and if you did I wouldn't know what to say. I like our relationship as it is. I do love you and I worry about you. We're happy enough, aren't we?'

'Possibly. Yes, but it could be better, more permanent and I think if we were married we'd both feel more committed. I know I would. Don't decide now. Come back to Higham with me and see the new house. It's only partly furnished because I wanted you to choose whatever you want.'

Helen didn't say anything so I continued, 'If you don't like it, we'll live here – or anywhere else you prefer. If you want to continue working that's all right, but if you don't we can live almost anywhere. Please think about it.'

'Oh, I will. I promise and thank you for asking.' Then she hugged me.

The bell at the front door rang and Helen asked me to answer it. Joyce and her fiancé were there. She said hello and kissed me. John and I shook hands and soon we were all in the sitting room chatting like old friends. 'Thanks for the invitation. Did you get my reply? I'm definitely coming and will be honoured to give you away but you must let me know what you'd like for a wedding present. I'll save my fatherly talk to John for later. I gather you've moved into the house at Pegwell Bay. Are the windows all right now?'

'They're absolutely fine. Mrs Bull is like a mother hen. We've told her we're getting married and will be sending her and her husband an invitation.'

We chatted about world events and then things much closer to home, then about the smugglers and inevitably Mike Jevons' name cropped up. Somehow it all seemed old news and of no consequence to us. From what was said it certainly seemed that the smugglers and my involvement with them would soon be nothing but a distant memory.

I managed to get Helen on her own. 'How long are Joyce and John likely to stay this evening? Only I thought it might be nice if we all walked down to the pub for a celebration drink. It's my treat.'

'What a good idea,' was Helen's comment and she suggested it to the others. John and Joyce walked ahead of us, arm in arm. Helen and I followed, holding hands. I glanced sideways at her occasionally. She seemed happy enough, and when once she caught me she smiled and squeezed my hand. I felt 20, no 30 years younger.

The landlord was pleased to see us, and when I explained the reason for the visit he insisted on giving us champagne on the house. He actually brought it over and poured it himself. It was a pleasant interlude. As we left the landlord came over and said, 'We've taken your advice and bought ourselves a motor home. It should be delivered this weekend. Do come round and give it the once-over.' I said I'd love to see it.

We started out on the way home, linked arms and walked four abreast until we reached Northdown Way, where the pavements are too narrow, so we continued in pairs. Joyce stayed behind with me while John and Helen walked ahead. I ventured a 'Nice young man you've got there, Joyce.' To which she replied, 'I think my mum also has a nice young man.' My answer was, 'Well, young at heart if not in body, but there's still a bit of life yet.'

Soon we were sitting down in the lounge having coffee, and not long after that the young couple left to return to Pegwell Bay.

As we got ready for bed Helen said, 'Thanks for taking us to the Wheatsheaf. It's been a happy day. Let's go to bed and tomorrow you can begin to make an honest woman of me.'